I0563756

Phantoms
and Other Cruel Tales

Phantoms
and Other Cruel Tales

by
Charles-Marie Flor O'Squarr

Translated, annotated and introduced by
Brian Stableford

A Black Coat Press Book

English adaptation and introduction Copyright © 2017 by Brian Stableford.
Cover illustration Copyright © 2017 by Phil Cohen.

Visit our website at www.blackcoatpress.com

ISBN 978-1-61227-586-4. First Printing. January 2017. Published by Black Coat Press, an imprint of Hollywood Comics.com, LLC, P.O. Box 17270, Encino, CA 91416. All rights reserved. Except for review purposes, no part of this book may be reproduced or transmitted in any form or by any means, electronic or mechanical, including photocopying, recording, or by any information storage and retrieval system, without permission in writing from the publisher. The stories and characters depicted in this novel are entirely fictional. Printed in the United States of America.

Table of Contents

Introduction

Les Fantômes [Phantoms], by-lined Ch.-M. Flor O'Squarr, was first published by Jules Lévy in 1885. The additional novelette added herein to the contents of that collection, "Mon Enterrement," translated as "My Interment," was first published in *La Grande Revue de Paris et Saint-Petersbourg* in three parts in January-March 1893.

Bibliographical information relating to the author of *Les Fantômes* can be a trifle confusing, because the journalist Joseph-Charles Flor (1830-1830), who later sometimes signed himself "Flor O'Squarr," is sometimes confused with his son Charles-Marie Flor (c1850-1921), who also sometimes signed himself "Flor O'Squarr." The latter is the author of *Les Fantômes* and "Mon Enterrement."

The original Flor O'Squarr was born in Brussels but spent the greater part of his life in Paris, where he worked as a journalist for numerous radical periodicals as well as working for major newspapers, most notably *Le Figaro*, as an art and theater critic, and where he used various pseudonymous by-lines, including "Oscar," of which "O'Squarr" is a deliberate corruption. He had several plays produced, mostly vaudevilles, and also worked as a translator. The Bibliothèque Nationale credits J.-C. Flor with being one of two possible authors—the other being (very improbably) Napoléon III—of a curious satirical pamphlet entitled *La Révision de la carte de l'Europe* [The Revision of the Map of Europe] ostensibly published in London in 1854, and also with a account of the Crimean War published in the same year. The most successful book credited to either of the Flors O'Squarr is, however, *Les Coulisses de l'anarchie* [In the Wings of Anarchism] by his son, which was first published in 1892, and went through numerous editions thereafter. The confusion between the two is doubtless encouraged by the fact that much of J.-C. Flor's work for far-left periodicals, especially during the Second Empire, was clandestine, and his similarly radical son undoubtedly continued the policy of masking some of his own political writings.

Very little is recorded in readily available sources about the biography of Charles-Marie Flor, even his birth-date remaining mysterious, but he employs himself as the narrator of "Mon Enterrement," and presumably does not stray too far from the truth in reporting background biographical data in that story, which records that he fought in the Franco-Prussian War not long after his twentieth birthday; that probably places his birth-date in 1850 or thereabouts, when his father would have been twenty years old. He saw action during the Prussian invasion before being transferred to Paris in time for the siege and the Commune. One of the first-person narratives in *Les Fantômes* provides a little more detail about that narrator's postings, which might reflect the author's, although the story itself is obviously fictitious and contains other data that seem chronologically confused. The biography cites the narrator's place of residence as a region of the South of France close to the Italian border, and two of the longer stories in *Les Fantômes* transplant their protagonists from Paris to that region in a fashion that strongly suggests an intimate acquaintance with it on the part of the author.

The datum might simply have been omitted, but the biography sketched in "Mon Enterrement" makes no mention of the narrator ever having been married, and all of the stories in *Les Fantômes* give a very strong impression of a man deeply but regretfully disillusioned by his experience of amour; much of the energy and idiosyncrasy of the work apparently stems from that circumstance.

The title story of the collection is subtitled "étude cruelle" [a cruel study] deliberately linking it to the tradition of *contes cruels* that had been given that label by a classic collection Villiers de l'Isle-Adam. Most of the works in *Les Fantômes* share the invariable cynical fascination with "the

8

irony of fate" that is definitive of all classic *contes cruels*, although they are various in their themes and narrative methods. Although most *fin de siècle contes cruels* were written for newspaper feuilleton slots, and thus tend to be short and snappy, Flor O'Squarr's are much longer, except for the vignettes grouped as "Fantômes amoureux" and thus permit much more leisurely in-depth analyses of their central ironies, thus licensing the variant generic description of "*études cruelles*."

"Les Fantômes" (tr. as "Phantoms: A Cruel Study") is, as its title suggests, a classic study of a haunting, featuring a highly unreliable narrator whose account of himself and the harassment in question is deeply questionable. In most stories of that type the narrator presents the apparitions by which he in confronted as frankly supernatural, and it is left to the reader to determine whether or not they might actually be figments of his imagination. Flor O'Squarr's story, by contrast, inverts that strategy completely; the narrator flatly refuses to admit that the apparitions from which he suffers can be anything but hallucinations, but then ties himself in extraordinary knots trying to explain them in terms of his own psychology, which he claims insistently, but unconvincingly, to be entirely free from remorse and guilt. The story thus becomes one of the most interesting and elaborate nineteenth-century developments of the theme of an essentially ambiguous haunting, notable for its acidic artistry.

The second novelette in the collection, "La Source Prégamain" (tr. as "The Prégamain Spring") is an outright comedy, whose humor only turns black at the end, as is typical of comedic *contes cruel*, but it is highly unusual, and perhaps unique, in the configuration of the double twist that gives an extra turn of the screw to the eventual psychological demolition of its hero. It contrasts very sharply with the third story in the collection, "La Petite" (tr. as "The Girl"), which is a love story that certainly has its cruel and deeply ironic aspects, but also has a philosophical dimension that calls into interesting question both the conventional mythology of sentimental fiction and the quality of its own cruelty. Although it is distinctly clipped in its later phases, giving the impression that it was finished off in something of a hurry, and thus falls short of being a masterpiece in terms of its form and structure, it is certainly a remarkable item, in its passion as well as its peculiarity.

The items contained in the section headed "Fantômes amoureux" (tr. as "Amorous Phantoms") extend the spectrum of variety established by the three novelettes vastly, and although they certainly adopt the essentially jaundiced and disenchanted view of amour typical of *contes cruels* they take it in unusual directions to unfamiliar extremes, and some of them hardly qualify as *contes* at all, seeming more akin to meditations. They range in manner from the blatant farce of "Vision" to the seemingly heartfelt sentimental romance of "Le Portrait de Bébé" (tr. as "The Baby Portrait") via the enterprising bizarrerie of "Le Téléphone"—surely the first story every written about phone sex—but they nevertheless retain a certain integrity as a set. Their disillusionment is given a further twist by their elaborate dedication; if they really were written with the intention of entertaining a potential fiancée, one can hardly be surprised by the implication that the ultimate result of the endeavor was that their author's suit was rejected.

The story added to the present collection as a supplement, "Mon Enterrement," provides an interesting counterpart to "Les Fantômes" in similarly developing one of the classic motifs of horror fiction, ostensibly in a thoroughly naturalistic fashion. It poses, and might really have been intended, as an item of social propaganda, but its real fascination is the imaginative intensity of the author's attempt to put himself in a hypothetical situation and to describe its psychological development with all due conviction. It is certainly more impressive, as well as more compelling, viewed as an item of melodramatic fiction rather than as the quasi-documentary item of autobiography that it pretends to be, and it neatly fills out a set of stories remarkable for their range and enterprise, and their relentless quest for originality in their narrative strategies. *Les*

Fantômes was published just as the Decadent Movement was getting under way in fin-de-siècle Paris, and it provides an intriguing kaleidoscopic display of the world-view embraced and perversely celebrated by the members of that Movement.

The translations of the stories in *Les Fantômes* were made from the version of the Lévy edition reproduced on the Bibliothèque Nationale's gallica website. The translation of "Mon Enterrement" was made from the relevant volume of *La Grande Revue de Paris et Saint-Petersbourg* reproduced on the same website.

Brian Stableford

PHANTOMS: A CRUEL STUDY

To Monsieur le Marquis de Cherville,
Homage and Respectful Sympathy[1]

I

For three years, I had for a mistress the wife of my best friend. Yes, the best. I would search my past in vain for an individual who was more attentively faithful and more spontaneously devoted to me. Several times, in the grave crises of my life, I had appealed to his affection, and he had generously offered me his aid, his time and his purse. I had always simply exploited his good will and congratulated myself on it. He had replaced the lost affections of my youth and watched over my dying mother. If I underwent an ordeal, or a chagrin, he wept with me—even more than me, for nature protected me against the effects of facile compassion.

It is freely and voluntarily that I render him that homage. Who, after all, could constrain me to do it? I intend to prove, by inclining before that venerated memory, that I am not blinded by any egotism, that I possess an elevated notion of the just and the unjust, of good and evil. Others, in my place, might strive ingeniously to circumvent opinion by means of a different conduct, or employ a more dissimulated language; I scorn those hypocrisies because I disdain everything that is petty. I say what I think, I report exactly things exactly as they are, without lingering over the objections the certain minds

---

[1] The writer Gaspard de Cherville (1819-1898), one of Alexandre Dumas' numerous collaborators and the author of many volumes about hunting and animals.

falsified by conventional doctrines might think they ought to address to me.

Similarly, I reject any appreciation that would tend to represent me as capable of or susceptible to timidity. If I praise my dear and regretted friend Félicien to the skies, it is not because my soul has been solicited by repentance or bruised by remorse. I am not yielding to the belated whim—fatally sterile, in any case—of covering up the extent of my sin by means of sentimental demonstrations. It is perfectly evident that in consenting to take Henriette as my mistress I committed the greatest of crimes, the most cowardly of treasons.

Nor am I thinking of bringing in extenuating circumstances based on the physical charms and mental seductions of my accomplice. Henriette was a very ordinary woman, bad rather than good, vain, well brought-up and plump.

I hesitate to draw a severe portrait of her, for most of the time, the judgments of men regarding women are only those of servants without employment, but I have imposed the task upon myself for my personal satisfaction and for the instruction of my fellows. I cannot neglect it, and it is necessary, in spite of my reluctance, to tell the truth about Félicien's wife.

She was, I repeat, a sturdy, ordinary individual, not pretty, with a mediocre education, stuffed with old-fashioned prejudices and bourgeois errors, having gleaned from poorly chosen and poorly understood reading the formulae of an outmoded sentimentality. She had doubtless aspired since youth to a romantic ideal, a confused ideal but invariably placed outside the precisely delimited circle of duties that religion had taught her. To the extent that she lost her footing in her banal dreams, she believed in good faith that she was taking flight for some promised land, some planet of a new beauty.

Poor woman! How many times have I heard her express the belief, typical of young dressmakers led astray by romanticism, that she was of a superior nature, of a privileged race, of a rare species, and that she would die misunderstood!

Oh, her girlish dreams! Did she fatigue my ears enough with them? She was not born to associate her life with that of a grave, pensive individual always curbed over captivating problems, that of a man devoid of ideals and passion, who took for a guide in life one knew not what dubious light that he confessed himself having only glimpsed. She, created for amour and passion, suffered from being thus abandoned, neglected for chimeras. And so on, and so on.

I never paid the slightest attention to such nonsense. Women who take passion for a guide resemble navigators who count on flashes of lightning to find their route instead of seeking it in the stars; they are certainly mistaken, but at least they require some energy in the soul and an appreciable dose of heroism in the spirit. Any passion supposes grandeur, even in the humblest individualities. Now, Henriette lacked a true vocation for premiere roles, just as she had lacked the courage for action. Her sentimentalism offered reminiscences of serial novels and reflections of romance.

Her heart had experienced nothing, her mind would have been, I firmly believe, incapable of conceiving anything outside the fabulous inventions, poetic monstrosities, heresies and fictions with which her mind had been stuffed since childhood. The imprint of that intellectual disorder was evident here and there in the platitudes of her conversation, sometime as stupidly melancholy as a ray of moonlight on the dormant water of a canal, sometimes spiced with the worldly slang—a kind of inverted pedantry—whose expressions apply an informality to all subjects and which serves as the superiority of inferior beings.

Henriette was not pretty and she suffered from it. A woman can have—exceptionally—enough intelligence to cause it to be forgotten that she is ugly, but she can never have enough to make herself forget it. The sentiment that Henriette had of her inferiority, by comparison with numerous other women prettier, younger or more gracious, was profound to the extent of spoiling all her impressions. For instance, she had never been able to believe that her husband could love her, that he could have married her by virtue of a sincere determined attachment, an exclusive desire of possession, and that he had not acted since before their union with the hidden agenda, outrageously wounding for her, of completing his domesticity with the presence of a tranquil, vulgar, insignificant wife to whom no one would deign to pay court, and on whom no approach, even by chance, would be able to compromise the conjugal honor.

That suspicion was absurd, but it did not enter my role to undeceive Henriette by repeating to her the confidences with which Félicien had honored my friendship at the time of his marriage. Then, I had seen dear Félicien happy, confident and, in advance, like the wolf in the fable, forging a felicity that made him weep with tenderness. He loved Henriette honestly, but I fear that, after a few months of communal life, he had had reason to lament, in discovering the negligibility, the sickening stupidity of the creature to whom he had devoted his life, his fortune and his most noble ambitions.

It must have astonished him to the point of alarm—him, the prestigious analyst who had consigned his marvelous studies of the human mind to books in which posterity would seek the summary of physiological and psychological science—to the point of horror, that he had committed an error so redoubtable, that he had associated with his thought that petty schoolgirl with a narrow mind, a paltry soul, limited ambitions and slow and stupid desires.

How could he, impeccably clear-sighted, have deceived himself to that extent? Worthy and proud, as was his custom, he did not breathe a word of that terrible misadventure, even to me, his best friend. If I had an intuition of it, it is because I saw him, for several weeks, somber, discouraged and idle, weary of all work, as if under the depression of mourning.

Then, a transfiguration took place; Félicien returned to his labor with a new determination. I thought I understood that, disdainful of a deceptive dream, scandalized by having gone temporarily astray, having neglected for subaltern enjoyments the source of his primary voluptuousness, deceived and forever cured by the deceptive proof into which his heart had fallen, he was setting forth again, definitively free this time, toward the superior, pure, starry regions in which, far from the pettiness and hypocrisies that are sufficient for the crowd, his great mind was going to float again, shaking its dust-stained wings, facing the sun, like an eagle in flight.

Henriette had no suspicion of that drama. She only observed in her husband a sudden distancing from her, a kind of impassive indifference that her coquetries could not disturb. I suppose that from then on, vain as I know her to be, she sensed dully within her, with an angry resentment, the preoccupation of a vengeance.

Yes, it was entirely and uniquely by virtue of vengeance that she became my mistress. Félicien's chilly attitude imposed on Henriette's vanity the need for revenge. She would have hastened to listen to any flattering voice, sincere or not, so long as it was loud, disposed to repeat to her all the good things she thought about herself. The homages of her pride, which she was obliged to confuse for the necessities of the moment with her conscience, became insufficient for her. Having observed me, she did me the honor of thinking that I would not hesitate to accept my share of her infamy in exchange for the abandonment that she granted me of her person.

When she had made me party to that hideous project, I believe I was skillful in not discouraging her to begin with, and contented myself with smiling, reserving myself the delay necessary to the examination of the risks to be run. Shortly thereafter, I consented. Our fall was vulgar and brutal. The next day, the sentiment that dominated my mind was that of surprise—a double surprise; I was astonished to have become Henriette's lover, and astonished not to have done so much sooner.

Certainly, poor Henriette might have been better favored by fortune. With a little patience, with the slightest discernment, it would not have been difficult for her to encounter a handsome, rich and elegant young man capable of loving her nobly and making her happy. For, after all, if I do not have the

17

excuse if having yielded to the charm of an irresistibly beautiful woman. Henriette could not explain her enticement and fall by the omnipotence of my prestige.

I am of medium height, short rather than tall. I have a coarse ruddy face, thick lips, ears as big as veal cutlets, eyes as red and damp as cherries in brandy, a bristly and untidy beard and thinning hair—and in addition to all, very young with a bad stomach. The habit I adopted since early youth of smoking a pipe—little clay pipes, black and very short; they are the best—gives all my garments an unbearably stuffy odor. Mentally, I know myself to be authoritarian, abrupt, obstinate, intolerant of the slightest contradiction and little disposed to suffer feminine caprices, even if the caprices are charming and the woman adorable.

And yet, our adulterous commerce was prolonged for three years; it would still be going on if circumstances permitted and if I could still, without offending convention, approach Henriette.

Now, did we love one another?

Did amour ever exist between us, even for a day, an hour, or even a minute? That is not the point that concerns me, but I want to pause upon it.

I admit that it troubles me. For my part, I believe that I never loved Henriette and, the day after our rupture—an entirely accidental rupture, since it was not occasioned by her or by me—I'm certain that I did not experience any regret for that lost mistress. If, for three years, I had not ceased to maintain regular relations with her, I put my constancy down to the great facility of the liaison. I did not deceive her, but that was probably out of laziness, indifference or even economy. Amour in Paris has become a colossal enterprise, which has its docks and its counters and in which, after having loved solidly, at a premium, one arrives at loving at the closing price, and even loving at a discount. Henriette cost me nothing, or almost nothing: cabs and bouquets from time to time. All things considered, there was no amour on my side; I believe I can affirm that.

As for Henriette...no, I shall not be conceited. She was vicious, perverse; she thought herself abandoned. She took me because I was there, without preference, hastily, by virtue of a gluttonous rage to behave badly. O mystery! Were we, then, subject solely to the attraction of our vices? Were we brought together by a mutual criminal curiosity, a common taste for treason, baseness and villainy? Had we no other goal and motive than the satisfaction of our worst instincts?

One question.

How is it, then—I ask of moralists—that our criminal, hateful union, dishonoring for the mistress and lover alike, gave us such sensualities, such profound intoxications that we could not have obtained any more troubling if it had been legitimate? If we did not love one another, if we were two cowardly and bestial creatures rushing to the lure of who known what unspeakable and ridiculous spasmodic convulsions, why did the combination of our two perversities hurl us into un unforgettable exaltation of the mind and the senses: an exaltation that we savored so infinitely, so delightfully, that it is impossible to imagine what more genuinely divine joy might be reserved for the august communion of two quivering chastities?

Oh, I congratulate myself on having thrown down that challenge to all religious morality as to all natural morality, dogmas, philosophies, theories and systems of thought! These enunciated facts permit me to affirm in total security that one is perfectly free if one wishes, and finds pleasure therein, to argue about the ideal, but one can only rely with certainty on the material.

Perhaps I will come back to this, for the problem is immense; it is as interesting as the sum of consideration due to God. (I shall explain the importance of that word in due course.) For the moment, I do not want to venture into it further; that would lack logic, since I cannot find any response therein to the question posed: Did Henriette and I love one another amorously?

Once again, I doubt it.

What is certain is that, since our separation, she has not taken another lover.

Poor woman! She must lack energy, then, even in curiosity. The rule is that a woman takes a first lover to see, and the others to look. Henriette must have thought that she ought to limit herself to her one excursion. However, I have not, so far as I know, sensibly enlarged the gray horizons within which her banal nature moves...

II

You might suppose that I yielded to the vainglory of deceiving a superior man.

What do you take me for?

A consideration of that sort might, in truth, tempt a vulgar mind; I was not preoccupied with it at all. Félicien could have been anyone at all and I would have betrayed in the same way.

To imagine that the greater number of deceived husbands are imbeciles, idiots and cretins is the greatest error. The words imbecile, idiot and cretin are much abused. That is a mistake; men more stupid than others are exceedingly rare. Then again, it is necessary not to lose sight of the fact that the cleverness of husbands constantly runs into the cleverness of wives, which is much more redoubtable. All in all, husbands are not, and never will be in accord on the very nature of the facts that engage the responsibility of the latter, while they justify the severity, or at least the anxiety, of the former.

I shall explain.

For several thousand years, man, always on the alert, always active, has created, invented, constructed, imagined, built, planned, raised and perfected a host of things, some of which merit praise. Woman, indolent, ecstatic, too frail to construct and too nervous to invent, has given herself the task of perfecting her virtue. That work of perfection is probably not yet complete at present.

Let us suppose that, in the beginning, the virtue of women could be represented by a rather vast circle, capable of containing an honest number of duties. Women initially pulled a face, but, as ancient legislation opposed an effective severity to them that is not to be feared in modern legal codes, they were patient, gnawing their bit, and waited for the advent of a more liberal state of affairs, more favorable to the spirit of reform. When that moment, for which several generations had looked forward, arrived, they did not waste and time. That was, if I am not mistaken, as insofar as one can assign a date to that great historic event, in the first half of the eighteenth century. Women then examined the circle in question, judged it too large, and with a common accord, without a single voice rising up among them to propose an amendment—Jeanne d'Arc had taken her secret to the tomb—they decreed its shrinkage.

The great circle became, in consequence, a circle of mediocre dimension, which, naturally, did not contain as many duties as its predecessor. That was already quite audacious for the epoch. Men, our ancestors, would gladly have shown themselves reactionary at that point, but women assured them so tenderly that the diminution in question would not be followed by any other, that they would hold it there, that if they neglected the duties now placed outside the circle they were not fail in any of those contained within it, and were, in sum, so persuasive, that the measure passed.

We know to what fatal consequences the regime of concessions can lead. That one cost the strong sex dear. Women, having got the taste, let a few decades go by and returned to the assault. A second time, the circle was narrowed, and then a third, and then a fourth, the number of duties imposed on the weaker sex diminishing with the circumference—with the result that today, that famous circle, continually shrunk, is no more than a dot, and can no longer contain more than one single, lone duty. Of course, having arrived at that point, women have declared that therein lies their virtue, and that nothing henceforth can lead them to let go of it.

For a long time, men have tried to react, to return the circle to its original volume, but they are not the stronger. In any case, can one turn back the tide of progress?

The result of the perfections brought by the feminine species to the dimensions of their virtue, that in our day a woman only thinks herself culpable when she fails in the sole remaining duty. For her, adultery has no commencements. The preliminaries of a criminal liaison—exchanged glances, furtive embraces, *billets doux*, mysterious rendezvous, al the precursory incidents that a husband night easily perceive since they generally happen under his nose—escape his jurisdiction. He would be ill-advised to take any anxiety therefrom, or to seek any motive for recrimination and reproach. The wife will always reply to him, in all good faith, that all of that is perfectly innocent, and that she has not failed in her duties. Out of habit and tradition she will have conserved the plural. Now, when the fatal day comes on which she will fail in all her duties, nothing will modify her attitude, and the finesse of the husband will already have been put to sleep by the monotony of the aforementioned precursory incidents "in which, I swear to you, my love, that there is nothing that is not perfectly innocent."

After our sin, Henriette had no need to have recourse to any ruse. Félicien never interrogated her, never suspected her going out, was never anxious about her frequent absences. My mistress was probably further enraged by that. Our liaison gradually slid into our habits and took on the insipid tedium, the sickening regularity, of a marriage. That consideration is perhaps sufficient to explain its duration.

We could see one another every day at times deftly selected in order not to inconvenience either of us. Félicien lived in a superb apartment near the Église de la Madeleine; I had a small house built at the extremity of the Avenue de Villiers, where superb habitations begin to replace the solitudes of the Plaine Monceau. Every day after lunch, Henriette boarded in a respectable fashion the tram that stopped at the bottom of the Boulevard Malesherbes, and came to spend a few hours with me. She occupied my idle existence and populated my house, taking an interest in its furniture and decoration. In the evening, three times a week, I had tea at Félicien's house. At other times we met at the theater, in her box, by fortunate coincidence.

There was talk in society about our affair, but with indulgence. Society is governed by regulations very similar to those of the Church, which is tolerant of sinners and only excommunicates heretics. What is shameful in irregular liaisons is not so much vice as scandal. Conventional, correct vices, neatly gloved and guaranteed by shares quoted on the Bourse, do not displease it. Henriette, like myself, made it a rule never to offend anyone's sentiment of propriety. I render her the justice that, in the critical circumstances we have traversed, she was always perfect in that regard.

Henriette had been my mistress for a year when God took the trouble to bless our criminal amours. After a painful pregnancy, followed by a difficult labor, she gave birth to a child of the female sex, who was registered at the Mairie under the names Henriette Camille Pauline. It was very emotional for Félicien; naturally, he appointed me as the little girl's godfather, had a superb baptism celebrated, and had a resurgence of affection for his wife, but in such a fashion as to let it be understood that the affection was primarily compounded of gratitude and a kind of tender compassion for the tribulations of childbirth, I generously offered the requisite gifts, unsparingly. The bill for boxes of chocolates rose to six hundred francs.

Henriette did not share her husband's delight. Maternity had been an abrupt disruption of her habits and the regularity of her culpable life. She was desolate from the first day and was never entirely consoled. One dread preoccupied her above all, which was that her graces would be further diminished, perhaps completely ruined; that her figure would remain thickened and deformed. She got up again pale, fatigued and dead-faced, and it was quite a long time before she took the tram to the Boulevard Malesherbes again. But as soon as her

23

strength returned, she fell back into the monotony of our adultery without anything subsisting in her of the supreme crisis from which she had emerged. That proof, which even transfigures young women and puts something celestial into the souls of the worst, had no purchase on that disquieting creature. She made no more mention of the child than if she had remained sterile, gave no evidence of interest in her, and only visited the nurse as much as she felt constrained to do by the rules of convention.

She was a very correct little woman.

Félicien was happy now. Of the child that he believed to be his daughter by blood, he counted on making a daughter in spirit. He attached himself to the frail little creature with the love that he would so gladly have devoted to Henriette had she been capable of meriting it, or even comprehending it. He adored the child, was incessantly occupied with her, dreaming of fortune and happiness for her.

Internally, I was amused by that error of a great character. Let anyone come to me after that to talk to me about the voice of the blood, a father's instinct, and everything that poets invent to deify the humblest and most bestial of human functions. Pitiful, utterly pitiful, all that! The child was mine, I had no doubt of that, and yet, my certainty was not mingled with any emotion. Perhaps that was because it was not permissible for me to let any be seen. To show affection for Félicien's child would have been a deplorable lack of tact, a scandalous failure of good taste. Now, emotion is worthless in itself, but only in terms of its expression. In any case, as I have already had occasion to say, I am not very impressionable. I consider that egotism is a natural and social law. Sensibility is a currency that has no value in society; to spend it is to ruin oneself without enriching anyone.

I became accustomed to thinking that nothing would happen to disturb that shameful but comfortable existence. Henriette and I had a right to expect a long security and, in case with lost our appetite for one another, an eternal impunity.

How could we foresee that a futile, absurd and rival circumstance would determine our doom?

If things have turned out badly, it is not my fault. At the very most, I have to reproach myself for having abstained, for once in my life, from reading the evening newspapers—but the emotions of the day render that neglect forgivable, or at least explain it.

You can judge for yourselves.

III

That morning, the *Journal Officiel* published a presidential decree, in the terms of which Félicien was raised to the rank of grand-officier in the national order of the Légion d'honneur, by exceptional entitlement; order of the day 15 August 1878.[2]

It was a day of celebration for us, even though we were fully prepared for the event. The newspapers had been announcing it or weeks, and Félicien had been notified officially by one of his colleagues in the Académie Française, who was a minister at the time and President of the Council. For a long time, in any case, that high recompense had been due to our friend, who would have obtained it sooner if he had not been accused of coldness toward the new regime.

Félicien greeted his promotion with a feigned indifference. He constantly affected disdain for human vanities, but I had always suspected him of not being indifferent to them. On the evening of that happy day, I dined at his home in intimate company, with Henriette and Félicien's secretary.

The secretary obtained permission to leave before dessert. Immediately, I advised my friend to go to the Palais de

---

[2] The original text has 1868, but abundant subsequent detail demonstrates that the date intended must be 1878, when Maréchal Patrice de MacMahon was Président du Conseil (General Jean-Louis Borel, presumably the general mentioned below, had previously been his aide-de-camp).

l'Élysée in order to offer his thanks, according to custom, to the Maréchal. I added that there was a ball that evening at the presidency, and that, in consequence, the step would be entirely natural. He hesitated on the pretext of fatigue, the need for rest and the desire not to go out, but I insisted so much that he made the decision.

He put on his coat and hat and left. I remained alone with Henriette. But I had not read the evening papers, and all our troubles stemmed from that.

That same morning, one of the daughters of Her Majesty Queen Victoria had been removed from the affection of the English people after a brief and painful illness.[3] Immediately, in London and all the other cities of the three kingdoms, all the shops had closed. England was in mourning. And, by virtue of an absurd custom, the governments of the two worlds, as soon as they were informed by telegraph, had hastened to renounce all earthly joys. In consequence, the ball offered that evening to the elite of Parisian society by the President of the Republic was postponed, as etiquette required.

At the Élysée, Félicien was received by an orderly officer of General Borel, who explained to him that his promotion in the Légion d'honneur had not prevented the young English princess from dying, and that in that circumstance, the Maréchal-Président had been able to postpone for a week the *cavaliers seuls* and polkas already ordered from Desgranges and his orchestra. He offered his congratulations to the new dignitary and escorted him with enthusiastic salutations to the threshold of the Aides-de-Camp's hall. Félicien, annoyed by his futile journey, hastened to go home.

At that moment, I was just yielding to the unfortunate coquetries of my accomplice. Were we not counting on at least two good hours of solitude? When we perceived Félicien's return, it was too late; we heard him traverse the dining room,

---

[3] None of Queen Victoria's daughters died in 1868 but Princess Alice did die in 1878, although in December rather than August.

and then the drawing room. The door opened and he appeared on the threshold, surprised and utterly amazed.

My position was as perilous as it was ridiculous. Félicien had all the advantages. For a start, he was correctly dressed, in a dinner jacket and white cravat, with his new medal on the right, partly hidden by the lapel, two others round his neck, a cross in his buttonhole, and white gloves. I was in my chemise, sitting on the edge of the bed, with my naked legs dangling, getting ready to dress myself again.

A ridiculous, ridiculous situation.

I confess that I was afraid.

Félicien's face had just been invaded by a mortal pallor. Nothing in him stirred. He stood there staring, frozen, haggard, stupidly holding a lighted candle in a tray, at which I would probably have laughed but for the solemnity of the occasion. He covered us with a terrible gaze, his eyes dilated by the amazement and anger directed at me and my accomplice, who had made the decision to faint. That did not last long—a second or a century. I waited, motionless and indecisive, but telling myself that, after all, the situation could not last forever.

With his left hand, Félicien seized a chair that was set against the wall near the door. For sure, that chair was about to become a redoubtable weapon; he would raise it over my head, would march toward me and split my skull with a single blow.

But no. Félicien let himself fall into that chair and dissolved in tears. I can still see him, weeping, with his candle-tray in his hand.

It was not a moment to waste time. Rapidly, without ceasing to watch Félicien, none of whose movements escaped me, I put on my clothes one by one, and I went home. Never, perhaps, had I dressed so quickly. After a few seconds, I found myself in the middle of the bedroom, my hat on my head and my cane in hand.

The other was still sobbing.

A ridiculous, ridiculous situation.

Perilous too.

To get out it was necessary for me to pass close—very close—to Félicien, so close that it might be impossible or my overcoat not to brush his knee. I did not hesitate, even thought I was convinced that this time, he was about to hurl himself upon me, try to strangle me, and start a fight, a savage fight with punches, kicks and bites, a battle of coachmen or cut-throats.

I went by, not without bowing correctly, because, in the worst circumstances, I remain a man of the world. He did not budge. I traversed the drawing room, the dining room and the antechamber. There I paused momentarily, my hand on the knob of the exit door. Félicien was still weeping, and through the doors that I had left open behind me, I could still see the light of his candle. Why did I stop in the antechamber? Why did I pause? What was I waiting for? I have never been able to explain it to myself. Finally, I understood the utter futility of my presence. I opened the last door, which I was very careful to close behind me, and found myself on the staircase.

A minute later I was striding rapidly along the Boulevard Malesherbes. The last tram had just gone, and there were no cabs.

It was an evening of annoyances.

My first impression was entirely one of relief. I was de-lighted—delighted—to have got out of the pickle without a punch being thrown. It was only then that I thought about Henriette. In what situation was she about to find herself? What perils would she have to confront? What difficulties would she have to overcome?

To think that if I had, as usual, cast an eye, even distract-edly, over the *National*, the *France* and the *Temps*, none of that would have happened! For the evening papers, as I was able to assure myself on returning home, announced, along with the death of the English princess, the postponement of the ball to be held at his Palais by the Maréchal-Président.

A fatal omission! It had required the joyful emotion caused by my friend's new success to occasion that neglect, in me, the most orderly and most routine-bound man in the world!

What would become of Henriette? Félicien had not seemed disposed to slake a homicidal rage on her—or perhaps it was waiting for my departure to burst forth. No, my ears were still full of the echo of his distant sobs, stupid moans and infantile, idiotic tears.

It was all right—not very reckless, friend Félicien. Another would have been upset, seen red, spoke of killing everyone, roused the whole household. All the same I could count on receiving a challenge the following day, to the necessary duel, with a puerile cause that would not fool anyone; a serious duel for an apparently futile pretext. Although denuded of scandal, the adventure had to be concluded. Félicien would not dare leave things as they were, swallowing the insult, under penalty of passing in my eyes or the least of good-for-nothings.

I went home on foot, lost in a world of unpleasant reflections. Fundamentally, I would have preferred it if all that had not happened.

To be caught like that—how stupid!

What a lesson for the future!

It was the first time that I had yielded imprudently. Ordinarily, I remained on my guard, in spite of Henriette's provocations, always audacious to the point of folly. Women are all the same, fear never holds them back. Henriette often displayed frightening temerity, squeezing my hand under the table, seeking my lips rapidly between two doors, one step away from a drawing room full of visitors. When I made observations she was scandalized by the cowardice of men and protested the bravery of women; there was no means of making her listen to reason. In the end, I always gave in, abruptly pushed beyond my prudence by a self-esteem that was, in my eyes chivalrous.

An accursed point of honor that had caused me to weaken again that evening! Henriette, all of whose resources of coquetry I thought I knew, had surprised me with unexpected seductions. With what end, and for what reason? She had spent two hours in my home, and I thought we had nothing more to say. In exhorting Félicien to go to the ball at the Élysée I had been acting in good faith I had give him excellent advice, perfectly innocently, with a perfectly disinterested intention. I had not had the slightest hidden motive—word of honor! To what pernicious and fatal desire had Henriette yielded, then? I cannot say it in complete certainty, but I think she was, in fact, impatient to deceive a grand-officier of the Légion d'honneur. That explanation might seem absurd and ludicrous to many practical men; for me it is one more reason to admit it as unique and veritable.

Poor Félicien! I would have given a great deal for that adventure to have crushed another of my friends, one of those that I encountered with indifference and at intervals. Apart from the fact that I shared his chagrin to a considerable degree, I had not lost sight of the fact that the incident, unfortunate in every respect, was about to upset my existence completely. Where would I go now to smoke my pipe in the evening and drink a cup of tea?

As I had passed the exterior boulevard and found myself between the houses of the painter Édouard Detaille and that of Mademoiselle Louise Valtesse, an even darker idea occurred to me.[4]

Certainly, I could count on a duel with Félicien, but, on careful reflection, another danger threatened me against which I would remain completely disarmed. Henriette might come to find me, expelled, ashamed, without a trunk and without a sou, and propose that I run away with her, to depart for Italy, Egypt or America, for some country glimpsed in her bourgeois dreams. What could I do in that case? To respond with a refusal would be unworthy of a gallant man. To comply would

---

[4] The references are to the painter Édouard Detaille (1848-1912), who made his name during the Franco-Prussian War, and the courtesan Comtesse Valtesse de la Bigne (Émilie-Louise Delabigne (1848-1910).

become a whole new matter, an exile, a change of residence. And I calculated in thought the turmoil, the fatigues and the sense of a life, errant at first, continually complicated by the dread of an encounter, the need to hide, to go from city to city, hotel to hotel, finally to run aground in some remote little commune, a hole, sheltered from tourist excursions and far enough away from a railway line!

I had, however, organized my life sanely, rid myself of unnecessary friendships, cumbersome mistresses and grave occupations. A fine advance if, nearing forty, I had to find myself torn away from my habits and seeing myself with a woman on my arm!

A limpet, no more and more less! The expression is harsh, but I could not put it any better.

Scarcely had that thought come into my mind than it pitilessly expelled all the others. The Henriette question, which, at the beginning of the crisis had appeared to me to be a negligible quantity, became the important question, the capital question. All the rest—Félicien, the evenings scene, my troubled life, the obligation of finding another household for an evening cup of tea—appeared secondary. The wife frightened me much more than the husband, and I would have liked to be able to quit Paris in all haste, by the first morning train, in order to escape—even by a dubious means—the emotional visit that Henriette was doubtless preparing for the stroke of nine o'clock.

But there was nothing to be done about it. I resigned myself to it. In any case, let it be said without vanity, I have never declined any responsibility. The wine was uncorked, it was necessary to drink it. So much the worse for me.

Very preoccupied, I was late going to sleep. It was nearly three o'clock in the morning by the time I felt slumber overtaking me.

My valet came to wake me up at ten, as usual. On awakening, my appreciation of the previous evening's events remained fundamentally the same. In form, I found it colder and more rational. Perhaps Félicien had reflected for his part, and he would not send seconds to me, for fear of scandal and the malignity of society. After all, he could not act like just any husband, having a situation to maintain. He would doubtless decide not to broadcast his disaster. In any case, that remained to be seen.

As for Henriette, perhaps she would have the idea of going back to her family. In hours of affliction, what safer refuge is there than a mother's bosom? What environment is more favorable to repentance than the paternal hearth? In any case, if she did not comprehend the necessity of that course of action her own accord, my duty as an honest man required me to enlighten her, to indicated to her the path to follow. Was it appropriate that I should take advantage of her distress to doom her to my own profit? Could I abuse the circumstances to accept the sacrifice of her reputation, of her entire life?

No, I could not. No, I must not.

It is the prerogative of timorous spirits, of weak consciences, to yield to the first approach of attraction, to abandon oneself to temptation. Serious characters resist to begin with, regain possession of their individual resources, and then measure, calculate, weigh the pros and cons, examine the good and bad side of things. If Henriette abandoned herself, I would retain her on the edge of the precipice and show her its depth. It would not need lengthy argument to make her understand that, all things considered, our adventure was banal, ordinary, and did not justify any extreme measures.

Was a broken household a great novelty, was a ruined hearth very original? Were we the first people in that situation? No, certainly not. Separated women are longer scarce, and all of them find, when a few weeks have gone by—the interval of the heart's mourning—a center of relations, indulgent salons, faithful friends, and even a respect of good enough quality. As for tested husbands, no one keeps count of them any longer; the statistics would make one go pale.

Of course! Nothing was lost if the mater were taken seriously, if one did not lose one's head. Decidedly, whether the duel with Félicien took place or not, Henriette would get out of the affair in accordance with reason, in accordance with wisdom.

And I finally arrived at the realization that, of the three interested parties, I was the only one seriously injured, the only one irrevocably deprived of something, the only one profoundly afflicted. In fact, not only could I not return to Félicien's house, but it would be necessary for me to take care to avoid him, to cease to frequent certain salons where he might appear—a stupid obligation, in truth, since it was not me that the events rendered ridiculous.

All in all, it was necessary to wait and see.

At about eleven o'clock, as I was beginning to be astonished, a groom arrived—Henriette's groom—with a letter.

I had hardly cast my eyes over the paper than I dissolved in tears.

Félicien was no more.

In the course of the fatal night, about an hour after my departure, the poor fellow had succumbed to an attack of apoplexy. He had been found lying on the floor of his study, black in the face, with blood on his lips and beard.

A thunderbolt.

Henriette informed me of the great misfortune and invited me to call and see her as soon as possible.

I had the groom come up and asked him from a few minor details.

It was in the middle of the night, at about one o'clock in the morning—it must, in fact, have been one o'clock—when the domestics had been woken up by Madame's cries and the furious ringing of a bell. The cadaver was still warm. Madame had been very ill, a prolonged crisis of nerves that had only been calmed by the arrival of the physician. The whole house was in turmoil. Monsieur's brother and Madame's parents had been informed, and had arrived very quickly. What a misfortune! Such a good master!

The groom left.

I was overwhelmed by stupor.

Poor Félicien! A friend, a true one! We had quit one another so badly. To depart thus, still young, in full glory, without my being able to shake his hand one last time! What a shock! None of the dolors suffered in the past had struck me so rudely. There was no one in the world for whom I would have wept as much.

I do not know why, and cannot explain why, but I had never wept as much as I did that day.

IV

Three days later—the burial had been scheduled for midday—I got up early in order to think about the short speech that I was to make at the cemetery, in response to a general plea. The day before, all the arrangements for the funeral ceremony had been settled. The number of speeches became considerable, and it was necessary to take into account the unexpected: the arrival of delegations from provincial scientific societies of which Félicien was the honorary president, of students from the Schools, always so eager to attend the funerals of great men. My mission was limited to pronouncing a few words on behalf of the dead man's most intimate friends—fifteen or twenty lines at the most.

Not being very eloquent by nature, I took rigorous precautions—which is to say that I traced on a piece of paper the gist of my little speech, intending to engrave the terms in my memory in the course of the morning. I had reason to be satisfied with my work. It was simple, grave, moving, and not banal: a perfectly adequate funeral oration.

Oh, it was a beautiful burial. I held one of the cordons of the bier; the other five were held by a member of the Académie Française, a member of the Académie des Inscriptions et Belles-lettres, the cabinet chief of the Minister of Public Education and Fine Arts, a député from the département of the Orne, and a former pupil of the École Normale, which counted the departed among its most brilliant laureates.

34

Behind the catafalque with the great mourning veils sown with silver stars, folded under palms and crowns, came, after the masters of ceremonies bearing the dead man's decorations, veiled, on violet velvet cushions:

The family;

One of the Maréchal-Président's aides-de-camp;

The bureau of the Académie Française;

The delegations of the Institut;

The Societé des Gens de Lettres, led by Emmanuel Gonzales;[5]

The members of the Societé des Auteurs Dramatiques;

The representatives of numerous scientific societies in which Félicien had shown a protective zeal;

Artists, scientists, journalists, and an impressive cortege of admirers, disciples and faithful followers.

And we filed through the piously silent crowd, between two ranks of soldiers in dress uniform, to the strains of the band of the Republican Guard, whose silences were marked by the protracted roll of rums muffled beneath the unreal drapery.

In Paris there was a kind of meditation. Heads were bared as we passed by. Oh, France had lost one of those on whom she counted for her glory, a sublime intelligence, a great heart. The soul of the crowd seemed to be praying.

A magnificent spectacle, that will never be effaced from my sight!

At the Madeleine the mass was sung by Bosquin and Melchissedec of the Opéra, and Mesdames Mézeray and Vidal of the Opéra-Comique. Alexandre Georges played the organ.

At Père-Lachaise cemetery, the burial took place in a temporary vault offered by the city of Paris. When the bier had been taken down into the tomb, the orators, designated in turn

---

[5] The popular novelist and dramatist Emmanuel Gonzalès (1815-1887) was president of the Societé des Gens de Lettres from 1863 onwards.

by the master of ceremonies, advanced and spoke. It was lengthy, but beautiful. Finally, my turn arrived.

I took two steps forward, stopping at the edge of the tomb, and I pronounced:

"The venerated friend that we have lost, the great thinker, the..."

But it was impossible for me to finish, not because I was uncertain of my lines or became emotion took my by the throat...no, it was not that...but a memory returned to me that completely changed the course of my ideas. I forgot the ceremony, the mourning of all those assiduous hearts, the meditative crowd awaiting my words, and I no longer saw anything but the scene, the ridiculous scene of the other evening: me in my chemise, in the middle of the bedroom, Henriette fainted, my garment scattered, and him, Félicien, in formal dress, with is candle-tray in his hand, weeping like a calf. At that furtive vision, I was very close momentarily to bursting into laughter. I closed my eyes, fearing suddenly to discover Félicien sitting in the depths of his tomb, his candle-tray in his hand. Someone took my by the arm and drew me aside. I heard vague words in the crowd:

"Poor fellow..."

"The emotion, no doubt..."

"Just think, that was his best friend..."

"What a loss!"

But I pulled myself together immediately, and, while I was old away, I did not miss any of the words of the orator who had taken my place..."

"On behalf of the literary and artistic society of Alençon, I bring to this still-open tomb..."

Half an hour later I left the cemetery, pursued by reporters in quest of intimate information about Félicien. I replied to them as best I could, obligingly, glad to contribute by my revelations to the glory of the dead man. I told them about my friend's difficult, poverty-stricken early days, his courageous struggle against adversity, his family life, so simple and to touching, his wife, his only amour, and his daughter, an adorable child as beautiful as the angels. I kept quiet about a few eccentric or ridiculous manias of the deceased. In brief, I acquitted that concern marvelously.

At about five o'clock I went to pay my respects to Henriette, surrounded by her family: an inevitable visit.

Henriette put on an accomplished distinction, neither too emotional nor too glacial. She accepted my condolences with a sad smile—one of those smiles that one encounters in the illustrations in romances—and informed me of her departure the following day. She was going to spend a few weeks at her parents' home in Saumur.

An excellent idea.

I replied to her that, for my part, I intended to get away from Paris immediately, where I had been harassed for several days by so many and such dolorous memories.

That was all. She did not attempt to speak to me in private, nor ask me where I was going, nor breathe a word about a possible correspondence. It seemed that everything was finished between us, completely finished, without any word of farewell being necessary, that we were going to live henceforth as strangers to one another, even more than strangers: unknown to one another.

Thus, I simply took my leave of that insignificant creature, the mother of my daughter. I went out after having responded to the grateful embraces of the family. Just think! I had given myself so much trouble, occupying myself with all the preparations, replacing the relatives in the somber chores of those funereal days. I had screwed all the knobs personally on to the bier in which I had buried Félicien.

Well, believe me if you will, if I loved Henriette for an instant, or, to put it better, if for an instant I ardently desired her, desired her madly, desired her with anguish, desired her dolorously, it was that day, that last day, when I saw her so white, so pale, so cold in long, sinister vestments, with her dark eyes, hard and staring, dilated by insomnia, in which the fascination of an infernal flame was gleaming!

V

Where to go?

I had traveled very little, but I did not feel any instinctive taste for one country rather than another. At first I had the idea of going to lose myself in some desolate and empty country, but I renounced that immediately, for the reason that the voyage would serve no purpose if, in taking me away from my home, it did not draw me out of myself. The goal ought, therefore, to occupy all the vital forces of my mind with new objects, landscapes that would continually renew the emotion of surprise. In that regard, I had a choice, but I lacked the elements of a preference.

Fortunately, I recalled one country about which Félicien had often talked in my presence: Italy.

In his youth, on leaving the École Normale, Félicien, attached as secretary to a commission of the Ministry of Public Education sent to the environs of Naples for some sort of scientific excavations, had been so profoundly smitten with the great Latin fatherland that when his mission was concluded he had solicited and obtained authorization to prolog his voyage. For a year, he had traveled the great peninsula from north to south, marveling, delighted, and quivering with emotion.

Often, in the evening, between Henriette and me, he returned gladly to the thousand incidents of that voyage, of which he had conserved a kind of dazzlement. He told us about his interminable wanderings in Rome, his travels in Sicily, the three months he had stayed in Florence, unable to tear himself away, going through hard time' living on two lire a day, sleeping in the mansards of *trattorias* in order to stretch out his sojourn a little. And Pisa, Bologna, Ferrara, Venice and Naples!

On his return he had published is first two works: *The Soul of Rome* and *The Fathers of Florence*, superb books whose success is still universally remembered.

How many times had not Félicien said to me: "One of these days, we'll make that voyage together. You'll see!"

I decided upon Italy, and, having made all my preparations, I took care to squeeze Félicien's two books, each enriched with a fraternal dedication, into my valise.

The following day, at eight o'clock in the morning, I took the train to Marseille, with the intention of going to Italy via Ventimiglia.

How soon I congratulated myself for having left Paris. It was so intense that I was astonished not to have had the idea of traveling sooner and more often. For years I had remained confined in Paris, as if blocked in by snow or by an invincible besieging army. Throughout the time of my liaison with Henriette, I had not felt any appetite, any desire, sharper than a furtive caprice—to the point that I believe that I understand, today, that the singular charm of that woman had brought about a kind of suspension of life, an interruption of the presence of mind, a dreamlike absence in which my idle instincts languished. And I acquired the conviction that, but for the deplorable adventure, I might perhaps never have separated from Henriette, and that in the end, fortified in habitude, out criminal attachment would have become a respectable bond thanks to the years. In the early days of my voyage, I sometimes missed Henriette, especially on rainy days.

Gradually, the enchantments of the route sufficed to absorb me. I gazed and I studied ardently, with a profound, patient, obstinate interest that I had never previously brought to the objects of art and nature. One might veritably have thought that the recent crisis had developed an unhealthy nervousness in me, a hectic susceptibility to all external manifestations, a previously unsuspected faculty of sensing quickly and profoundly. It was as if I experienced new tastes, a constant anxiety of impressions, of sudden, inexplicable tremors in the presence of an idea or an object indifferent until then. To that transformation of my temperament was added a perfect clarity of mind that enabled me to conceive and express, not without eloquence, thoughts that blossomed unexpectedly within me. I became more irritable, but I also became more clear-sighted. In sum, a whole world of sensations awakened and sang, a new world more populous, if not more interesting, than the first. Is it necessary to believe that the mind is subject to transformations, like the body, which renews its atoms every seven years?

A probable hypothesis. How many men die in a man before his death!

I would have difficulty saying what pleased me most in my voyage...

Perhaps Rome.

I arrived there with an impatient curiosity, over-excited by a laborious study of Félicien's book, *The Soul of Rome*, a superhuman work with which I had impregnated my memory. Thus was verified, albeit in strange conditions, the project that Félicien and I had formed to visit Italy together. In truth, he never quit me. I heard, mentally, thoughts that would have been his personal responses to certain questions that I addressed to myself; I discovered in myself a way of seeing more fortunate and more elevated, as if the echo of his thought were resonating constantly behind my brow. I recognized, without anyone being there to name them for me, certain monuments and certain sites of which his book contained magical descriptions. I was, so to speak, seeing Italy again, and I experienced the sweet enjoyment received from people and places rediscovered after a long absence.

At certain times, that illusion carried me away to the extent that I turned around abruptly, in the certainty that Félicien was there, to my right, walking beside me as a faithful companion, whispering the most judicious reflections to me. And, which was particularly striking, I did not imagine an ordinary Félicien in a traveling costume, but I represented him as I had seen him on the supreme evening, in a dinner jacket, white cravat, white gloves, with the medal of a grand-officer on the right side, orders around his neck, and a cluster of little crosses pinned to the lapel of his coat.

The sincere amity that I had avowed to Félicien, and which I continued in my memory, presented the preoccupation of is presence becoming disagreeable to me. Far from proscribing his memory, I came back to it constantly, and began to make appeal to it. My situation as an intimate friend of the illustrious writer opened many doors to me; in the noblest salons of Roman society I was surrounded, questioned, overwhelmed with respect, and more than one evening was dedicated to the apotheosis of the dead man, me talking abundantly, full of my subject, and the entourage, attentive to my words, suspended from my lips.

It was thus for a year...I don't know exactly.

In the end, weary of my continual displacements and living in inns, I withdrew to a village in the French Alps, Sospel, the small administrative center of a canon half way along the mountain road that links Nice to Coni. I rented a small villa there on the estate of the Commande, not far from the torrent of the Bévéra. I brought my valet, my cook and some furniture from Paris, and, once installed set to work.

An idea had occurred to me on the way. Why should I not write a biography of Félicien?

In good faith, without having made any decision, I had asked which of his faithful followers might take on that pious mission, that difficult task. One by one, I had judged all those who might seem capable of such a task, and I had concluded that I alone could succeed in it.

In fact, I fulfilled absolutely all the desirable conditions for that object.

What is rarer than a good biographical work, truly complete and truly accurate? In the great majority of cases, the biographer, addressing himself directly to the man who ought to be its subject—or if the man is dead, to his descendants—receives notes that are naturally suspect of partiality or confidences that impose the double duty of discretion and gratitude. He brings such a base attachment to the service of the man he is recounting that one would willingly take him for a kind of lackey of his immortality. In other, rarer cases, the biographer is a dogged enemy, an adversary carried away by passion or led astray by jealousy. Eugène Jacquot, alias Mirecourt, published many of those biographies inspired by the most detesta-

41

ble spirit, and which can also be reproached for a frightful number of capital errors.[6] The happy medium, the true biography, does not exist, so to speak.

My situation in the past and in the present permitted me to act not only in total liberty but with complete assurance. I had been the dead man's oldest friend, his childhood friend, his schoolfellow at Bonaparte. I had known his father and mother, had lived for a long time in his intimacy, received his intimacies, witnessed his struggles, known his judgment of the people and events of his time, sounded his conscience, read his thoughts like an open book; I knew the man, the writer, the poet, the citizen, all the aspects of his personality; I possessed the elements of a powerfully interesting correspondence; a thousand anecdotes that had not appeared worthy to me of being recorded in the past came back to me as precisely as if they had been events of the day before.

I was the perfect, designated, fatal biographer.

None of the duties of the biographer could escape me. In addition to my own testimony, did I not have Henriette's? And would it not be permitted to me to make use of it? Oh, discreetly! It has often been said that no man is great to his valet; that is indisputable. For very good reason, is not the spouse more directly and more immediately informed, for one hides from a domestic?

Now, Henriette possessed one great quality: she was false, but she was not a liar. She did not always tell the whole truth, but she only told the truth. By a religion of truth? No, out of pride. Pride is a sin that prevents us from committing base actions. She brought me on a daily basis the photographic reflection of her husband, the story of little interior scenes

---

[6] Eugène de Mirecourt [Eugène Jacquot] (1812-1880) denounced Alexandre Dumas for hiring others (including himself) to write his books, and went on to publish a *Galerie de Contemporains* (1854-57), followed by a fortnightly periodical, *Les Contemporains*, the biographical articles in which provoked a blizzard of complaint and lawsuits.

provoked by his manias rather than his moods; she brought me up to date with his intimate habits, often joking as she recounted to me, on the pillow, in moments of calm, the ridiculous and puerile vexations from which the greatest minds are not exempt. In consequence, I possessed Félicien from head to toe, as no one else could have known him.

And then again, was that not a duty for me? I ought to preoccupy myself with it, having never compromised with duty. Yes it was my duty to write Félicien's biography: his life and his works. Posterity had an interest in knowing the man from whom it received the most precious information. Given that no excuse could dispense me from rendering that sincere testimony to the future, I could not escape it. To be sure, it would be a difficult, long and laborious task, a labor to which it would be necessary for me to apply all my faculties, the power of memory, the religion of the past. I needed a long time to meditate upon it before writing a line, and a long time to write after having meditated.

No matter.

On my instructions, my valet brought to Sospel all the letters that Félicien had written to me. I took pleasure in re-reading them, slowly, reading them over and over again, thinking, not without anxiety, of the honor that their publication would bring me—for protestations of amity and mages were not spared therein.

I absorbed myself in that study for several months.

Sospel is a very old own, traversed by the torrent of the Bévéra and surrounded as if by a ring of high mountains: Mont Braus, the Barbonnet, the Magiabo, the Testa di Cane, the hill of Saint-Lucia. It is a picturesque corner, but long dead. One finds oneself five hundred meters above sea level there, between olive groves—the region's only resource—and a few vines. Foreigners do not come there, passers-by are rare, the inhabitants speak a language as different from Italian as it is from French, a kind of deformed and violent patois in which traces of peasant naivety are found and the harshness that great solitudes give to the human voice as well as the song of birds and the accents of beasts. The life one can lead there is either a bestial life or a contemplative life—gazing at the soil from which one's pasture is taken, or admiring the snowy summits that haunts dreams; there is no other alternative. Be a poet or a ruminant. The local people ruminate; a few people pass through who dream; the latter the inhabitants exploit.

In a hour, if one follows the Bévéra along a mule-track, one descends into Italy between two Ligurian villages, La Piena and Olivetta, the first perched on a high crag like an eagle's nest, the second hidden in the verdure like a refuge of turtle-doves. By the main road one climbs over the Brouis pass to descend thereafter toward a succession of singular locales: Breil, with its feet in the torrent of the Roya; La Giondola, surrounded by sheer glaciers; Saorge, clinging to the flanks of the mountain over a five-hundred-foot precipice; Fontan, the Italian frontier, with its population of deserters, customs-men and smugglers.

It takes about four hours to reach the railway, which extends along beneath the coast road between Nice and Genoa. The paths are poor, which stops tourists. In winter they disappear under three feet of snow, which even stops the postal service.

I stayed there…for how long?

I no longer recall, exactly.

What is certain is that I arrived in the first days of November and was only comfortably settled at the end of January.

My first weeks were devoted to walking. Every day, after lunch, I climbed to the summit of Saint-Lucia where the ruined wall of an ancient Saracen fortress still existed. Sitting in the grass, my back turned to the sun, I traced the first notes of my labor, devoting myself to arranging them in an orderly manner, for more often than not, the memories flooded my brain in a tumult of stormy inspiration. The facts presented themselves in a host, with the chaos and complicated movement of crowds. There was a struggle between my memory, sensitized by the work, and my violently activated energy.

I organized, I organized...

One curious thing is that on returning from those walks I experienced a hindrance, a heaviness in all my limbs, an overwhelming cerebral fatigue, the absorption of all my vital force by the unique preoccupation of my work. The portrait of Félicien, hung in my improvised study, appeared to me to fill the entire room and to make the objects by which it was surrounded pale. My excessively persistent application to rereading the dead man's correspondence led to sentences already formed coming to my lips as soon as I opened my mouth and I pronounced those sentences involuntarily, with no motive, in the solitude. My mind was evidently extended toward the various aspects of the same image, a single idea, and had grown accustomed to that premeditated tension. There is a gymnastics of the brain just as there is a gymnastics of the muscles. The mind gladly bends to the discipline that it had imagined itself. It is simply a matter of will. I wanted to think about Félicien, I thought about Félicien. If I had not wanted to think about Félicien, I would soon have forgotten.

There is no doubt about that.

The proof is that, Henriette having no part, even minimal, in my work, was only recalled to my memory feebly and at distant intervals. I evoked her apathetically, without regret and without desire, as I might have evoked a vague camaraderie. No news of her had reached me since my departure from Paris, and I was neither afflicted nor offended by that obstinate silence.

Definitely, in that direction, everything was completely finished. The time elapsed had even weakened the precision of her memory. I only saw her any longer floating indecisively, without personal form, without proper color, without intimate character, pell-mell with the other women that I had possessed.

It is necessary to arrive at a certain age in order to know how easily the past evaporates. A day comes when a man summarizes his dead impressions by means of a cipher of heart-breaking humility; and, as in exhumations, he can pack

all of his memories—amours, amities, ambitions and miseries—into a very tiny coffin.

To forget! That must be good! I had beneficent evenings
at Sospel. It was at the confused hour when the sun, near to
disappearing behind the eternal snows of Turini, allows the
red gold of its last light to fall into the valley, while in the distance, beyond the Alpine rocks, the quiver of if lunar rays rise.
What peace! What serenity! What soft cradling of the hour!

Light azure vapors rose up from the torrent toward the
frail olive-trees on the hills. The transparency of the air was
iridescent with charming demi-tints, delicate shades of an exquisite tenderness. They closed over the haste of flocks and lit
up with the glow of fires.

I contemplated on the terrace on my villa. Everything fell
silent. The night soon opened the richness of its blue jewel-
cases over nature. It seemed that I could see the stars weeping,
so delightfully pale at that moment. Spasmodically, the cry of
a hawk traversed the sonorous tranquility of the evening like a
lugubrious plaint. It was almost death—which is to say, the
most complete and the most sincere impression of nature; for
what the attraction of the countryside does is to make one feel
that one in dying a little there.

On those evenings, sleep overcame me more rapidly.
Sleep, death: two terms that are linked, the second of which
completes the first. Sleeping often consoles living. If people
did not sleep, a temporary death, and absolute suspension of
dolors and chagrins, perhaps they would not have the patience
to wait until death!

VI

I had not yet written a single line of my book when, abruptly, I abandoned the project of writing it.

Why?

It was because my initial enthusiasm had become my
perpetual fatigue. I had had enough of it, and I interrogated
myself seriously regarding my state of mind.

Furthermore, I was falling ill. Doubtless the fatigue. Irresistible insomnias left me exhausted and aching in the morning. I experienced continual headaches that baffled the expertise of the modest physician of Sospel and caused me to suffer cruelly. None of the known remedies serve to relieve me. In order to achieve a few hours of respite, I had no other means than undertaking long excursions on foot, in all weathers, on all routes, until, exhausted by fatigue, I had killed within me even the strength to feel. And there were interminable walks every day, furious climbs from which I returned famished and unsteady on my feet, to let myself fall into bed after having gluttonously devoured a little poor village food.

Of the biography of Félicien there was no further question, but I did not forget the husband of my mistress for that. I thought about him a great deal, often; I reread his books and his letters; I learned with satisfaction of the success of a subscription opened in Paris with a view to building a monumental tomb for him in the cemetery of Père-Lachaise.

Do not suppose, at least, that the memory of Félicien had anything to do with my suffering; you would be in error. My suffering was purely physical, you understand: purely physical. My intellectual faculties exerted themselves easily, even better, with more application, than in the past.

And it was not so much a malady as a cure. Nature is submissive to rules, notably a need for equilibrium. A long inaction in Paris had favored the beginnings of a plumpness that could have led, as it developed, to all the inconveniences of obesity. I walked, I took exercise, for hygienic reasons, to combat the unhealthy principles resulting from the detestable atmosphere of a big city. That gave rise to my fatigues; but my mentality, I repeat, was not attained.

I was master of myself.

In the contrary case, if I were, for example, experiencing suffering caused by a mental illness, it would have been caused by...what?

Depression?

Chagrin?

No.

Remorse?

Ah! There we have it. Remorse! Everyone's first impulse would be to suppose that I was remorseful. It's a mania.

But, I ask you, with regard to what would I have had remorse?

I'm not a saint, it's necessary to admit. I know my qualities and am not unaware of my faults. I have committed a great crime, a treason, a cowardice—whatever you wish—but I affirm that I know no remorse, that I have never experienced remorse, and that it is impossible for me to experience it. There are absolute reasons for that, reasons of the highest order.

I shall enumerate them.

Man has the superiority of the animals and over woman of being a reasonable and prudent creature. He has devoted innumerable hours to decreeing measures of self-preservation, of limiting his actions, of building dykes in the open domain of his appetites—which appetites claim to be natural and seem, at first, to be law. Those appetites are not only revealed in themselves—which is to say, by the desire that man has to satisfy them; they are complicated by the sentiment of preference that modifies them and often denatures them at the whim of singular influences that we may call, if you wish, and for want of a better word, psychological.

Preference is redoubtable. If man never had preference, he would be perfect. His ambitions would be moderate, his desires would be reasonable, his tastes would be sensate, and even his follies would have a frontier: facile resignation or indolent indifference. The secret of all virtue is therein; and the powerful minds of the day, poring over the study of public welfare, inventors of theories and elaborators of laws, would sagely not seek elsewhere the unknown of social reforms whose belated realization torments peoples.

Can they do anything? No. The harm is done; man has preference. He has eaten the fruit of the tree of the knowledge of good and evil; he discerns, he compares, he chooses, without perceiving that he is thus becoming his own enemy, and that, from each of his settled choices, a torture emerges, or the seed of a new weakness, a virgin appetite. For between man and his desire there is always disproportion.

It is from preference—in the state of appetite in some, passion in many others—that scrupulous concerns are born in man and the attraction of evil. Civilization has tried to extend a regimentation over the ensemble of those various contradictory forces, whose elements, initially scattered in the depths of conscience, have subsequently been gradually combined, in the form of laws and the unity of codes.

In that regard, there has never been absolute accord or universal agreement. It is sufficient to cast a glance over the different legislations that govern the world to observe the alarm of human judgment. Here, the law is inspired by the broad lines of a religion, the Gospel, for example, and is applied in the most extensive interpretation of the divine word. Elsewhere, it takes its source and its prestige from the caprices of an autocrat, and, in spite of any brake, as of any logic, imposes an absolute domination all the more stupidly observed and sensed as it is weighed more stupidly and more ferociously. Elsewhere, again. it responds to certain particular conditions of climate and geographical position; it arises from politics and hygiene. Elsewhere, finally, it seems to be the unworthy heritage of legend and draws its strength from fable. Sometimes it is just, too often it is merely strong. It is important not to forget that it was always dictated by masters.

In the meantime—this is my point—it is diverse.

Here, in Europe, the family is a sacred institution. Among the Pucchana, a tribe in the Oceanic isles, it is normal for a son to kill his aged parents on the day when they become incapable of supplying their own needs by hunting and fishing.

Among us, marriage is indissoluble, we are monogamous; polygamy is the law in Turkey, and the Mohammedan husbands expels like a slave whichever is his wives has ceased to please him.

A Parisian husband whose conjugal harmony has been troubled by some scandalous adventure becomes an object of ridicule or pity; on the banks of the Red River, the mortal fortunate enough to have someone steal his wife becomes an object of envy, jealousy and admiration.

One considers as infamous the European capable of delivering his wife to someone else; in Persia, the traveler sufficiently ill-inspired to reject the adulterous offers of is host runs the risk of seeing his nose and ears cut off.

Theft was punished in Rome, recompensed in Sparta.

In brief, at all times, the human mind has been groping. It is impossible for it really to elevate itself, to attain the great and splendid verities before which the totality of the species would kneel. It has made laws, but has not discovered the Law. Hence an illusion with which the generations flatter themselves one after another. People believe, benevolently, in progress, in conquests. Alas, in all times things have been as bad, they only appear a little better to the pride of the living, and that consoles them.

National self-esteem apart, I proclaim that the most equitable of these bad laws is French law. I find the proof of that in the constant testimony of Europe; we are followed, we are imitated. The few ameliorations of which foreigners can boast have passed via our codes, have originated as verities among us, and if we have become poorer, it is necessary to blame for that the extreme mobility of our political institutions. We have been chosen as the model, rightly or wrongly. Legislations that are respected depart from the Napoleonic code or come back to it. That is not an appreciation, it is a fact.

Well, I am a faithful observer of French law.

It is truly admirable that men have, since the earliest times, sought a rule outside or beyond the proclaimed law. Why is that? With what end? For what motive? Is it by virtue of a perversity of their nature or a consequence of the instinct of revolt by which every thinking being is afflicted? In that score there are philosophies as various and contradictory as laws, progressive and reactionary moral theories, systems and coteries. From that mass of formulae human genius has been unable to draw anything indisputable. We are still in chaos, and that chaos no longer counts its victims. Man only has what he deserves. It befits him. With a little reason, by the renunciation of that sentiment of preference, the source of all his torments, he might arrive, if not at juridical unity—which would imply the impossible reign of universal fraternity—at least a kind of harmony between legislations. It would have been sufficient, for that, to kill within him the pretension of persona superiority, to submit, to recognize honestly, in the age of reason, accomplished facts, and to abandon his conscience only to judgments that obtain a consecration.

It is necessary to be stupid to torture oneself deliberately, when everything is in accord for your tranquility. They are evidently sick, men who are feeble enough to impose an imaginary tribunal upon themselves as fictitious punishments. Is life not difficult enough? Are its effective penalties not heavy enough for those exposed to them by ill-fortune? Is it not proof of madness, that insistence on questioning oneself, on striking oneself with one's own hand?

You might say to me: the conscience!

I do not contradict that. Conscience is not a vain word. I have a conscience, you have a conscience, we all have a conscience. Only animals have not.

The conscience! That is a very positive term; it offers nothing vague, it comprises a series of obligations, duties and responsibilities. It is one of the most beautiful words in the human language.

But it is also necessary to understand it.

Where does the conscience take you?

What is its essence?

Or, to put it better, what are its laws?

Your conscience might perhaps differ from mine; you might then be mistaken. If you do not retain as the basis for all your judgments a certain rule, invariable at least immediately before and immediately after your judgment, you expose yourself to the risk of continual errors, you cannot reach anything absolute.

There is the conscience of Christians, the conscience of Muslims, the conscience of Mormons, the conscience of the anthropophagous warriors off Bouloupari. There is the morality that a man creates himself, that he draws from his reflections, from his experience; and there is the conscience collected from the lessons of childhood, received ready-made, which belongs to the scholarly baggage of every duly certified graduate. There is the conscience of men and the conscience of women, very dissimilar, the man pronouncing most often according to his interest and the woman according to her passion. There is the implacable conscience and that open to attenuating circumstances. What was Robespierre? A conscience, but terrible. What was Vincent de Paul? A conscience, but charitable. Should a sculptor represent conscience as impassive, austere, with an arm lifted to punish, or gentle, smiling, a hand extended in a gesture of forgiveness?

What diverse images? How subject to error!

In these conditions, every man concerned for his repose—repose is the sole wellbeing worthy of purchase—ought to subordinate his conscience to the realities of the law. Thus, all peril is avoided in advance; one is no longer deceived, one marches through life with certainty, with a firm footing, supported by a savant conscience that has foreseen everything and punishes everything.

That conscience does not only say to you: "Theft is a crime, murder is a crime, adultery is a crime, forgery is a crime," it goes further, it adds: "If you steal, you will be punished by these penalties, if you kill, take someone else's wife or become a forger, by some other penalty."

Nothing unexpected, no groping. The responsibilities are defined and measured. Justice, sheltered from the caprices engendered by differences in temperament and the mobility of impressions, had weighed every sin in advance by assigning it its ranking in the scale of punishments. Let us also note that, in that case, the judgments of conscience are not lost, that the events ensure that they are consecrated. If some individual merits the loss of his liberty, he is imprisoned for a lapse of time calculated according to the gravity of his sin. If he merits death, the public conscience—one says "the public conscience" precisely because it is the conscience of everyone—receives immediate satisfaction. In any case, it will not allow the culpable to escape voluntarily. In that regard, it is superior to relative consciences, inspired by churches or philosophies, which permit scoundrels to die In peace, with respects inclined around their death-bed—which constitutes a dangerous example as well as a scandalous spectacle.

That said, I admit—in any case, I have never denied it—having violated the law in committing the misdemeanor of adultery, which is only a misdemeanor, in complicity with Henriette.

No one knows it, but my conscience reproaches me for it, and I listen attentively to that interior voice.

I am culpable, and I know in what measure. I judge myself severely. Why? Because it is necessary, because I am human.

Let us examine the case.

I transgressed the law in committing adultery, evidently. I ought to reproach myself for that, but I can only veritably reproach myself for that. The accessory circumstances remain accessory; only the fact is worth examining.

Félicien is dead; that is unfortunate; but nothing demonstrates a link between that death and my sin. A physician was summoned who explained the death by a devastating attack of apoplexy. That is the truth, the only truth.

There would be no shortage of people capable of imagining, and others of wondering, for example, whether a brutal surprise, a chagrin too violent for human strength, might have led in Félicien to a mortal congestion. Let us seek, compare, and, in sum, take account! Not a day passes when a husband does not catch his wife in the act of adultery—I am only talking about those who are not ashamed to have the fact noted by the police. How many of those tested husbands have died at

53

the spectacle of their misfortune? None. Not a single one can be cited. But those, the objection might he raised, might have been able to prepare themselves for the irritating apparition; they has suspected, spied, discovered. So be it; let us take the others. Let us take the classic husband, the one who has missed the evening train or returns from a journey without giving prior notice. Does he die? No. Never. If he has a weapon, he kills; if he does not, he screams. But not a single one has ever been encountered who dropped dead.

Félicien suffered from a predisposition to apoplexy. He had a short neck, a face that often went red. The habit of remaining seated for several hours a day at his desk had rendered him stout and sanguine. He had to end as he did. Sooner or later. one cannot escape the fatalities of one's temperament. I can therefore speak freely about that death, because it does not weigh on my conscience. No one can ever prove, even after reading this honest confession, that the terrible scene of that evening had anything to do with that tragic end.

If, by some temerity of the upholders of the law, I had to answer in court for Félicien's decease, there would be only one voice among the jurors and the members of the court to acquit me of any accusation. There was no poisoning, no murder, no violence, but merely a phenomenon familiar to physicians. At the moment when he succumbed, Félicien was alone in his stuffy, after a rather agitated day. It is necessary not to forget that he had just been appointed a grand-officer of the Légion d'honneur, that he had dined well, perhaps drunk a little more than usual; add that on leaving his apartment he had walked through the streets on a rather cold evening. No more than that is necessary to bring about a revolution in the organism, especially when digestion is incomplete.

Any physician will tell you that.

There remains the fact of adultery.

Oh, that I don't deny.

But what is the penalty for adultery? Three months in prison, neither more nor less. I merited three months in prison.

And I should forge chimeras for myself, create terrors, harass my thoughts, shiver, sweat with fear, for a hundred wretched days of imprisonment?

What! I should hurl myself full tilt into crazy ramblings, constantly and obstinately gaze, even with closed eyes, at a lamentable figure, the grotesque Félicien that I brought out of his tomb by the force of will and memory? I should have atrocious insomnia, hallucinations of a macabre round-dance, visions of the cemetery? I should feel my head standing up on my head, in the dark, my head coming to life, sensitive; I should hear sobs rising from the inferno to assault my ears, like the howling of a dog before a charnel-house?

No, no, no! That cannot be! If some mental torment has to be inflicted on me, it ought not to exceed, in all justice, that which I would have suffered from an imprisonment of three months.

I reject remorse as an iniquity. I protest. I do not want bloody apparitions, icy fingers that pose invisibly on the foreheads of the damned and leave the crimson stigmata of an ineffaceable burn there.

Get away!

Nightmares, all that!

Once, I don't deny, things like that were possible. Orestes fled under the persecution of the Erinnyes, ran like a madman hurling at nature entire the furious cries of his terror. But that was in an era when humans, incapable as yet of reason, needed to contemplate images in order to understand, to give a visible form and color of invisible realities. Ignorant and poetic, they lived in the heart of mythology; they required statues, incarnation. Then it was impossible to isolate themselves from external influences; they entered into the mind through the eyes.

Today we have cast own the old idols. In the morose desert where we march, we can trample underfoot the marmoreal dust of fallen gods. The symbols whose aspect troubled the human brain so perniciously have crumbled one by one into the past. No more statues. The great rivers where their reflections trembled for centuries have dried up, as if exhausted by time, and dead waters flow sadly over their desiccated torrents. Soon, all trace of the ancient world will have disappeared definitively; we shall be cured of allegories and will no longer risk moaning under unknown torments.

Once the sky was populated by menacing divinities; at least, people believed so. Science and reason have killed, successively, all of the chimeras that cast a shadow over our thought. We know that there is nothing up there above our heads—nothing, not even breathable air. We can grow old in all security.

In order to conceive remorse, it would therefore be necessary for me to be going mad, veritably.

And I am not mad.

I take you as a witness that I am not mad!

VII

5 November.

Yesterday, I received a note of announcement that had been addressed to me in Paris and that my concierge had forwarded to me.

Henriette has remarried.

She has married Léonard V****, the celebrated geographer, one of Félicien's friends, one of the regulars of the Madeleine salon. V**** is certainly the man she needed, heaped with honors, inconceivably stupid with regard to everything that is not narrowly linked to geographical science. He is not yet too old, and quite presentable. It is a perfect match.

I appreciate the notification. Henriette has remained a tactful woman. After a lapse of more than two years without a letter she reappears with regard to the first notable incident.

Very correct.

All is well; it upset me at first. The first impression was a shock. I immediately thought that I ought to have been able to marry Henriette myself. One sees many such unions, and society approves them. But for the decision we both immediately made to leave Paris, things might have worked out that way. I would have seen Henriette again, infrequently at first, then regularly, and one fine morning, our marriage would have become a necessity. Our entourage would have pushed us into it invincibly.

Thus I would have entered one evening as master into that dwelling full of memories, of the presence of the other; I would have been able to install myself in the dead man's study, sit down in his place in the dining room, take his armchair beside the fire, and, finally, go back into Henriette's bedroom, the room with the mauve curtains into which I have not penetrated since the horrible evening.

That, I agree, would have been impossible for me.

Oh, no, not that! Anything, the solitude here, exile, my long troubles, my fatigue, my unbearable neuralgia, the acuity of which increases every day, my abandoned relations, my lost life, anything, all of it, but not that!

Since yesterday, Henriette has become an object of hatred for me. What a cowardly creature! I'm certain that she has been afraid, that she too has seen the phantom, the dead man, the vengeful apparition. She has had nightmares, nights devastated by insomnia; she has turned over and over on her dishonored bed for hours, breathless, seating, her wide-open eyes seeking infernal protectors in the darkness.

I can see all that from here. She has been terrified.

For two years she struggles vainly against the shadow. She sees Féliciens everywhere.

When she is asleep Félicien comes into the mauve room, climbs on to the bed and comes to lie down on her breast; he is livid, there is an acrid humidity on his face, blood in the black holes of his eyes and on his discolored beard.

And she sees him, the wretch! She looks at him, she cannot help looking at him. Sometimes the specter is dressed, sometimes he is naked; and when he is naked, Henriette follows, trebling with fever and horror, the slow and sure labor of the filthy worms devouring that cold flesh. Now the eyes have been eaten; one sees the profound and sinister location, two cavities into which one could plunge two fingers. On the shoulders, a dirty bone appears, fleshless; the toenails and fingernails have fallen off, allowing the sight of little withered stumps.

And Henriette has to share her bed with that infamous putrescence; she feels it next to her. Sometimes she attempts a desperate movement; then the cadaver rolls off her, with the slap of a dangling arm, and, abruptly thrust away, falls to the floor, ragging the satin eiderdowns and lacy pillows with it. Then Henriette dares not get down, no longer dares budge. She stays there, overwhelmed, half-naked, on the bed, and waists, shivering, for the dawn.

During meals, the dead man sits silently in the place the living man once occupied, or comes up behind Henriette stealthily and sly tugs the hem of her skirt. In the evening he installs himself be the fireside and smiles—which is frightful. His skeletal feet flop in carpet-slippers. All his teeth are visible now instead of the lips devoured by the worms.

And all around floats an odor of the tomb.

That, for sure, has been Henriette's life since the fatal evening. The dead man has taken possession of her, of her days, of her nights, of everyone's face,

So she has remarried in order no longer to be alone with the dead man. There will henceforth be beside her, at night, a distraction, caresses, a protective intervention. The dead man will no longer dare to enter the mauve room, or, if he comes, the new husband will throw him out of the widow. At table, he will no longer be able to sit down, his place being occupied by the living husband. A new, real presence will be substituted for the imaginary one. There will merely be a question of habits to lose.

So, she is protected, saved, the wretch a hundred times more culpable than me. For, after all, she enticed me, provoked me—me, who had no thought of anything.

She is married. And I remain alone, alone, all alone.

6 November.

The physician has come, with another physician established in Menton.

They have conversed privately

My neuralgia has become complicated, it appears; I am to go to bed and take care of myself seriously. I attribute the terrible headaches from which I am suffering to the seasonal heat.

Besides which…

VIII

The Expert Medico-Legal Report of Dr. Solognot

I, the undersigned, Edmond-Albert Solognot, doctor in medicine of the Faculté of Paris, have been charged by Monsieur des Aubrais, the examining magistrate, by virtue of a special commission, with presenting a report on the mental state of Henri Laverdin, accused of the attempted murder of Madame Henriette V****.

I had myself transported to the Mazas detention center, where the aforementioned Monsieur Laverdin is being held.

Monsieur Laverdin, although he is only forty years old, resembles an old man. His hair, once thick and black, is now completely white and thinning. The chest is sunken, the limbs thin and weak, the hands agitated by a continual nervous tremor. He received us mildly, and has responded appropriately to the questions that were put to him.

The accused complains of intense pains in the head, a persistent ringing in the ears, and a general weakness that, after the slightest effort, engenders overwhelming lassitudes. Thus, he spends the greater part of his time, by day and by night, huddled on the bed in his cell, in spite of the impressions of terror that he experiences there. In fact, Laverdin claims that as soon as he lies down, it is necessary for him to engage in a struggle against a cadaver that forcibly occupies his bed and only leaves him a very small space.

He does not remember the circumstances that preceded, accompanied or followed his criminal attempt. He only remembers having returned from Sospel in the Alpes-Martitimes to Paris in the course of last month, with the resolution to seek out Madame Henriette V**** in order to reproach her for her recent marriage. What he had told us about the incidents of his journey is in conformity with the facts ascertained by the examining magistrate. But the accused memory stops there. He has no memory of having entered the home of Monsieur and Madame V**** while brandishing a knife, or of having pursued Madame V**** into her bedroom, or of having been disarmed by the domestics, to whom he announced the intention to take off his clothes.

The manuscript written by Monsieur Laverdin, communicated by the examining magistrate, which we have attached to the present report, is sufficient to explain the tragic past that was able to disturb the intellectual faculties of the unfortunate. One discovers there the persecution mania by which Laverdin is now incurably afflicted, and which is degenerating into general paralysis.

The detainee is repulsively dirty. During our first visit we were obliged to prescribe baths for him and to instruct the warders of the section to see to the cleaning of his cell.

From our various observations, it results that Henri Laverdin was not responsible for his actions when he accomplished the deeds that led to his incarceration, but that his release would present the most redoubtable danger to public safety.

For these reasons, and as it is important that the detainee receives immediate care, we propose to the examining magistrate to have him urgently admitted, by order of the court, to the hospice of Bicêtre.

THE PRÉGAMAIN SPRING
A Parliamentary Fantasy

To Aurélien Scholl, my great colleague and great friend.[7]

I

On the evening of 5 January 1879, one would have searched Paris in vain in Paris, as well as the suburbs and even the départements, for a man more completely satisfied than Gédéon Prégamain.

That very morning, he had conducted to the cemetery on the heights of Père Lachaise his uncle, Babylas-Clod-Fracre Prégamain, carried off in a matter of days by an indigestion of turnips, after eighty-two years of an obscure and futile existence. The deceased bequeathed to Gédéon, his sole heir, his entire fortune, which, according to the notary, could be evaluated at five million francs, as much in excellent shares and bonds as in easily realizable immovable assets. Now, if one considers that Babylas had shown throughout his life the most sordid stinginess and the good humor of a sergeant major riddled with rheumatism, and if one reflects that Gédéon had received nothing but a little mocking advice from him in response to urgent solicitation, one can understand, without necessarily approving of it, the immoral hilarity that the heir could not help displaying.

Every time that Gédéon, harassed by debts or pushed by some covetousness, had elected to take seriously the modern

---

[7] The journalist, writer and dramatist Aurélien Scholl (1833-1902), who wrote an obituary of Charles-Marie' Flor's father for *Le Matin*.

axiom by virtue of which uncles are nature's cash-registers, the old man had opposed to him a visage and a strong-box firmly locked, softening his stubborn refusals with phrases such as: "Patience, my boy; I'm not giving you anything because I love you and understand your interests better than you do," and "Patience, you'll be glad to find the money still there when I'm dead..."

Having savored that kind of consolation for ten or twelve years, and tried in vain to slake the thirst of his suppliers, Gédéon did not believe that he was failing the memory of his uncle by manifesting a joy of which the deceased himself had had a presentiment. In fact, as Babylas had announced to him many a time, Gédéon was delighted to find a fortune, and the first confidences of the notary had effaced the bitterness of old disappointments.

Five million! A fine figure! Gédéon now possessed five million, and an annual income of two hundred and fifty thousand francs—which is to say, starting tomorrow, a luxurious dwelling, a large château in a beautiful region, paintings by masters, marble statues, horses, carriages, mistresses, a sumptuous table and vintage wines.

Tomorrow would bring back the old comrades, smiling henceforth, envious and humble; tomorrow would see a thousand women's smiles blooming, and a thousand provocative gazes radiating. Tomorrow, he would be handsome, powerful, surrounded; he would have the right to be stupid, and even to be insolent. His creditors yesterday arrogant and fierce, would bow down, and pretend to have forgotten their bills. The old furniture, accumulated piece by piece from the auction rooms in ground-floor hovels, would be sold, or given away, or abandoned. Jackets would be replaced by frock-coats, battered old hats by new ones, shoes by boots, the local eatery by the Café Anglais, the wine-merchants by the Café Riche, the petty bordeaux by the *nec plus ultra* of H. Upmann.[8]

---

[8] The reference is to cigars, H. Upmann being one of the oldest and most esteemed Cuban brands.

Five million! A fairy tale! In his days of tribulation, Gédéon had sometimes despaired of the future. He had thought: "That old man is immortal!" A frightful suspicion had occurred to him that Uncle Babylas might have invested his entire fortune in a life-annuity. He had glimpsed strange smiles on the stubborn old man's face, the smiles of a perverse individual congratulating himself secretly for having pulled off some vast hoax.

But not at all. What was all that? A dream, a chimera—imagination! Babylas was definitely buried; Gédéon had no fear of his being resurrected once or twice, like the Emperor Frederick Barbarossa. The family vault had closed on the old man's bier, and tomorrow, the notary would put the heir in possession of the inheritance.

Five million! At the very most, Gédéon would have wagered on four. He had expected four, neither more nor less. The fifth million surprised and delighted him. He considered it as compensation.

"My uncle owed me that," he said.

Five million! Thus far, Gédéon Prégamain had lived miserably, without ever possessing everything that truly belonged to him. Having passed his baccalaureate in early youth, full of ambition and dreaming of attaining the highest summits of the social ladder, he had been picked up by an advocate who paid him a monthly sum of fifty francs in exchange for twelve hours work a day. In those conditions it was necessary for him to renounce dazzling his contemporaries with the luxury of his carriages and trips on a whim to some town on the Mediterranean coast.

He often wore a black suit borrowed from some comrade; he went to the theater thanks to free tickets extracted from the benevolence of a wine-merchant; he read books that belonged to anyone and everyone. The Temple market was his tailor, boot-maker and shirt-maker. He lived in sordid mansard in shady streets and frequented twenty-one-sou eateries where passers by were served with aliments that never passed muster. As ingenious as all paupers, he had learned the art of restoring a luster of youth to old clothes by means of Indian ink and concealing the lamentable wounds of worn-out footwear by covering them with wax. He had rarely gone hungry, but many of his menus had been reduced to two hard-boiled eggs. He was familiar with the coffee that is manufactured with burned beans, the butter that is margarine, the fine champagne that is proof spirit, the cigars composed of potato-leaves, fuschined[9] wine, milk with sheep's-brain additives, gelatin consommé. Lobster appeared to him to be a chimera, pheasant an allegory; he treated truffled *foie gras* as a paradox and Champagne wine as a utopia.

How many times, in contemplating is antique jacket with leather buttons, had he cried: "When will I be able to put a new coat on those buttons?"

How many times had he thought, like Dante, that the stairway to the other world is difficult to climb![10] How many times, pale and hungry, he had groaned, wept, raged and ground his teeth thinking about old Babylas' millions!

He had those millions now.

So he felt happy. From the practical point of view, he saw himself rich and free; from the familial viewpoint, given the unsupportable character of the deceased, he no longer saw anything in that death than one of those unpleasant things to which one gets accustomed, like, for example, living above a locksmith or opposite a packer.

Running over the world in louis, napoleons, dollars, doubloons, espagnols, Dutch ducats, pounds sterling, Austrian kemnitz, Turkish kitzes, American eagles, German or Danish fredericks and Brazilian piastres, there are slightly more than sixty billion gold coins. That gold passes from hand to hand, warming up, getting tired and worn away. Effigies are flattened and effaced, the sharp ridges of letters and numbers are softened and seem, after a number of years, to have emerged

---

[9] Fuschine, or rosaniline chloride is a magenta dye when dissolved in water.

[10] Dante's *Purgatorio* is replete with awkward stairways.

from a mold rather than the formidable strike of the die. A little gold falls, flies away and drops into the bottom of strong-boxes or sticks to human fingers. That metal dust, invisible and impalpable, floats in the air, mingles with the breeze, fills space, is breathed in by the rich, whom it hardens, and the poor, whom it exasperates. Passions, angers, jealousies, temptations, opulence devoid of generosity, poverty devoid of resignation, contained rage below and insolent scorn above, avidity and revolt: the respired gold causes all of that to germinate. We all experience, more or less, a grim thirst drunk with the soul of louis that fly away.

Gédéon Prégamain had, so to speak, no knowledge of that unhealthy thirst. The habit of long privation had adapted him to a mediocre life. In spite of his firm determination to neglect nothing to assure the revenge of the poor dinners of old, he applied himself gladly to reasonable projects. Anyone might easily have lost his head in confrontation with that fortune abruptly acquired; the least foolish might have lost themselves in extravagant or absurd schemes, like the peasant who, after winning a hundred thousand francs in a lottery, cries: "Finally! I'll be able to eat mutton stew every day!"

Gédéon was radiant, but the perspective of the material enjoyments that wealth provides did not enter significantly into his delight.

On the evening of the burial, at the moment when this story begins, he dined soberly, contenting himself with adding to his usual meager fare a solid morsel and two or three gasses of a generous wine. After a short stroll perfumed by a good cigar he went home, had a fire lit by his concierge and, with his feet on the fire-irons, his stomach full and his mind free, he gave free rein to his thoughts.

"Finally," he exclaimed, "people are going to talk about me!"

He lit a second cigar, and, with his head tilted back and his arms dangling, he stretched himself out in his armchair.

"Yes, people will talk about me. When? Soon. What will they say? I don't know. But they'll talk about me, that's certain. Oh, my dream! Oh, my goal! Since leaving school I've been vegetating, lost in the crowd, languishing unknown and obscure. For ten years I've been gnawing my bit, awaiting the fortune that I'd have the strength to scorn if it weren't to be the instrument, the lever of my glory. Yes, to be one of the men whom the world admires and salutes, to hear my name flying from mouth to mouth, sensing in passing the curious and intimated gaze of passers-by, reading stories in newspapers and magazines of which I'll be the hero, seeing collected as so many important notes for the future the slightest incidents of my day, becoming the focal point of jealousies and praise, knowing that I'm famous—that's where I want to get to!

"Marble palaces, gilded drawing rooms, flowered carpets, rich estates, feasts, horses, mistresses, enjoyments—what need have I of all that? Have I not lived without banquets, carriages, kisses, almost without shelter? And when my youthful years have submitted to austere fasting, when my by body and my pride have been buckled forever, how can a poverty-stricken future frighten me? Get away! Is it hunger, thirst, cold and ennui from which I've suffered? No what I've suffered from is that no one knew that Gédéon Prégamain was hungry, thirsty and cold!

"I felt that I was nothing, nothing at all, that there would never be any mention of me in the newspapers, that not even a cat would come to my funeral. I said to myself: Is that possible? What, in a time when the humblest become notorious, when it's sufficient to attain celebrity to write a book, to say something stupid, to sell a medicament, to manufacture chocolate, to go up in a balloon, to be run through with an épée or go into a cage with Monsieur Bidel where his gouty old lions are dying! When Amerigo Vespucci is famous for a world he didn't discover and Nordenskjold for a pole he didn't get near! When everyone is known, whether they succeed or fail, Skobelev for his victories, Benedek for his defeats! When one sees the paltriest individual bearing a popular name, when one knows, for example, that Gambetta's chef is named

Trompette, that Dr. Véron's cook is named Sophie, that the Jockey Club's florist is named Isabelle, I, Gédéon Prégamain remain unknown and forgotten!

"Paris is occupied with a host of people of no value. A newsvendor, Gabrielle de la Périne, was famous for six months simply for having sold newspapers! There are reporters to celebrate the big nose of the actor Hyacinthe, Daubray's belly, the sickening puns of the comic Hamburger, Jeanne Samary's teeth, the Duchesse de Pourtalès' dresses, the acrobat Océana's legs, Comte Lagrange's horses! For there are famous horses—Gladiator, Vermouth, Saltarelle, etc., are names that the public knows and repeats. Oh, shame! At Franconi's there was a donkey named Rigolo, the recollection of which is still in everyone's memory. People know the name of the goat that appeared at the Opéra-Comique in *Le Pardon de Ploërmel*, and the elephant featured in *Le Tour du Monde* at the Porte-Saint Martin. The hippopotamus at the Jardin des Plantes that died recently was favored by an obituary in *L'Évènement*. People know his name! But who knows mine? No one."

There Gédéon stopped, and closed his eyes as if to be unable to look the negligibility of his own existence in the face, and he remained thoughtful for a few moments, his forehead hidden by his hands.

"But that's going to change!" he cried, raising his head. "That's going to change! I'm no longer the mercenary doomed to ignoble toil, the wretch bound to quotidian labor, trembling night and day for his salary. I'm no longer the prisoner of poverty. Henceforth, I'll be able to work, not for my bread, but for my glory, nor to satisfy my hunger but to appease my soul."

He got to his feet, already drawn by a necessity to act, and continued pacing back and forth in his narrow room.

"Right! Let's examine ways and means a little. I have a choice. I can, at my whim, found an annual prize for the laureates of the Institut, follow the burials of well-known people, write a drama and have it staged at my own expense, create a newspaper, explore Central Africa, pierce an isthmus, become a great artist or commit some frightful crime. Let's see...

"An academic prize? No, people would only talk about me once a year at the most. They would say: 'The Prégamain Prize had been awarded to Monsieur X...' And every year would bring me a rival, a schemer who would steal half my glory. Sensational burials? It's facile, but over-used; the least writer who has had recourse to that means of publicity has gained the soubriquet of 'man of letters for hire.' The theater? What if I'm whistled? What if the public split their sides laughing at my tragedies or yawns at my vaudevilles? Create a newspaper? Oh, fie! A vulgar expedient. Everyone has a newspaper nowadays.

"Commit a great crime? Well, the idea isn't stupid. Do you see that millionaire who cuts throats, shoots or poisons, not out of cupidity, not for vengeance, but for nothing, for pleasure, for sport, out of the idleness of the great lord? That would be an original crime that would interest the entire world. But afterwards? I mentioned piercing an isthmus. There are better things to do; what if I formed a company for filling in the Suez Canal? No, keep looking...

"A voyage of exploration in Africa? Yes, that's it. Discover a world, like Columbus. Give my named to a new country, like Kerguelen, or a strait, like Bering or Magellan. Prégamain Island! Port Prégamain! The kingdom of Prégamain! Or simply Prégamainville. Add my name to the list of celebrated voyagers and great explorers; make history say: Gunbiorn, Usodimare, Juan de Sanboron, Pierre Escovar, Dias, Columbus, Vasco da Gama, Ojeda, Vespucci, Fernand d'Andrada, Magellan, Jacques Cartier, Cortès, Jamoto, Willoughby, Barentz, Jacob Lemaire, Abel Tasman, Bougainville and Gédéon Prégamain!

"Yes, that's it. What's stopping me? I'm free, rich, I have millions; with millions one can equip caravans and pay men. Virgin lands still remain; Central Africa figures on maps as blank space. I'll go; I'll march; I want to reach Timbuktu, the inviolate capital of the Sudan. There, Europeans have not yet penetrated; there, I shall make my name illustrious."

Midnight chimed, and Gédéon was still talking, giving himself his word of honor that he would discover a world and accomplish some illustrious deed.

Slumber did not put an end to the visions sketched in wakefulness; Gédéon saw magical lands in his dreams, immense deserts populated by elephants of every color, scintillating birds, monsters, naked men and enormous women. He recognized himself, Gédéon Prégamain, traveling the solitudes at the head of his valiant caravan, making speeches in the midst of savages, and apostle of civilization and absolute master. No obstacle. With a shot from his fine carbine, he felled roaring wild beasts at his feet; with a stride he scaled mountains and crossed rivers.

The he had a triumphant vision of the return, his reentry to the port of Marseille or Bordeaux, the authorities gathered on the disembarkation quay, the recompenses, the incense of bravos and homages. The Institut would open its doors to him; London, Vienna, Rome and Saint Petersburg would dispute the honor of his presence. Finally, he found himself transported to Paris, before the entrance to the Champs-Élysées. There, workmen were laboring, and when they came down from their scaffolding, they uncovered a brand new enamel plaque bearing the words: *Avenue Gédéon Prégamain.*

II

The next day, Gédéon ran to the notary's office, and without wasting time in idle explanations, instructed him to send a sum of two million five hundred thousand francs to Saint-Louis du Sénégal, of which he said he had the most urgent need.

At that confidence, the lawyer turned three colors with surprise. For a moment he suspected that Babylas' nephew had gone mad. Two millions! Senegal! He would not have been more consternated on seeing penetrate into his study one of those characters of Hervé's, who, on encountering an old magistrate, shout: "Bonjour, Joséphine. My name is Fromage de Gruyère."

But seeing Gédéon calm, cold and serious, his gaze frank and his visage tranquil, he recovered slowly from the terror of the confidence and, anticipating some hazardous project, tried to draw the future explorer of the Congo into the path of explanations.

"My dear Monsieur," he said, "I will make arrangements for that large sun to each you in the designated location, but before then, permit to remind you that I possessed all the confidence of your venerable uncle, that he never made a placement without my advice, and that I would be happy, even proud, to see myself thus honored by you. I dare, therefore, to ask you—excuse my boldness—what destination you count on giving that capital..."

Gédéon frowned.

"Please believe," the notary hastened to add, "that in all this, your interest is my only motive..."

And he waited, not daring to say any more, as timid as a hunter who, in despair of salvation, has thrown a piece of rye-bread to a bear.

"Monsieur," Gédéon commenced, "I don't believe I have to congratulate myself, regarding the advice that you lavished on my uncle with regard to his placements, for every time I proposed to him a placement to my advantage he refused it, doubtless on your advice. However, I can imagine your attachment to a fortune long abandoned to your management, and by virtue of that consideration, I will consent to inform you as to my projects."

Then, as a captain exposes a battle plan, he explained to the ministerial officer the motive for his imminent departure, his desire to discover new countries and to attach his name to great things.

The notary pretended to enter into his views. Certainly, the goal was praiseworthy, and grandiose, and Africa a beautiful land.

"For two pins, I'd accompany you," he added. "But I know myself; I'd cut a sorry figure on such a voyage, and I can't really see myself in the streets of Timbuktu, a frightful city, they say..."

"They?" interrogated Prégamain. "Who are they? No one has penetrated there as yet."

"Timbuktu, my dear Monsieur? What an error!"

"Can it be?"

"Listen. In 1824, a scullion, or a cook, I don't know exactly, named René Caillé, quite Saint-Louis du Sénégal with the intention of reaching Tombouctou, as Timbuktu was called in those days. Caillé easily covered sixty kilometers in a day, of which you're probably not capable; he was endowed with eyesight so piercing that he could distinguish the satellites of Jupiter with the naked eye; you can't do that. He knew how to cook and you don't; if necessary, he could go for five days without food with impunity; he spoke Arabic, and you don't; he knew the entire Koran by heart, and you don't know a single line. In spite of all those advantages, it took him two years to reach Timbuktu and two years to return."

Gédéon smiled, and replied: "I shall have horses, carts, food supplies, weapons, interpreters, baggage..."

"Permit me," the notary interrupted. "In 1830, Major Gray of the English Navy left Sierra Leone to go to Timbuktu. He had horses, carts, food supplies, weapons, interpreters and baggage. On arriving at Boulibaba, on the frontier of Fouta-Toro, he found neither a stream not a well, and died of thirst in the desert with his entire caravan."

"I shall take water," pronounced Gédéon.

"In 1841, Adrien Partarrieu took water. At Boudou, near Fouta-Djalon, he was surrounded, wounded, captured and put to death by Hottentots."

"Damn!"

"As for Monsieur Leduc de Blairot, who set forth in 1850, his fate was different."

"Oh?"

"Yes. Monsieur Leduc de Blairot encountered not Hottentots but Kaffirs. They dug a hole and lowered the explorer into it, then replaced the earth in such a fashion that Monsieur Leduc was buried alive, with his head above ground. Then the Kaffirs emptied on to his head a basket containing two hundred parched and hungry rats."

"Damn!"

"Now, Monsieur, *bon voyage*…and good luck."

"For a moment, Gédéon had been meditating the necessity of installing a railway in the Congo, all the way to the Upper Niger. His knowledge of Arabic only extended to a few words that had entered into Parisian argot, such as *macache, bézef, mouquère, bono turco* and *maboul*, and would not have permitted him to sustain a conversation with an emir. Ten years devoted to copying documents in a study in the Rue Joquelet had only given a very vague idea of the Koran, and, on thinking about the privations imposed by the enterprise on René Caillé, who could do without eating as one does without going to the Odéon, the millionaire told himself that after having eaten badly when he was poor, it would be ridiculous no longer to eat anything at all now that he was rich.

In brief, the notary did not have great difficulty making him understand that one can occupy a nice place in history without having oneself devoured alive by rats for the greater distraction of a few primitive humans.

"Not to mention," he added, "that there would be no guarantee of a beautiful burial and a monumental tomb. The natives of the Congo generally like their European brethren as we like eggs—which is to say, fresh and lightly boiled, in the morning. In the probable case that you would be utilized out there for a wedding feat or a dinner party, it would be impossible for your admirers, however zealous they might be, to render the last duties to your mortal remains. I wouldn't want to discourage you, but let's see—hand on heart—do you really believe that there are fanatics to be found who will go to wear crowns of immortelles on All Saints' Day and make speeches over the belly of the cannibal who has swallowed you? Let's be reasonable, damn it!"

Gédéon was no longer listening. While the notary was perorating, he was thinking about the various means of achieving celebrity: the isthmus to be pierced, the canal to be filled in, the book to be written, the drama to be staged, etc., etc.

Fundamentally, the notary was reasoning accurately; Minerva was speaking through his mouth. The Congo, Timbuktu, Central Africa...an absurd project, a tenebrous adventure. One could easily count the explorers of the Congo, but the names of men who had become famous without ever having set foot in Timbuktu would furnish an interminable list—for example, Moses, Homer, Gutenberg, the Chevalier Bayard, Hamlet, François I, Van Dyck, Corneille, Madame de Sévigné, Monsieur Guizot, Labiche and so many others! Damn it, there was plenty of time to discover Africa; there was nothing urgent about it. One could easily do without it.

"Look," said the notary, "since you need noise, renown, why not go tranquilly into politics? That way, there's no danger to run, nothing to lose. According to circumstances, it might even be possible or you to augment your wealth. Perhaps, to begin with, a few sacrifices would be necessary, but a man disposed to spend two and a half million to follow in the tracks of a scullion won't recoil before an expense of two or three hundred thousand francs.

"In the times we're living in, my dear Monsieur, universal suffrage doesn't require superior intelligences; men of good will are sufficient for it. You have the resolution, the desire and the ambition to succeed. It's for the best. Would you like some sage advice? Buy an important property in a poor arrondissement, enlarge it, embellish it and show yourself; give prizes at agricultural shows and regional competitions. Become the benefactor of choirs, companies of firefighters, municipal fanfares and philanthropic societies. In a year, you'll be a councilor, in eighteen months Maire of the commune, and in two years a general councilor, and then a député at the next election. Who knows? Once in the

Chambre, could you not reach the Ministry? Anyway, take a look, examine the possibility. I remain your humble servant..."

Gédéon replied: "Notary, you've saved my life. So be it: I'll consent to become a Minister. One day, later, we'll settle the choice of the ministerial department that it's necessary for me to accept...what do you think of the navy?...but for the moment, it's a matter of taking care of the most urgent matter. I applaud your idea. Yes, by the means you indicate, an active, rich, determined man can make a name for himself in a short time. I renounce discovering the Congo, and I'll console myself for not being able to initiate my contemporaries into the mores and customs of the Mandingo peoples. You've opened my eyes. Speak, expound, dictate—what is it necessary to do? Where is the poor arrondissement? Where is the estate for sale to be found? Where do my future electors live? Buy, I'm ready—for you haven't told me all that without having something in mind?"

"Perhaps..."

"I'm listening."

"Here it is: among my clients there's a former page of King Charles X, well into his seventies, an old bachelor, who retired to a small village in the Basses-Alpes called Lathuile. It is, I believe, in the arrondissement of Sisteron. He's just died and his heirs want to sell the château, park, land, forests—everything, in sum. It's going for next to nothing: a hundred thousand francs. Buy Lathuile, repair the château, do a little good, occupy yourself with agriculture, give the peasants a fire-pump, a bridge, a fountain, a drinking-trough—it doesn't matter. I think I even recall that the estate includes a thermal or mineral spring, from which a profit might be gained. At any rate, I can ask for the dossier if you think the affair worth investigation..."

"I believe so!"

On the notary's order, a clerk brought the famous dossier.

"Here you are," the notary continued. "Domain of Lathuile, comprising: firstly, a château constructed toward the end of the last century, with dependencies, commons, stables, garages, etc.; secondly, a park of three hundred hectares surrounded by walls; thirdly, a forest known as de la Gardule, comprising an area of sic hundred and fifty-seven hectares. The whole has a registered value of four thousand francs. No mortgage. No charges. Entry to immediate enjoyment."

"I'll buy it," Gédéon interrupted.

"One more thing. The mineral spring is situated in the park; it's said to be rich in salts of all kinds. Perhaps you'll be able to exploit it. If Lathuile becomes a spa, you'll enrich the locale and your affair is settled."

"I'll buy it." Gédéon replied.

He did, in fact, buy it. The evening train took his to the Basses-Alpes, and a week had not gone by before an army of workmen descended upon the humble village to restore the château, repair the roads and renew everything. Renowned gardeners were given responsibility for the park; one of the great cabinet-makers of the Faubourg Saint-Antoine supplied the furniture; and a chemist and physicians were occupied in analyzing the spring, which an engineer made haste to capture.

The notary was not mistaken; the affair promised to be excellent. The repairs could be completed rapidly without overmuch expense. The water of the spring was judged precious. The park was overflowing with furred and feathered game. The vicinity offered interesting excursions; there was an old manor built by the Templars, a cave-system containing a number of picturesque grottoes; Roman remains, including a circus and a triumphal arch; high mountains charged with green fir trees and gracious valleys along which ran a fast-flowing steam where trout were quivering.

On the advice of the notary Gédéon did not hesitate to push forward with his glory and his affairs. Not far from the château he built a superb hotel on the model of the Cauterets Cosmopolite, and surrounded the spring with a complex of bath-house, swimming-baths, inhalation-rooms, showers, etc. Lathuile saw two or three lovely inns spring from the ground, a few shops finer than those in Sisteron and Digne, a casino whose banqueting hall and theater were praised in advance, and capacious cafés modeled on the most luxurious establishments.

Gédéon was everywhere. He made a gift to the commune of a superb pump bought from the supplier of the firemen of London. Thanks to his liberalities, the municipal council was able to revive the primary school, construct an old people's home, and plant a few mulberry-bushes in front of the church. The curé received his share: a chasuble embroidered in gold and two pictures commissioned from a serious painter. Gédéon provided the local policeman with a new outfit and distributed the employments at the thermal establishment between the least ignorant of the young people of the district.

Three physicians from the Faculté de Paris were attached to the exploitation. An orchestra took possession of the casino and was soon followed by a troupe of actors and singers. In brief, by the first of September, about nine months after the death of old Babylas, the following advertisement could be read on the fourth page of the major newspapers:

PRÉGAMAIN SPRING
Near Lathuile (Basses Alpes)
First-Class Establishment

The details followed.

Gédéon recommended his hotel, the Grand Hôtel de Lathuile, the largest and most imposing in the département, with a large southern garden, surrounded by salons, restaurants, a hydraulic elevator serving all the floor, rooms, suites, *table d'hôte*, lecture room and music room, smoking rooms, billiard tables, an omnibus meeting all trains, and moderate prices.

A long description recommended the casino and the local excursions.

The analysis of the spring came next:

Water: 1 liter; carbonic acid, 42 centigrams.

Calcium sulfate	1.5010
Magnesium sulfate	0.3080
Sodium sulfate	0.0180
Calcium carbonate	0.1300
Magnesium carbonate	0.0540
Iron oxide	0.0015
Aluminum	traces
Sodium chloride	0.0090
Calcium chloride	traces
Magnesium chloride	traces
Silica	0.0140
Iodine	traces
Phosphate	traces
Organic matter	traces
Total...	2.0385

"The water of the Prégamain Spring," the advertisements added, "can perhaps be utilized successfully to combat:

"1. Habitual congestion;

"2. Disposition to the inflammation of the principal organs;

"3. Chronic indisposition of the organs of respiration and circulation;

"4. Fatty deterioration of the heart;

"5. In general, any embarrassments caused by a superabundance of fat;

"6. The formation of gallstones

"7. Hemorrhoids

"8. In general, other maladies."

That enumeration was followed by an attestation signed by well-known scientists. We shall only quote the following passage:

"The properties of the Prégamain Spring include an incontestably aperient, diuretic and principally purgative effect, which is appropriate in numerous cases of acute or chronic maladies treatable by that important modification.

"Good effects can be obtained therefrom in cases of abdominal plethora, which provokes or maintains irritations of that cavity in the form of dyspepsia, constipation, flatulence, lumbar pain, aperitic jaundice with the swelling in the liver or the spleen, and principally in cases of intermittent fever of no matter what type, when the patient, falling from one relapse to another, no longer experiences the good results of quinine.

"Also, in maladies of the urinary tract, vesical catarrh, irritations of the kidneys, in certain forms of cutaneous maladies, with exaggerated irritability on the part of the subject by reason of age, temperament, or intemperate overstimulating treatment; and also palpitations of the heart, paralyses, rheumatic pains, sciatica, lumbago and articulatory swelling caused by trauma, etc. etc."

Gédéon had not recoiled before any expense. While in France the walls were covered with posters and the newspapers were overflowing with advertisements in which the name Prégamain was in enormous letters, the famous spring generated talk everywhere, in Spain, Italy, Russia and Austria.

The *Nordeutsch Allegemein Zeitung* praised the merits of "das natürliche Prégamain Biterwasser" and one could read in Rome's *Il Secolo* that "l'acqua minerale salina amina della fonte Prégamain si usa con successo spéciale per combattere tutti gli malattia."

It was an unprecedented triumph. The Académie de Médecine and the Académie des Sciences proclaimed the efficacy of the Prégamain Spring at Lathuile. Physicians, wonderstruck and seduced, abandoned customary remedies to the profit of the miraculous water. The vogue for purgative waters to which a solid reputation could be attributed was extinct. Those who ordinarily prescribed Royal-Hongroise water, Pülina water, flasks of Hunyadi Janos and Old Roger lemonade turned exclusively to the Lathuile establishment.

A superb affair! As soon as the season began it was necessary to think about enlarging the enterprise. A factory was built in which, in immense workshops, three thousand workers where occupied day and night in rinsing, filling, corking, sealing and labeling the bottles that were sent in truckloads to the four corners of the world. Illustrious individuals, dukes, princes, maréchals, ambassadors and bishops, brought the prestige of their clientele to the exploitation. Hotels multiplied around the park and a host of merchants set up shop, attracted by the abundance of customers.

To justify the enthusiasm of the public, Gédéon recruited for his casino the leading talent of the Parisian theaters. He had Judic, Théo, Granier, Dupuis, Baron and Lassouche. He put on real plays and had real operas sung. Lathuile became the height of fashion, and the entire world knew the name of Prégamain.

Finally, he was famous!

Finally, he no longer felt lost in the crowd. In Lathuile and its environs, he was the most important of the important people. He was fêted by the municipalities, and the sub-prefect of Sisteron lavished smiles upon him. He was awarded the place of honor at public festivals and the presidency at the distribution of school prizes.

Of that indigent little region he had made a magical realm. Land previously valued at four sous a meter was no longer sold for less than thirty francs. Cottages were transformed into houses, barns into farms, houses into palaces. Peasants once reduced to the slender income of their olive-groves now possessed bearer bonds and shares in railway companies. Shepherds became waiters in cafés and, before the twenty-five-louis tips of the season, smiled at the memory of the poor wages of old. Carters were revealed as garage-proprietors, goose-girls became perfect chambermaids, Poachers opened grocery stores, properly-dressed vagabonds served tourists as guides. Now the people of Lathuile ate meat every day, blessing the director of the thermal establishment. Gédéon was the father, the king, the God of that little society.

The Maire had handed in his resignation voluntarily, sensing his weakness, and Gédéon, yielding to the insistence of the notables, had generously advanced his candidature. No electoral success as enormous had ever been recorded by the *Journal Officiel*. The event was to remain unique, and we cannot neglect to relate it here. The counting of the ballots gave the following result:

Registered voters 884. Votes cast 884 (absolute majority 443). Monsieur Gédéon Prégamain (elected): votes 890.

As soon as he was elected to the municipal council, Gédéon was appointed Maire. It was a foot in the stirrup, the first rung on the ladder.

From that happy day onwards, the ambitious work of the millionaire progressed by measured stages. Certainly, the dazzling vision of the initial dream would not be realized overnight; it would be necessary to wait for several years before seeing the Avenue des Clamps-Élysées debaptized, his name given to an armchair, like Voltaire, a steel pen, like Humbolt or a fillet steak like Chateaubriand. Already, however, humble monuments attested to Gédéon's glory. On the square of the Mairie, now embellished and shaded, a majestic fountain stood, on the base of which passers-by could read:

In the year 1880
This fountain was built
under the municipal magistracy
of M. Gédéon Prégamain

The new bridge over the torrent of the Gapeau bore an analogous inscription. Even beyond the commune of Lathuile, Gédéon found means of having his name engraved in marble or bronze. Having conquered the commune, it was a matter of conquering the canton, and, without abandoning the Mairie of Lathuile, reaching the General Council.

By virtue of a providential stroke of luck, the seat became vacant, the holder having retired with his fortune made. Gédéon had disposed is batteries long ago, held discussions with the sub-prefect and gained influence with the party leaders. His candidature did not astonish anyone.

This time, however, it was necessary to take a position.

Which? That was the whole question.

The win the votes of the people of Lathuile there had been no need to write a manifesto or make any speeches. The neighbors of the thermal establishment had not wanted to know the candidate's color, whether blue, white or red, whether he regretted Louis-Philippe, Henri V or Napoléon III. They had voted for the owner of the big château, for the local benefactor.

But General Councils can have a political role to fill. In the case of an obligatory dissolution of Legislative Assemblies, they assemble immediately, without a decree of convocation, and take over, temporarily, the administration of the region. That extremity remains exceptional, to be sure, but it is written into the body of the law. Prégamain was therefore obliged to bring out his flag.

He thought about it for a week, prowling around men and ideas that had governed France, studying her laws, consulting history, rummaging through pamphleteers and commentators, agitating the pros and cons, seeking to discern among the opinions the opinion in favor, among the parties the party of the future.

By taking a position on the far right one was assured of flattering relations: there had washed up the sons of noble knights, the descendants of great families, the Rohans, the Léons, the La Rochefoucaulds, the Montmorencys. But those gentlemen enjoyed a frightful reputation in the Basses-Alpes; they were suspected of premeditating the reestablishment of the tithe, serfdom and the *droit de seigneur*.

On the extreme left, Gédéon feared the proximity of certain disquieting individuals, fierce republicans or reckless innovators.

In consequence, he opted for the politics of the center. There were seated the old parliamentarians, the liberals, the men of prudence and wisdom; there, the intolerable rigidity of principles was able to bend at need, according to the circumstances, and to fashion itself in complicity with interests.

He therefore chose none of the three colors, judging it more skillful to hoist all three in combination: no party politics, but a patriotic and veritably national politics! On the advice of his notary, however, Gédéon decided to lean slightly to the left. He intended to remain in the center, but not as close to the opposition as to the men in place. At the General Council he would adroitly support the prefecture, as a councilor jealous of his independence but truly impartial. Later, in the Chambre, he would hold himself at the disposition of the minister, without making any formal engagement, reserving the right, on days of battle, to move freely to the stronger side.

Thus resolved, he drafted his profession of faith, of which the exact text was as follows:

Dear taxpayers,

Responding to the appeal addressed to me by a considerable number among you, I put forward my candidature for the post of general councilor for the canton of Lathuile, which has become vacant by virtue of the resignation of Monsieur Cordenbois.

My name is known to you, the considerable works carried out in your arrondissement by my care are not unknown to anyone. A sincere and profound study of your needs causes me to hope that my efforts in the bosom of the departmental assembly will not be futile.

Concerned to contribute to the prosperity of the canton, the development of the agricultural and industrial wealth of this beautiful country, I shall strive to justify your suffrage by constant application.

From the political viewpoint, a friend of liberty and respectful of the law, I shall work for the affirmation of the present government and the institutions that rule us. Fatherland, liberty, morality and justice, such is my motto.

Vive la France!

Gédéon Prégamain, Maire de Lathuile.

There were, among the electors, a few mean spirits disposed to reject this program as too superficial. A veterinarian of the canton seized the opportunity to enter the lists and, relying on the advanced party of the population, inscribed at the head of his manifesto the reduction of taxes and the suppression of permanent armies. Gédéon parried the thrust by promising the separation of Church and State; to which the veterinarian, losing his head and his memory, responded with an engagement to vote for obligatory military service for priests and seminarists. That contradiction doomed him, but the struggle was prolonged and heated.

There were polemics. The veterinarian was supported by a radical newspaper in Sisteron; Prégamain founded a paper of his own *L'Écho de Lathuile*.

"What!" he cried in his first leading article, "do you think that a sick country can be cured like a horse with glanders or a sheep afflicted by scrapie?"

"What!" riposted the veterinarian, "do you dare to pretend that the canton has need of your purgative water?"

Gédéon spoke at a public meeting, covered his adversary with sarcasm and saw his candidature acclaimed.

At the count, he won by twelve hundred votes

When the general legislative elections arrived, the veterinarian returned to the charge, but once again it was to the shame of his impotent ambitions. In August 1881 Gédéon Prégamain was proclaimed député of the arrondissement of Sisteron (Basses-Alpes). In spite of his competitor's maneuvers he obtained an honorable majority and was able to count on an uncontested validation.

As soon as he was acquainted with the count proclaimed by the registration committee, he shut himself in his château, wanting to relax in peace, far from profane gazes.

Retiring to his study alone, quite alone, he measured in thought the road traveled, seeing himself as he had been before, an advocate's clerk, hungry and unknown, an obscure individual, a stray poor devil whom statistics alone would have called a soul, an infinitesimal earthworm. He compared his past with his present, as Murat, having become a kind, had been able to contemplate his postillion's whip beside his scepter, as Michel Ney, having become a Maréchal de France remembered having labored as a cooper. He thought: *I started from down there, I am pausing here, I shall go higher.*

"I'm getting there!" he cried, in a surge of noisy enthusiasm. "I'm within sight of the peak, I have set foot on the mountain. A few more steps, a few efforts, a few days, a little patience, and I shall be able to raise myself up to the heights of the most powerful. How right I was to trust in my star, to listen to the mysterious voices that sounded in my ear the fanfares of a glorious future! Yesterday I was nothing, today I am one of the seven hundred predestined who dictate the law to the fatherland. My vote contains the secret of tomorrow...

"With a speech I can change governments; with one word, 'Yes' or 'No,' I can summon the people to fraternal embraces or unleash war across Europe. My will is France great or small, humiliated or free, rich or ruined; it is our army conquering or vanquished, our railways radiating over the territory, our navy covering the two Oceans with its sails. And tomorrow? Today I am the man who decides, tomorrow I shall be the man who acts: a Minister!

"I shall become a Minister! I shall have the right to say: 'I want...!' Ambassadors will smile at me and strive to gain my benevolence, sovereigns will send me silken sashes and diamond crosses. My name will feature at the head of proclamations and the foot of treaties. An army of reporters will follow my voyagers, relate my speeches, worry about my health, copy the menu of my meals and comment on my slightest actions. With a frown I shall make commerce tremble and lower prices on the Bourse! My name will be known, repeated, admired, feared...

"Already, I'm famous. There is no corner of the world unreached by the water of my spring. All sick and healthy individuals, men and women, rich and poor, powerful and paltry, the happy and the melancholy, children and old people, think of me as a savior. In one respect, the world belongs to me. I have neither taught like Jesus, conquered like Charlemagne, subjugated like Napoléon, aggrandized like Columbus, renewed like Voltaire, not song like Homer, no—but I have purged worlds!"

III

The new député of Sisteron took full advantage of the three months of vacation by which he was permitted to commence his legislative labors.

He came to Paris, furnished from top to bottom a superb town house in the Avenue Marceau, moved in, married his notary's daughter, a charming child who drew like Paganini and played the piano like Monsieur Thiers. It was a rational marriage. A wife completes the domesticity of every intelligent political man. Certainly, Gédéon would have preferred to the notary's child the heiress of an illustrious stock, but in addition to the fact that, in the special circumstances in which he was placed, an alliance with the Rothschilds seemed difficult to conclude, Gédéon feared the inconveniences corollary to the proximity of a superior woman. He would have been royally displeased to pass in society for the fortunate spouse of an elite creature; he wanted a wife in the background, as negligible as possible, who would never have the audacity to claim a share of the conjugal glory. In that regard, the notary's daughter fit him like a glove.

Théodora was twenty years old, of good character and simple tastes. Without possessing the great beauty which is the despair of painters, she was pretty enough not to offend the vanity of a husband. She could be considered, from the political point of view, as a very passable legitimate wife. She loved her father, but without tenderness, pleasure, but without frenzy, clothes, but moderately; she loved her husband, but without passion. That was ideal.

Gédéon had formally sworn not to love his wife, for fear of squandering in amour time precious for glory. He kept his word, Madame Prégamain, from the day after the wedding, was invited to regulate her life according to her caprice and not to count on a husband capable of plucking a guitar, rhyming a madrigal or, after long kneeling contemplations, precipitating himself upon her like a tiger in order to crush her palpitating flesh in frightful embraces. She took the matter in good part, finding that quite natural and seeing nothing in the situation inferior to the ideal that her girlish dreams had formed of the marital state.

Without further delay, Gédéon occupied himself with his initial visits. The Minister of the Interior received him as one has to receive a man disposing of a vote. Gédéon was polite, but cold.

He deposited with the principal political personages, particularly those of the center left, visiting cards on which, by an innocent ruse, his name took on an allure of nobility. He thought he had observed that it is in good taste, in parliamentary society, to add something to proper names. The advocate Michel had called himself Michel (de Bourges), the clerical republican Arnaud had followed his name with that of his département, and only any longer responded to the appellation of Arnaud (de l'Ariège). Monsieur Martin, more demanding, had taken possession of a cardinal point and had become Martin (du Nord). By virtue of that tradition, the cards of the new député were thus inscribed:

Gédéon Prégamain de Lathuile
Député
Member of the General Council of the Basses-Alpes

It is a verity as old as the world that no one can flatter himself with being illustrious if he has not seen his renown consecrated by the suffrage of Paris. Tenors, financiers, vaudevillians, singers, musicians—no one has truly known success outside of success proclaimed in Paris. Those who lack that apotheosis are unconsoled. Richard Wagner could hear from the depths of Bavaria his triumphant fanfares clamoring over the battlefields of victorious German armies, but the regret of not having conquered Paris tortured him until his final hour. The provinces can furnish vainglory, but Paris alone dispenses true glory.

Gédéon had occasion to perceive that. The times of triumphal arches raised as he passed by dazed villagers, aubades played beneath his windows by the municipal fanfare, heads incessantly bared and bowed, seemed regrettable to him. The Parisian newspapers affected a veritably shocking indifference painful for a man accustomed to the daily homages of the *Écho de Lathuile*. Errant journalistic hacks continued to occupy the public with a thousand accessory incidents and fill the gazettes with cumbersome names. There was perpetual mention, in the public sheets, of Bismarck, Garibaldi, the Prince of Wales and Sarah Bernhardt, and Gédéon was reduced to the humiliating habit of searching for his name printed among the advertisements on the fourth page, between claims made for an ointment for traffic accidents and praise of a flour designed to exterminate tapeworms in less time than it takes to write the word.

In the salons where he was received, the pride of Sisteron encountered very amiable people assiduous in smiling at him, but, corrupted by the obsequiousness of the electors of Lathuile, he found the smiles insufficient. Often, in fact, he came to suspect a malicious intent on the part of his interlocutors. People talked too much about his spring and not enough of his career, said too much about his water and not enough about him. At every introduction, the same phrase was invariably addressed to him: "Monsieur Prégamain…oh yes, I know…a well-known name, indeed, indeed."

It was necessary for him to respond with modesty, to bow, to lower his gaze, adopt a satisfied expression; deep down, he was enraged. He often listened covertly to people he had just overheard pronouncing his name.

"That's Monsieur Prégamain, it's said."

"What Prégamain? Where do you get Prégamain?"

"The député."

"Oh, don't know it."

"Yes, you do know it: Prégamain water..."

"Right—got it! He's the fellow who sells the water that...he looks the part!"

But Gédéon was genuinely strong. When the first emotion had passed, he raised his head again.

"Patience!" he said. "Patience! Let's disdain these expressions of envy. These people are jealous of me and expressing it in malevolent irony. Patience! Let them enjoy their rest in peace. Soon the session will commence, soon I shall appear at the national tribunal, soon I shall impose silence on that impotent rabble..."

To dazzle his future colleagues and create innumerable relations in one day, he hosted a great political dinner. It was lugubrious. The guests, although numerous, maintained throughout the feast the silence of a mortuary chapel. At table, they looked at one another without daring to speak, all absorbed by the same disquieting and ludicrous thought. Several affected not to drink the water for fear of a mistake. After the meal, the drawing rooms of the Avenue Marceau were invaded by an elegant crowd, but the guests remained embarrassed and surly. An unpleasant idea haunted that rich dwelling, and, in spite of the old wines and the good food, in spite of the amiability of the hosts, it was a failed celebration.

Finally, in conformity with the presidential decree, the session of the Chambre commenced. Gédéon had himself inscribed on the center left and chose his place in the middle of the hall, behind the ministers' bench, facing the tribune. His colleagues welcomed him politely, but negligently, as an honorable man devoid of importance. The first sessions were uninteresting. Lots were drawn for membership of committees, elections for the committee of the Chambre, committee meetings precipitate votes on two or three hundred projects of local interest. For a week, the delegate of Sisteron wandered around the hemicycle and along the corridors like a soul in torment, saluted by ushers and orderlies, solicited by the immense host of beggars that besiege every man in position.

When that week had elapsed, however, Gédéon wanted to act. It was time. Sisteron and France were waiting.

Where to begin?

The debates of the order of the day did not lend themselves to his parliamentary debit. It was a matter of laws left unfinished by the last Assembly, a kind of liquidation. There was no means for Gédéon Prégamain to intervene, no resource. He was obliged to wait, to listen in silence, to limit himself sometimes to depositing a blue form in the tinplate urns, sometimes a white one.

He was forced to admit his impotence. In truth, parliamentary life required an apprenticeship. It was not sufficient to arrive in the Chambre, to lay out an electoral program on the green baize of the tribune, in order to make people listen and approve. Prudence, tact and skill dictated that it was appropriate to wait. Opportunities would arise of their own accord.

In fact, an opportunity presented itself. One evening, toward the end of an agitated session which brought the existence of the cabinet into question, Gédéon Prégamain saw one of his colleagues, Monsieur Devès, advancing toward him, armed with a sheet of paper. The paper bore the following words:

The Chambre,
Confident in the declarations of the government.
Passes the order of the day.

To be placed under discussion, an order of the day must, under the terms of regulation, be followed by twenty signatures. It was a signature that was being requested of Prégamain. With what joy he gave it, and how pleasant it was to hear the president read his name with those of the other authors of the motion!

What a debut!

The opposition newspapers affected to forget the other nineteen signatures of the order of the day in order only to retain the name of Prégamain, which gave rise to a thousand jokes in more or less severe taste. The Prégamain order of the day! The ministry treated and cured by the waters of Lathuile! One irreverent gazette put the incident in a vaudeville. Gédéon saw himself sung in verses of eight feet stuffed with allusions. The columnists came to the rescue of the reporters and for a week, there was no question in the public sheets of anything but Gédéon.

That ovation displeased him. He would have preferred something less raucous and more solid; so he promised himself not to engage his reputation lightly and to be suspicious of orders of the day. The idea then occurred to him to interrupt, and appeared excellent to him.

He could be heard from that day on, almost every day, with regard to no matter what. As soon as the session began to be troubled, Prégamain rose to his feet, mingled his cry with the general clamor, became animated, descended into the hemicycle, and gesticulated furiously. He came to fill a standard theatrical role in the Chambre, which posters generally described as: "Triple rank of men of the people...Monsieur Alexis."

Gradually, he assimilated the customary dictionary of interruptions, and becoming bolder, articulated them in a more distinct voice. He cried: "Closure! Put the question! Continue! Continue! Very good!" and, in general, the interjections that the official report summarizes under the formula: *Protestations from a large number of benches*.

To the right, he shouted: "Go back of Coblenz!" and to the impassioned of the left: "What of the fourth of September?"

One day, without knowing why, out of habit and instinct, he dared to interrupt alone, and the *Journal Officiel* bore in the extensive report these words thrown into the midst of a grave speech by Monsieur Freppel:

Monsieur Prégamain de Lathuile: "It's too much!"

But if he did not speak, he voted and showed himself. When Théodora, finishing reading a speech, read in the official report the words: *On descending from the tribune the orator received the congratulations of his colleagues*, Gédéon stopped her to say to her: "I was one of them!"

The work of committees offered him no opportunity to shine. On the day when the Chambre gathered in their offices to elect the members of the budget committee, Gédéon went to the Palais Bourbon, resolved to put forward his candidacy, but when he had taken his place among his colleagues he became circumspect again, admitted to himself that he would have nothing to say, and voted meekly with the majority of his group.

He did not lose courage, however. The day of his revenge would come eventually. Destiny could not have aided and served him so marvelously to abandon him half way, between the shameful past and the impossible future. All was not yet said, for sure. The député's mandate was a means, not an end.

"Patience!" he repeated. "Let's wait…!"

To the man who had said to him, four years earlier: "Would you like to become a député. You will be, within three years," he would have replied: "You were wrong to mock a poor advocate's clerk. Député! How do you expect that I could ever be elected? By what right? By what means?" Now he had a seat in the Chambre, he was suffering from seeing himself confounded with the other députés, as he had once suffered from living lost in the host of taxpayers.

He was indeed a député, but any député, an anonymous member of the Chambre. It would have been explained to him in vain that, with regard to vanity, one could already be proud of having obtained a place among the country's elect. Gédéon would not have taken comfort in that reasoning. Celebrity did not appear to him to be something relative, but absolute. In his eyes, a crowd of the elect remained a crowd, and that displeased him. From his député's bench he now wanted to leap to the ministerial bench. Certainly, it was impossible to act in Paris as in Lathuile, in theatrical gestures, lavishing millions and benefits; resignation and patience was required. Nothing was lost.

Did not the past answer for the future? Did not a great distance so rapidly taken prove that the member for Sisteron was marked for a higher destiny? Why be discouraged?

After all, he thought, *perhaps my hour has not yet come. The Republic is indecisive, it is groping. It has only really existed for a year, since the Maréchal's retirement. The ministers are now building temporary edifices, as it were, and dismantling them, like games of patience, if they don't fall down like houses of cards. Perhaps something definitive is in incubation. Let's wait.*

But the electors of Sisteron were growing impatient. Perpetually stirred up by the rancor of the veterinarian, they were beginning to think that their delegate was not doing them honor. Gédéon was warned of the danger and received advice to take action: a speech, just a speech, any speech. It did not have to be long or sublime, if necessary, people would be content with a hundred-line improvisation, but it was necessary to speak; reelection was at stake,

Damn! thought the député. *Let's not waste time.*

The Chambre had just concluded an important debate. The order of the day related to a projected law related to a question of mortgage loans, and fell within the acquaintance of the former advocate's clerk. He scanned the text of the project, analyzed the question, and, the day before the debate was due to open, requested to be inscribed by the president as a speaker.

The president appeared surprised, but did as he was asked. The news soon ran around the corridors and offices: Monsieur Prégamain de Lathuile was going up to the tribune.

"Bah!"

"It's official. He's just notified the office."

"When is it?"

"Tomorrow."

"I'll have to go to listen to that!"

A parliamentary debut is always an important event. The unknown, the newcomer who climbs the steps of the tribune for the first time might perhaps reveal himself as a Mirabeau. In brief, when Gédéon entered the hall the next day, with a enormous portfolio under his arm, he contemplated the tiers lines with representatives with amazement. The most inexact had turned up. Spectators were crowding the public benches in large numbers, as for a sensational debate.

Gédéon sat down in his usual place and put his hand on his heart to search for signs of anguish. No, the heart was beating regularly, the pulse was calm. No anxiety.

A secretary finished reading the legal formula.

The moment was approaching. A ringing bell put an end to private conversations and, in the bleak silence of the audience, the president pronounced: "The order of the day requires the discussion of the projected law relative to mortgage purges. The floor is given to Monsieur Prégamain de Lathuile."

Gédéon had risen to his feet at the first word. He passed into the central corridor on the steps and, as the president finished, he reached the bottom of the staircase to the tribune.

At that moment—an unforgettable session!—the thunder of five hundred bursts of laughter burst forth beneath the window of the austere hall. At first there had only been a few stifled chuckles, contained by the solemnity of the place and the dignity of the audience, but hilarity had abruptly spread through all the benches like a trail of gunpowder.

He députés were holding their sides, so true is it that sometimes only requires a wretched stupidity to cleanse the spleen of serious individuals. The simple phrase "mortgage purges," coupled with the justly famous name of Prégamain, had unleashed a tempest. In the hall, several honorable gentlemen tipped back in their benches, were laughing wholeheartedly; others, as red as poppies, were trying to soothe themselves by rapping on the lecterns; others were guffawing at length, only pausing to say: "No, it's idiotic! My God! Are we stupid to laugh like that?"

To the excitement of the national representation was added the delirium of the public benches; the spectators stamped their feet, throwing *double entendres* into the racket, coarse jokes about the question and the orator. Ladies, alarmed, turned modestly crimson and sought refuge behind the flexible branches of fans. Incapable of containing themselves and not daring to burst forth, the ushers had run away and were uttering such clamors in the corridors that they were audible in the Place de la Madeleine.

Bewildered, Gédéon contemplated the Chambre in folly and murmured: "What's got into them?"

The president was clinging to his desk, biting his lips, exhausting himself in superhuman efforts to preserve, at least in his own person, the dignity of the legislative body. He saw Gédéon turn toward him, pale and haggard, stammering:

"Monsieur le president…Monsieur le president…"

"What is it?"

"Repeat that I have the floor. They probably didn't hear."

"But yes! But yes!"

And the unfortunate president shook his hand-bell desperately.

Tears can easily be dried up, sobs caught in the throats of the afflicted, but it is something else entirely to extinguish the laughter of a crowd. If one isolated giggle bursts forth at the first moment of silence, the general laughter reawakens. Nothing is more contagious.

After a good five minutes, the hilarity calmed down, but, yielding to the persistence of the honorable delegate of the Basses-Alpes, and perhaps also out of malice, the president repeated the famous sentence: "The order of the day, etc."

He was not able to finish. On all sides the députés had risen to their feet and were shouting at Gédéon: "Get down! Get down!"

Prégamain saw himself surrounded by gesticulating arms and scarlet faces steaming with tears. He was begged to remove himself. A cry resounded from the public benches: "Take him away!"

Never had a political assembly laughed so much. It was a dementia, an epilepsy. The president had renounced reestablishing order. Abruptly, he seized his hat and put it on.

The session was suspended.

The députés quit the hall in tumult, abandoning the petrified Gédéon at the tribune.

The unfortunate had finally understood.

Hazard had only raised him up to fall from a higher point. The purgative spring to which he had attached his name, of which he had made the instrument of his notoriety and his glory, had now become a cause of derision. People had refused to see in him the representative and the legislator, to consider only the man who sold a purge. The pretext was absurd, but the catastrophe seemed irreparable.

Motionless before the deserted steps, he considered the portfolio stuffed with documents and notes, Bitter tears came to his eyes but he did not even permit himself to weep. An usher came to hand him his overcoat and hat. The hall was about to be closed.

He went out, determined to throw himself in the Seine. He would not have consented to return to the conjugal domicile at any price.

What would Théodora think? What might the notary have said?

Oh, that notary! With what joy would Prégamain have intoxicated himself on his blood! For he was that cause of it all, that man! Alone, he had thwarted the fine project of the voyage to the heart of Africa; alone, he had had the idea of the Lathuile domain and the mineral spring.

All in all...

But the veterinarian! He too would be laughing tomorrow, that poisoner of livestock, savoring in the newspapers the account of the session" He would be triumphant! He would say to the electors: "I told you so!"

Thus, so much effort accomplished, so many millions spent, had ended in a gigantic catastrophe. No man had ever reached that degree of ridicule. It was not a matter this time of

a small question of self-respect, a malicious intention suspected in an equivocal phrase. No, Gédéon sensed that he was
ridiculous before the universe. France entire, represented by
its territorial delegates, and those of Algeria, Guadeloupe,
Martinique and Cochinchina, had mocked him. He had heard
the formidable laughter of a nation. And tomorrow, thanks to
the telegraph, people would be laughing not only in France,
but everywhere, in Berlin, in Saint Petersburg, in New York,
and in Calcutta! History had not yet registered such a profound fall.

Wandering at random through the streets, he ran aground
in front of a restaurant, where he sat down in a corner, not so
much to eat as to rest; for, having emerged from the Palais
Bourbon at three o'clock, he had walked until seven in the
evening, Fearful of being recognized in the hall, he asked for a
private booth and, for the sake of appearances, ordered dinner.

When the first course arrived, he sent the waiter away.
"Leave me alone," he said. "I'll ring."

A great politician[11] once said; "It is necessary to take
everything seriously, and necessary to take nothing tragically."

Let's see, Gédéon thought. *It's a matter of examining
where we are tranquilly. I've been mocked, made to look a
fool, jeered and booed. So be it. Let's not dissimulate the fact
that today will have a tomorrow. At this moment, journalists
are putting me in songs. In the same way that Limayrac[12] has
been metamorphosed into a flower like Narcissus, perhaps I'll
be changed into a spring like Biblis. For a good week, I'll be
delivered as fodder to the chroniclers, to the gossip columnists, to the ferocity of jokes. All right... The people of Sisteron*

---

[11] Adolphe Thiers (1797-1877), first President of the Third
Republic. The description is probably sarcastic.

[12] Théodore Banville wrote a song mocking people who had a
poetic aspiration to be a flower, using the journalist Paul
Limayrac, an enemy of the Romantic Movement, as a hypothetical absurd example.

*will utter howls and my former competitor will be implacable.
Fine...*

But, all things considered, can this misadventure be qualified as original? No! I'll be attacked, but who has not been attacked? I'll be mocked, but who can flatter himself with escaping irony? People will go as far as to slander me, but are there not limits to the audacity of slanderers? If I can believe the testimony of history, celebrity generally gives birth to persecution; great men are for the most part, greatly calumniated. How they attacked Thiers! How they attack Gambetta! How they attack Bismarck! How they slander Garibaldi! How they mock Jules Simon! None of them has thought of throwing himself in the river. Confident in their destiny, those predestined men disdain the mockery, scorn the outrage. They go on, they march, they persist...

I shall follow that noble example; I too will be strong, valiant and disdainful. At the end of the day, they'll never make as many jokes about me as they have about Napoléon I!

He stopped in order to taste his soup, which he found to be excellent.

I was foolish to despair, he said to himself then. *Certainly, the assault has been rude; I'm still sweating and exhausted in consequence, but the pieces are intact. If I compare my situation with that of the wretch of whom no one takes any notice, I ought, on the contrary, to congratulate myself. All this is nothing but a proof. Until now, things have progressed too easily, I was threatened with arriving too quickly. Damn it! A stopover doesn't compromise a voyage. One rests, one meditates, one gathers one's strength in order to set forth again soon.*

"*The leave committee will understand my position and grant me a few weeks. The electors will read my speech in the* Écho de Lathuile *and I'll ruin my competitor by installing a veterinarian in the arrondissement whose consultations will be gratuitous. I'll be mocked for a week, but in two or three months, no one will think about the incident any longer. People forget so quickly in Paris! Besides which, my conscience is not reproaching me for anything, and I can affirm that in this affair, all the wrongs are on the side of my colleagues. I came as a serious man to discuss a serious question seriously; I was acting in good faith, with good will. They've been bestial and ferocious; they laughed at things that had nothing to do with the debate, and shut my mouth brutally. They alone have caused the scandal, they alone ought to blush at it. There will, I hope, be a newspaper that will present the matter under that aspect. Anyway, I have the* Écho de Lathuile, *and I count on making good use of it.*

In moments of crisis, the slightest consolation seems precious. In spite of his trouble, the unfortunate Gédéon had drawn up a first-rate menu and ordered a delicious meal. Solitude rendered him a little calm, good meat returned a little courage to his heart. He was glad to have avoided the Avenue Marceau, Théodora's ill-humor, the notary's chagrin, the possible arrival of visitors and petitioners. He decided to go back late, to distract himself, to go to a theater or a concert hall to pass the evening cheerfully and finish pulling himself together. For a long time he had not permitted himself the slightest distraction. This evening, he certainly deserved a little treat. Yes, but what if he were seen and recognized, and fingers were pointed at him?

Well, he would be recognized, that's all. People would see that he was showing himself without fear, being without reproach.

With that intention, he finished his meal more rapidly. Hope and confidence returned to him with his appetite. He drank a bottle of Chambertin and half a bottle of Roederer, in order to cheer himself up a little. Again, he saw everything looking rosy—pale, but rosy.

As he was lighting a third cigar and pouring a third glass of yellow Chartreuse, a voice made him shudder.

People were talking in the next booth, and the name of the delegate of Sisteron had just been pronounced. Gédéon pricked up his ears.

He soon distinguished two voices, male voices, voices that were not unknown to him. Who could they be? In vain he sought a little hole, a crack, a fissure in the partition, an opening that would permit him to recognize the diners. He had to resign himself to hearing without seeing anything.

Now, the neighbors—young men to judge by the sound of their voices—were chatting about indifferent things: theater, horses, women and baccarat. However, Gédéon could not doubt that his name had been pronounced. He persisted, and this is what he heard:

"Fundamentally, you see, my dear, it's all the same to me, but it's so absurd, your idea, that I'm amusing myself looking into it. You're surely the first..."

"Not at all. It's a human law. One loses one's taste for things because of those who obtain them, houses where one is received because of those who are received there, women by those who have loved them. A woman always conserves something of the man she deceives or whom she leaves; she has ideas and words that remain from the other."

"All right."

"Hence, it's prudent to choose. So, look, the woman we were talking about just now..."

"Little Madame Prégamain?"

"Yes...well, she's nice, she dresses well, she possess that slight air of candor that is exquisite in an adulterous woman. It's not difficult to divine that she's bored to death; I've put a finger on her heart and, word of honor, it promises to go quickly and well. Are you following me?"

"Yes, go on."

"Well, my dear, what can I say? She would no sooner throw her arms around me than I'd hasten to flee."

"Poor little woman!"

"Don't laugh. She'd be biting her thumbs. So, one doesn't marry a man like that Prégamain!"

"The fact is..."

"I'm sure that you'll share my opinion. No, but imagine being amorous of that woman, taking her hands, saying pretty things to her, trailing at her knees!"

"You're going a bit far."

"My demonstration will be more complete. Tell me, could you ever, even for a moment, forget the function of the husband in vulgar society, his medicinal water, the usage of that water, the role of that water? Pronounce the name Prégamain in a drawing room and you'd have committed what is known as a gaffe. One doesn't talk about such things..."

"Agreed."

"And the name that you don't want, even for a moment, in your conversation, you could engrave in your thought? With the word your ear doesn't want to hear, you could fill your heart? Get away! The name that produces laughter or evokes other sensations of a more unpleasant genre, you could produce with composure, with affection? You can put your soul into saying it? You could put passion into it?"

"Shut up, I beg you. What you're saying is abominable."

"Good, you've understood. It isn't only great arguments that engender strong convictions. In brief, old chap, one can take for a mistress the wife of a great man or a manual worker, but not the wife of a ridiculous man, not a Madame Prégamain. I imagine that she must reek of castor oil, that woman. There, frankly, is a mistress that would make one think of the tribulations of Monsieur de Pourceaugnac, or Monsieur Purgon, a mistress who would evoke ideas of the hospital."

"Oh, impossible!"

"Absolutely impossible!"

"It would be a horror!"

"An unspeakable horror!"

When he left the restaurant, Gédéon no longer resembled a man, but a specter. He was as pale as a wax candle, as cold as a sorbet, and, so to speak, an automaton. He walked without seeing anyone, without paying any heed to the noise of carriages, with a long and regular stride. Thus he reached the boulevards at the height of the Faubourg Montmartre and followed them in the direction of the Madeleine.

The Théâtre des Variétés was open, but he did not go in. He went passed the hall of the Nouveautés without perceiving the door, in front of the Opéra without distinguishing the illuminated façade.

The hopes conceived during the meal had fled into annihilation, the consolations glimpsed had disappeared. Prégamain no longer had the appearance of a man planning a hectic evening.

At the same pace he passed the Rue Royale and went up the Avenue des Champs-Élysées as far as the Arc de Triomphe and the Étoile. There he turned left and followed the Avenue Marceau as far as the door of his house.

The house was in turmoil because of the prolonged absence of the master. Théodora had not eaten and was weeping like a fountain, exhausted as she was by the hurricane of emotions: the session, the députe's disappearance. On hearing her husband come in she hurtled into the antechamber, threw her arms around him, glad to see him, to be finally reassured. But he rejected her brutally.

"Don't come near me!" he cried. "Don't come near me! Wretch!"

Frightened, she obeyed, and ran to take refuge in her boudoir, feeling that she was going mad.

Gédéon went into his study and locked the door.

His desk was laden with papers, letter, files, newspapers. He thrust it all away with a sweep of the fist, clearing the top. Then he took a blank sheet of paper and a pen and he wrote.

A quarter of an hour later, a loud detonation plunged the luxurious dwelling into terror. People ran to the study, forced the door, and found the député of Sisteron lying on the carpet with a bloody wound in his forehead.

The letter in which he explained his fatal determination was thus conceived:

In order to attain the first rank, I have expended two years of dogged labor and more than six million francs; I have enriched two hundred families and stirred up an entire region.

I wanted to become as illustrious as anyone else, and it has been proven to me that I can't even be deceived by my wife like anyone else.

I've had enough.

G.P.

It was universally believed that Prégamain had killed himself by virtue of despair, caused by his terrible parliamentary check.

What fools people are, eh?

THE GIRL

*To Hector Pessard, in testimony of my high esteem
and grateful affection.*[13]

"Damn, she's late..."

And Roland, anxious, asked for a newspaper.

"You're not dining?" a comrade interrogated.

"Yes...in a while."

He tried to read an evening paper, but without being able to interest himself in his reading. Around him, in the brasserie, the usual diners took their places, with a jovial racket of exchanged greetings. From time to time the door opened, giving passage to a newcomer. No Philistines. Everyone found his corner and his chair. At the back were the two tables of the painters, coupled by a sheet metal extension, and bearing the settings of Fernand Vermon, Michel Willine, David and old Legaz; to the right, Judey, Roucher, Charlerie, Valréau, the clan of journalists and poets; further away, the table where, twice a day, the engraver Reboureux sat on his own; to the left, under the spiral staircase, the places of the gamines, the models and the good girls devoid of social position: Nelly, Sarah, Mimi, Nana Merher, Victorine la Rousse and Bertha, a great pale caricature coiffed with superb black hair.

"Is it necessary to set a place for Monsieur?"

"Yes," said Roland."

Gradually, the brasserie filled up. Painters and sculptors, expelled from studios by the approach of evening, came down from Montmartre, from the Place Pigalle, from the Rue Lepic,

---

[13] The journalist Hector Pessard (1836-1895), best known as a theater critic.

from the Boulevard de Clichy, followed or joined by the mob of art-dealers anxious to broker some deal between the dessert and the coffee. Old comrades met up, amicably. Questions were asked:

"Going well, your big project?"

"So so..."

"By the way, I saw your two decorative panels at Bague's this morning; it's very good, you know…no, no, seriously, my compliments old chap."

"And Legendre?"

"Left for Rome yesterday evening; the whole Bouguereau[14] studio escorted him to the railway station."

"Let's see—five hundred francs? Can we make a deal for five hundred francs?"

"Go on! Dutil's going to be decorated? That's a bit stiff!"

"You can say what you like, but I believe that Cabanel..."

"No, I no longer prepare with bitumen, it's too expensive. Look at the Baudrys at the Opéra!"

"Have you looked at Detaille's water colors? That's bad."

"Bertauld? No one's seen him for three months!"

"Why, Jordeuil! How are things?"

"No, lad, no gum..."

Roland looked at the time. Seven o'clock already. Where could she have stayed so late? Let's see, after lunch, on quitting him, Gilberte was go to see Père Hermann, of the Institut,

---

[14] While the artists who feature as characters are fictitious, these merely named in passing are mostly real. This particular reference is to William-Adolphe Bouguereau (1825-1905), an academic painter immensely fond of painting female nudes titled for various mythological and legendary figures; he might well have been the model for Père Hermann.

who needed her for a Herodias.[15] Good. That was agreed; she'd promised him a sitting. She'd left at noon, in order to get to the Rue d'Assas at about one o'clock. How long was the sitting? Let's say until five. After five, no means of working; the light changing, changing, changing. So, at five o'clock— half past five—Gilberte was free. An hour to get back: six thirty. And it would soon be half past seven!

Then he remembered that Père Hermann was trifle garrulous. That old man lived more youthfully than the young, in spite of his sixty-five years. He'd conserved the manias of a neglectful and idle student, a rage for playing truant in the dubious eateries and shady cabarets of the Latin Quarter, the habit of swilling his absinthe at a corner of the banal table and listening to the new ones chat, the correct and gloved students of our epoch, while heaping with platonic madrigals the beautiful girls whom he regaled sumptuously with black coffee and cherries in brandy, striving to make them laugh when they had pretty teeth. And with that, tidy, as decently-clad as a perfect notary. He had probably taken Gilberte to some dive in the Boulevard Saint Michel or the Rue Soufflot, and they were both chattering away tranquilly, their elbows on the table. A delay, after all—a slight delay.

"Is it necessary to serve Monsieur?"

"In a while."

Meanwhile, the other models had arrived: Nelly, the plump English blonde who posed for Parisiennes at Nittis'. Victorine, the understudy of Sarah Bernhardt that Alfred Stevens employed; Nana Mehrer, the usual model of Jules Lefebvre, who had used her as the model for his *Vérité* for the Musée de Luxembourg; Gabrielle, Benjamin Constant's Moorish slave; Mimi, one of Corot's pale nymphs; Maria la Belge of the Gérome studio; Nini, the sculptor Suchetet's Biblis; Élise Fanet, Manet's model, and even Sarah the Eng-

---

[15] In French art and literature the names Salome and Herodias were often regarded as equivalent, so the reference is to a painting of the notorious dancer.

lishwoman, who always arrived after all the others, drunk on gin quaffed during the day in the taverns of the Pigalle quarter.

The clients were still coming in. Two or three times the door opened for a band announced by a tumult of joyful voices—the deep timbre of males and the fresh laugher of cheerful girls. They were the little fugitive troupes on the Rat Mort or the Nouvelle Athènes, comrades at table upstairs over their absinthe, with those from the Boulevard Rochechouart and the Avenue Trudaine, the colonists from the Clou and the Chat Noir, bringing new faces or keen to sample the atmosphere. Then there were people one saw at intervals, once or twice a month, musicians, engineers, men from the Bourse, gripped by an intermittent dilection for the little artists' estaminet. The latter took the trouble to sit down and drink something with plenty of water.

Irregulars passed through, leaning on a cast iron pillar or stopping at the corner of a table to exchange a "How goes it? *Au revoir!*" A few possessed a place in the models' corner; there was Eva, the mistress of a paint-seller in the Rue Fontaine; Louisa, separated from her husband—a former squadron leader, yes, my dear—and living on alms; Louise Dupin the second-hand dealer, with a packet of exquisite sketches from the studios under her arm, which she sold to naïve amateurs.

All the gas jets were lit now, and the room with the white and gold walls was ablaze in a heavy atmosphere of fuming stews and stale wine. A horror! It was stifling. The menu was passed around, a poor one with railway buffet dishes. The voices, languid and suspended at first, soon woke up again. People chatted with more enthusiasm, not only in the narrow vicinity delimited by the place-settings, but from table to table, and from one end of the room to the other. The conversation flowed in all directions, witty and disordered, ideas and follies colliding, touching on everything in fine surges of juvenile and sincere effrontery, from which a bizarre essence mingling hectic paradoxes and profound thoughts could be decanted. From that rumor of buzzing speech, freely voiced, flew the occasional lightning-flash of a neat phrase, a sane and accurate judgment, a delicate observation, a poetic formula, which gave the din an incomparable youthful grace.

In their corner, under the staircase, the gamines were cackling breathlessly, mouths full, through their twenty-year-old hunger. Some, serious, were talking painting, defending the painters who employed them and the pictures for which they had posed. A petite blonde of consumptive appearance remained dazed, sunk in the divan backed up against the wall, her head tilted back, with an expression of stupid and blissful contemplation. Other were quarreling, jealous and enraged, with dignified attitudes and pinching their lips to address one another as "my dear Madame."

Finally, the noise of a carriage was heard outside the brasserie, in the Rue de La Rochefoucauld; then the door opened and Gilberte appeared on the arm of a handsome, decorated old man, whom she was pushing slightly.

"Get in, then!"

There was an abrupt pause in the conversations. Everyone got up to salute.

"Monsieur Hermann!"

It was Père Hermann, radiant, blooming, with his face like an old river, his beautiful white beard, his broad-brimmed hat, his eternal black frock-coat buttoned up, ornamented with his commander's red rosette: Père Hermann very proud of giving his arm to the most beautiful girl in Paris.

There was a question of who would offer him a place.

"There!" he said. "I was sure of it! I'm disturbing them, I'm embarrassing them. Listen, I didn't want to; it's the girl who abducted me. At my age, eh!"

"Damn!" said Gilberte. "He wanted to take me to dinner at Foyot's; I preferred to bring you here." And addressing Roland, she added; "As you can imagine!"

Old Herman went from table to table, distributing *bonjours, bonsoirs* and *ça vas*, addressing everyone as "*tu*," the old, the young and the gamines.

"Well, Vermon, your medal of honor, when is it?... Bonjour Florin—oh, you can boast of getting me into a state with your Folies-Bergère water colors... Ah, my old Legaz, so you don't want to come to see me anymore? That's cowardice!... I no longer say bonjour to you, David, you have too much talent... Why, Willine, I was talking about you yesterday to Pothey. What, you don't know Pothey? Pothey of the Muette? Pothey who has so much hair? Right! I said so too... Bah! Nelly! And you had the cheek to write to me that you've been too ill to pose for days... *Bonjour*, Elise, *bonjour*... *Sacrebleu!* It does me good to see all this youth around me!"

He went to shake Roland's hand

"I'll tell you...we went to get something at the English tavern—you know, behind the Sorbonne. I wanted to keep her, she didn't want to. No hard feelings, eh? Come on, come on, where are you going to put me? Above all, I want to be beside the girl."

Roland advanced a chair for him, and while the others were finishing their meal, all three of them commenced dinner—a poor fifty-sou dinner served in coarse faience, on gunmetal place-settings. But with a good appetite, for sure! Old Hermann devoured one dish completely before the others had touched theirs, briskly emptied his glass and said to Gilberte:

"I ought to come here more often...seeing you, my girl, gives me back my appetite."

Roland listened, ill at ease, gnawing at his bit, showing a constrained and awkward politeness, having difficulty suppressing the desire that gripped him to leave abruptly, immediately, throwing down his napkin, at the risk of a big scandal. Why the devil had Gilberte brought that old fool? Couldn't she have got rid of him and come back on her own? Apart from the fact that he didn't know Père Hermann very well, he had a grudge against him—as he had against all those who employed Gilberte. It was a torture to find himself side by side with one of the great artists who, for a louis or two, bought the right to contemplate, at leisure and stark naked, the woman he loved. When one of those redoubted encounters took him by surprise, he felt himself reddening with anger and shame at the same time. His mind filled with disgusts, fears and desires.

More than any other, Père Hermann was odious to him. It was the old artist who had discovered—invented, as he put it—Gilberte and had made her famous. It would soon be two years ago. Modeled on that little seamstress, then common and poorly clad, Hermann had painted goddesses and empresses. That lucky find, toward the end of his career, had rendered the painter a renewal of youth and potency, had, so to speak, re-tempered his genius. So he loved the girl with a quasi-paternal tenderness into which entered an indefinable gratitude and a kind of jealousy. Yes, he was jealous, the old man, and jealous without amour, jealous only by virtue of artistic egotism. In the early days, after he had abducted Glberte from her dress-making workshop, he had imposed on himself the task of watching over her, of lodging her, of educating her, of giving her elegant tastes in harmony with her beauty. He also gave her good advice, like a true Papa; and he was afflicted and angry, like a lover, when he learned that, yielding to persistence or promises, she had gone to pose for others.

"She's being unfaithful to me," he said, then.

That singular jealousy did not stop at the concerns of the painter; it went much further, weighed upon the young man's actions, movements, preferences and habits. For a long time, for instance, he had been suspicious of Roland, in whom he suspected a lover, and had followed, watched, and spied in the girl, only being reassured on the day when he was conscious of the fact that the young poet was simply a rejected lover.

For that too, Roland detested him; but, knowing Gilberte's admiration for the master, he suppressed his rancor. Every time he found himself in the old man's presence, he strove to put on a brave face, to salute him with a humble veneration.

This evening, the ordeal was ruder, complicated by Gilberte's presence. Thus far, Roland had only bumped into the old academician in neutral and severe salons where chatter could be more easily avoided. When Gilberte said to him: "I have a sitting with Père Hermann. Come and pick me up there at five o'clock; he likes you and often asks me what's become of you," he had always made up excuses to refuse. To know that Gilberte was going to the Rue d'Assas was a torture for him; to hear her talk about the master displeased and aggravated him. He avoided meeting him. For the first time, he found himself between the old man and the girl.

The dinner would have been lugubrious without the inexhaustible loquacity of Hermann, for whom it was a treat to cross the bridges and climb up to the quarters in which our painters and sculptors—who would have lacked light in the old narrow streets of the left bank, and peace and quiet in the frenetic movement of the boulevard—have aggregated for some years. Certainly, it was pleasant to find young talents there, nascent renowns, valiant and bold spirits, but his greatest satisfaction was to be able to contemplate again, even in that narrow and vulgar frame, the adorable model to whom he owed his recent successes.

To employ a trivial expression, he ate her with his eyes, granting little or no attention to Roland and the others, disdaining the flirting of the gamines. And he went on, and on...

As nine o'clock sounded he drank his coffee in a single draught and stood up, saying:

"This is the hour that fellows of my age go to bed. If you would care to, Roland, we'll take this child home, and then you can walk me to the end of the street."

Gilberte lived a few paces away, in the Rue de Laval, at the corner of the Rue Bréda. Having arrived at her door, she held out her two hands to her friends, and disappeared.

Hermann lit a cigarette and took the poet's arm in a familiar fashion.

"What a princess, eh!" he said, while walking, gesturing over his shoulder at the house that they were leaving behind.

After a pause, he went on: "You see, Roland, my lad, that child isn't a woman, she's a world. Two years ago I was empty, used up, finished! An old Salon beard, an old man with palms, something lamentable and comic. I painted as a matter of routine, without pleasure; I made portraits of magistrates and women of the world, tiresome types. Well, from the day when I unearthed that marvel, a change of vision! I rediscovered my talent, word of honor, which hadn't happened to me since 1865. I began to love my art again, frankly, passionately, naively, as I had loved it at twenty, when I was twenty, when I arrived in Paris. Absolutely as at twenty! All the beauties that I dreamed then and of which my heart and head were full, that child has given me...and unstintingly, royally.

"I owe to her having known Juno and contemplated Cleopatra. That concierge's daughter seems the issue of a race of gods. She alone is as beautiful as Semiramis, Pasiphae, Imperia and Princess Borghèse, perhaps more beautiful, for she combines and summarizes the beauties scattered between thousands of women. I haven't yet arrived at seizing her own head, the expression of her face; she has them all. At the slightest indication, she strikes the pose, of her own accord, naturally, so to speak, with a facility and a rapidity of assimilation that is a gift. I haven't found it in anyone else.

"She isn't a model, she's *the* model, the only one. A wrinkle in the forehead, a movement of the lips, a gleam or a languor in the gaze, and she transforms herself, transfigures herself, dresses herself in a new beauty, an unexpected splendor, an unknown charm. She isn't only the pure form, created for the contemplation and intoxication of artists; she isn't only the divine cup from which the ideal spills, she's the spirit, she's the soul, my dear, she creates thought. An admirable creature and a sublime actress. It's necessary not to be enticed; what will survive her in my work will have been inspired by her. You've seen my Ophelia? Well, you'll see my Herodias...a blonde Herodias, that's bold, isn't it? Well, one would swear that it was another woman! Nothing of Ophelia any longer survives in the model; she's wild, she's terrible, it's an allure of sacred horror! Would you give me a light?"

They took a few steps in silence, then the old man resumed.

"By the way, I read your volume of verse, the last one, the *Tendresses*. It's fine, it's very fine, but it doesn't please me. Don't defend your work, I'll explain; at least I'll try to

111

explain it to you. First of all, you have talent, a great deal of talent, and sincerity, something honest and naïve, which seduces the reader and makes him your friend from the first pages. But do you think it's sufficient in art to do well? It's a theory; many think that one responds to all the demands of the spirit by limiting oneself to deploying a masterly skill. But I also have my theory, and this is it: one is only an artist on condition of embracing nature entirely. Do you understand? For example, an animal painter is an animal painter, but he isn't a painter. If he isn't moved either before humans or before the sea, if he reserves all the resources of his personality to the cult of little sheep and English horses, that's sufficient, he's classified. Possibly, he shows talent and is counted as a great man, but he's not an artist, he's a specialist. You Roland, are perhaps not a specialist, but you're certainly an egotist."

"I don't understand," said Roland.

"Wait…in art, one becomes an egotist by accident. That's your case, and it's the case of many others, even among the foremost. Look, take, for example, Beethoven having gone deaf. That's where you are. In the same way that Beethoven could no longer hear the song of the woods, the plaint of the wind, the eternal and profound symphony of nature, and he then listened to the melodies of his heart weeping within him, you've lost all tenderness for the things and creatures that surround you. You're listening within your breast to the singing of a young bird intoxicated by amour, which is cooing your refrains and weeping your own tears; if a hope reaches you, a suffering afflicts you, a joy enlightens you, you consent to be moved. You, always you, you alone—or, rather, the amour that is within you. Apart from that, beyond that, nothing exists. The world could crumble and you wouldn't quiver; at the most, you'd regret what the world might have produced to ornament your idol. You want more? You're in love, my poor fried, which is to say, a prisoner. You're living locked within one thought, one sole ambition, one sole desire, in a unique dream, in a narrow servitude; and you're walking with little infantile steps when you could be traversing the world with great strides and sensing, palpitating within your breast in its entirety, immense humanity!"

There was another moment of silence. Roland was no longer thinking of interrupting the academician now; on the contrary, he was listening attentively.

The old man stopped to relight his cigar, and taking the young man's arm again, he continued:

"If that amour were even alive in your book—but no. Between us, there isn't a single line in your *Tendresses* that isn't addressed to Gilberte is there? Yes? Good. Well, Gilberte no longer exists in the poem, she's absent from it. Your work might have been inspired by any other woman, anyone that's pretty, Nana Mehrer or Bertha. You're so preoccupied with your sensations, the care of giving a form to your melancholies, of putting blood into the veins of your images, that you've forgotten...what? The idol herself...who is, however, far more beautiful than your dreams, child! Look, the great sentiment of the artist, the one that makes great artists, isn't amour, it isn't an ambitious desire—no, it's the one from which he suffers and that makes him bleed; it's sacrifice. Would you care to give me a light?"

They had arrived beside the Seine, in the Place du Châtelet, and they had stopped between the two theaters, as if they had tacitly agreed to separate there. But Père Hermann had not finished.

"Come this way, young man. I know a glass of Hungarian beer in this quarter, of which you can give me your opinion..."

When they were at table on the sidewalk of the Avenue Victoria, in front of a large brasserie all ablaze with light, the master, changing his tone abruptly, said: "I'm boring you, aren't I?"

"No, no!"

"Yes! It's a privilege, at my age; it's necessary not to hold it against me. It's quite probable that I'm talking drivel, but I have my idea and I speak my mind. If you were a painter, you'd understand me better. It's so rare, a woman veritably and perfectly beautiful. I've only known one of them before encountering the girl: she was a bit-part player at the Théâtre Historique—you didn't know that one, a masterpiece. She posed for Ingres' *Source* and Ary Scheffer's *Marguerite*.[16] She turned out badly. The misfortune of these queens is that one evening they encounter handsome fellows and they start to love them. Then, *bonsoir!* The goddess is embroiled in domestic habits, she smells the stew and isn't afraid of blackening her hands. Two months later, she's finished. Her waist thickens, her breasts sag, her hips are deformed. If a kid arrives, that puts the lid on it. The day after the birth the woman is still pretty, but she isn't beautiful. Model the *Source* on a mother! Use a sitting with Mère Gigogne in order to resurrect Leda or Salammbô! That was the history of the actress in question. I related it to Gilberte and I believe it's had its effect. Oh dear! Now it's starting to rain. I just have time to get home, I'm running away!"

They were about to separate on the sidewalk at the street corner when the master, looking Roland in the face, put both hands on his shoulders.

"My son," he said, "remember this: the day when Gilberte has a lover might perhaps be good business for industry, but it will be an irreparable loss for art. Love that child as an artist, as a great courageous and devoted artist; love her without desire, as you might love an empress or a woman who died before having been able to give herself to you. Believe me, creatures like her are worth more than a kiss; they merit masterpieces. The girl is born for art and for artists, not for life itself. Her role is merely to traverse life in order to enter the

---

[16] Ingres' *Source*—his most famous painting and a classic female nude—was completed in 1856, but is said to have been begun in Florence in 1820, obviously employing a different model. Nor is the model employed likely to be any of those employed by Ary Scheffer in his various (fully clad) depictions of the character of Marguerite from Goethe's *Faust*, painted between 1831 and 1856.

glory of immortals. One doesn't fall in love with Minerva, you see. One sings her praises, one celebrates her. Would you be any further forward if you made a child? Bah! Write her an ode! Enable her to climb Parnassus and let's try to open the doors of the Louvre to her, where she'll be enthroned among the most radiant and the purest. Young women like that are too beautiful for men. Give me a light, will you? There. I'm going to get soaked. *Bonsoir*."

"*Au revoir*, Master."

An hour later, Gilberte, having put out her lamp and screened the hearth where the logs were reduced to pink embers, came back to her window and perceived, through the slats of the blinds, Roland, drenched with rain, swathed in his ulster, his hat pulled down over his ears, stubbornly holding form under the downpour. He was pacing back and forth, hugging the walls, with the gait of a policeman on the beat or a sentry, filling the quarter with the sound of his boots, considered anxiously by the passers-by whom the weather and the hour were making scarce. Sometimes he marched toward the Rue Frochot, stopped at the corner of the square, and raised his head toward the girl's windows; sometimes he returned to the Rue de La Rochefoucauld, sheltered under a coaching entrance, and then came back toward the Rue Bréda.

One by one, the shops closed, leaving the pavement dark and sad. The Rue de Laval was now completely dark. There was no sound, or almost none—from time to time the heavy thud of a door closing behind the hasty footfalls of a belated tenant, or the tremor of a carriage traversing the causeway in a scintillation of jolting lanterns and splashing puddles.

Finally, after one final glance at Gilberte's windows, Roland turned the corner of the Rue Frochot, and disappeared.

The girl let her curtain fall back.

Perhaps it had been repeated to her too often that she was pretty.

While still a little girl she had developed a strange and wild pride. At the age when girls still cherish dolls and learn simultaneously, from the coins they are given, the redoubtable arts of coquetry and the august solicitude of mothers, Gilberte liked ribbons for their own sake. In the house in the Rue des Martyrs where her mother kept the lodge, there were those among the tenants who spoiled her, giving her bonbons and silver coins. She possessed a full box of bright cast-off ribbons with which her precocious art made adornments, and her greatest chagrin was to see the box confiscated by Mère Bonvilain in her fits of red wrath.

The day when it was necessary to go into the dressmaker's workshop she wept. At first, the idea had made her smile, of going out, of having an escapade in the streets every day, through the passers-by, going past the opulent boutiques of the prosperous quarters, but when she came home on the first evening, she found her hands dirty, the fingers pricked with little black marks; when she felt tired out, exhausted, suffering, the horror of work gripped her and she applied herself to her labor thereafter with the sly rancor of the proud slave. The only good moment of the day remained the interval of idling after lunch. The whole workshop went out in a band, running around the butchers' shops and the fruiterers.

Six sous' worth of salt pork; two sous' worth of green apples that set the teeth on edge and gave a warm vivacity to the carmine of the lips; they ate on a bench on the boulevard, near the omnibus office, with the morsels on their lap. When the little meal was finished, the seamstresses shook out their lustrine aprons and, arm in arm, strolled along the boulevard, harassed in passing by the stupid provocations and lewd laughter of clerks on their lunch break.

At one o'clock they went back in, bringing back to the morose and disciplined workshop more good humor and courage for the work, subjects for gossip at which to laugh behind the boss's back, vague and slow refrains emitted by a hurdy-gurdy at the nearby crossroads. But then the servitude and repulsiveness of the quotidian labor reappeared, the long curbed sorrows, and Gilberte sank into mute rage.

In her eighteenth year, she had an adventure. Irma, her comrade in the workshop, a large jovial girl for whom the employees of the neighborhood lay in wait every evening when she left work, proposed a trip to the country. They would go to eat fries at Asnières with Monsieur André, an employee at the Bon Marché, who would bring one of his friends. The girl consented apathetically, being neither repulsed not tempted, but promised herself to be prudent.

The excursion took place the following Sunday, a stupid stroll in an area covered in stinking factories and ridiculous villas, along a river troubled by drain-water with dead cats bobbing in its muddy waters. It was ugly and dirty. The day was spent almost entirely in waterside cafes occupied by noisy boatmen and frightful young women made up like chorus-girls in café-concerts. After lunch, they crossed the Seine to reach the Île des Ravageurs, where a coarse Bohemia of shop-workers and prostitutes had invaded the playgrounds and the worm-eaten booths. Dinner was served on the terrace of a cheap eatery on which the dust of the towpath descended. Down below, on the roadway, ambulant musicians succeeded one another, blind accordion players, comic singers with white hair, and little Italian pifferari scraping tunes from that nation on poor violins. And all around the hubbub of violent gibes rose from the bank, interrupted every two minutes by the whistles of locomotives and the dull rumble of trains passing over the iron bridge.

Gilberte was bored. At about ten o'clock in the evening, as they were going into the Bal des Canotiers, she perceived that Monsieur André and his friend Édouard were slightly drunk. She refused to dance, in spite of the insistence of her cavalier, who had become singularly gallant, and the example of Irma, who never missed a quadrille. The three young people manifested a turbulent and nervous gaiety, running from one end of the ballroom to the other, talking to strangers, uttering abuse of a calculated and heavy absurdity, offering glasses of beer and talking familiarly to passers-by. They had encountered comrades and formed a merry band, agitated by the orchestra in the luminous haze. Gilberte, being a poseur and a prude, according to Édouard, remained in an obscure corner of the garden, beside a painted sheet-metal table, with an empty glass.

Suddenly, there was a tumult of exasperated voices, cries and insults. The child, climbing on to her chair, perceived Monsieur André in the middle of the ballroom, gesticulating in the middle of a group. He was pale, sweating and furious, struggling against four big boatmen with bare arms and enormous biceps, who were throwing punches at him. André, hatless, his cravat torn away, a long bloody streak on his forehead, was howling, calling them all "filthy swine" and shouting for the police—then an abrupt silence, municipal guardsmen falling into the mob, separating the combatants, arresting everyone. Trembling, she saw Monsieur André, the boatman and the weeping Irma taken away, while the crowd followed, sniggering, leaving the hall empty.

As she was going out, Édouard caught up with her. It was nothing, the affair. A fuss, caused by a boatman who had kissed Irma. André was annoyed. Bang! A slap! Wasn't it stupid? To get into a fight because of pleasantries like that, at a party, on a Sunday. He put his friend squarely in the wrong. As for him, he had had enough of that part of the country, and he was going home to bed. Oh yes!

When Gilberte talked about waiting for Irma, he protested. What for? Go to the commissariat, get roped in with the others. No way!

"It's better to go home, my girl, you see. They'll only let them go for the last train."

Very sad, frightened of remaining alone, Gilberte went with the young man. In any case, she was impatient to get away from that crowd. A fiacre was going along the road to Paris, returning empty. Édouard pushed her into it, got in beside her—and the carriage pulled away.

First, a silence; Édouard had lowered a window and was smoking beside the door, vaguely looking out at the road. Gilberte, fearful, was huddled in her corner, tucking in her shirts, making herself small, Fear was galloping through her heard, and the memory of that sickening day ended by a savage brawl rendered her tremulous. The carriage was not traveling fast enough for her liking, she wanted to be home already, back in her mansard, definitively separated by the coaching door from the bacchanal into which she regretted having ventured.

Oh, it would be a long time before she did it again, for sure! Fortunately, Édouard was still there, ready to take her home; but for that, what would have become of her in the midst of the hooligans and drunkards of Asnières? And Irma? And André? What was happening to them back there, at the commissariat?

Edward threw away his cigarette, closed the window and turned round. Without anything allowing her to foresee the attack, Gilberte felt a robust hand slide around her waist between her dress and the upholstery of the cab. With a rapid movement, the hand advanced, seized her forcefully, drew her toward him, while another hand in front seized her throat and she felt passing over her face, near her mouth, a large rough moustache impregnated with tobacco and alcohol.

She tried to push the shop-clerk away, but in vain. He held her with the massive solidity of a vice, grabbing her arms and twisting her wrists roughly, assaulting her in silence and with a kind of rage, like a brute. And he talked to her in a low voice, hissing: "Come on baby, come on, don't be stupid, be nice. Never seen such a thing! Some manners! Why did you come, then?"

She struggled with all her strength.

"Let go of me! Let go of me, I tell you! Will you let me go! Let me go, or I'll scream!"

"Go on, scream!"

Redoubling his effort, he succeeded in maintaining her with one hand, while holding her two arms dolorously joined behind her waist. In order better to master her he was standing up in the fiacre, and with one knee bent on the seat, he was trying with his free hand to tip her head backwards. She was trapped. A gluttony of gross kisses, delivered like bites, descended on her face, wetting her cheeks, her eyelids, her forehead, the nape of her neck, fell forcefully upon her mouth, with shocks of wild brutality.

She had the horrible sensation of being simultaneously compressed and gagged by those filthy and hairy lips, imposing upon her to the point of making her feel ill, and while she gasped nervously under that bestial caress, Édouard's other hand, rapid and violent, attacked her corsage, tearing away the buttons, ripping the enlarged buttonholes, breaking the threads, and descended over her neck, clutching her breasts like an enormous and heavy spider.

She tried to scream, but no cry emerged from her throat desiccated by fear; nothing except the dull, monotonous gasp that was weakening, weakening...

And that mouth, still stuck invincibly to her mouth, that hot breath inflaming her face, that brow damp with sweat that she could feel dripping onto her forehead. A concussion gripped her, as if she had been struck on the head; it seemed that everything around her was spinning vertiginously, the fiacre, the shielded lanterns with green flames, the houses that she divined along the two sides of the road, and the road itself, everything was trembling. A gut-wrenching turn made her feel sick, rendering her inert and half-intoxicated. Édouard would have been able to let go of her without having to fear the slightest resistance.

In spite of the sanguine fury that had taken possession of him, Édouard perceived that weakness. It had required all his strength until then to tame the beautiful girl, and he was getting to the end. Without a jolt of the vehicle that had thrown the child sideways, perhaps it would have been impossible for him to mater her, for she had defended herself rudely. When he saw her thus, relaxed, defeated, when he divined the fatigue in the slack enervation of her bruised wrists and the slowed rise of her chest, he made gentler caresses, calculated, savant caresses, and gave her less violent kisses—still maintaining her, however. Then, by degrees, believing it a hypocrisy of a debauched grisette, or taking cowardly advantage of his victory, he became bolder.

Then she uttered a heart-rending scream, a ferocious howl. She bounded. got up, squeezing her knees and gripping the shop-clerk's hair with both hands, and, as he still dared to persist, she leaned over him, furious, maddened, and bit his ear cruelly.

"Oh! Damn it!

He was about to strike her with his fist when the carriage stopped dead, in a broad circle of light traversed by men in uniform and formed by a long railing between two thick walls. It was the customs post at the gate to Paris on the Avenue de Clichy.

Gilberte and Édouard hastily resumed a correct attitude, she adjusting her torn and crumpled corsage, he wiping away with a handkerchief a trickle of blood that was running from his ear over the collar of his shirt.

A man came to open the door. "Have you anything to declare?"

Édouard replied, in a curt voice: "No."

But the girl did not wait for the vehicle to move off again. She leapt down to the ground, leaving the furious shop-clerk in the depths of his fiacre. And as he got up to follow her, she looked at him fixedly, with a harsh, hateful stare, and said to him in a voice that anger rendered tremulous: "If you get out, I'll have you arrested."

The young man was afraid—afraid of a bad affair and also afraid of ridicule. He departed, hurling a crapulous insult at the child.

The first tram that passed took Gilberte home.

That night, it was impossible for her to sleep. For hours she stood in her chemise in front of the mirror on her chest of drawers, looking at the traces of the wretch's fingers and the marks of his kisses on her neck, her face and her breasts.

The fingers had hollowed out red furrows, a dirty, violet-tinted red, with thin bloody streaks where the skin had ceded beneath the contraction of the nails; the kisses had left thin signs, elongated like cuts, leaving blood ready to spurt transparent beneath the skin. She saw her arms, humiliated and blackly marbled with frightful patches, and her painful wrists, one of which—the left—was bleeding, scratched by a thin silver bracelet that had broken in the struggle.

For a long time she went from the mirror to the sink, sponge in hand, covering herself with water in order to efface the stigmata. The stains reappeared more vividly, reignited by that freshness, and Gilberte, chagrined, felt an infinite wrath swelling within her.

The red furrows on her breast exasperated her, they burst forth on her skin, as white as young ivory, like the imprint of a branding tattoo. Furthermore, her flesh as burning, suffering everywhere that the coward had put his hands. Was she going to fall ill now because of that man? That was all she needed. She saw herself confined to bed, put on a diet, covered with compresses. Oh, the wretch!

In the hope of sleep, of repose, she blew out her candle and went to bed. But no: a sovereign overexcitement kept her eyes open in the night. She remained crouched on her bed until dawn, her elbows on her knees, and her chin in her two closed fists. She saw again the scene in the fiacre, the struggle, Édouard leaning over her, the head of the red-faced, sweating man, illuminated by fantastic lights, the lanterns of the carriage and the gas-jets fleeing along the roadway. She shivered at the memory of the contacts that had soiled her, the filthy words that she had heard, the danger avoided, her bruised and painful skin.

A hundred times, she repeated: "So that's it? That's it, then?"

The incidents of the evening whirled in her mind like a macabre phantasmagoria. So it was for those base satisfactions that she saw so many girls around her going to the bad: false pleasures, tedious excursions, dirty restaurants, vile dance-halls, absinthe, beer, eau-de-vie and the police station. And the men? Brutes. So, she had the devil in her body, that Irma, with her rage for getaways every Sunday? And her André…another fine fellow, that one!

"So that's it? That's it, then?"

Oh, that fiacre…and to think that, all day long, that wretch Édouard had been repeating that he was in love with her, and that Irma had talked about him as a very nice fellow. In love…amour…

"So that's it? That's it, then?"

And during the desolation of that mute night, Gilberte, humiliated, sensed flowering within her, like a clump of wild red immortelles, hatred, fear and an insurmountable disgust for men.

It was via the painter on the third floor that she met Père Hermann shortly thereafter. Initially she had been asked for sittings of an hour or two, out of pure kindness, to paint her portrait.

The first louis the gentleman offered her—for her trouble—she refused, very surprised to be recompensed for so little, but the old man insisted, declaring that he did not intend to make her waste her time, and added that he might need her again, and often. Then, as she did not understand, he explained to her that it was a métier, to be a model, and cited women who earned four, five or six francs a month by posing.

"Then, if I wanted…?"

"You, child, could make a fortune."

"Oh?"

He had no great difficulty convincing her. In any case, Gilberte detested her work as a seamstress, that obscure and fatiguing labor. On the assurance that she would lack for nothing, she ran away from the maternal home with her poor bundle of clothes and the precious box full of brightly-colored ribbons.

With Hermann she did not experience any dread. Apart from the fact that the old academician was very old, he reassured the girl with his behavior, mingling tenderness, solicitude and a strange respect. He did not grab her by the waist, never tried to stun her with promises, and when he kissed her it was, to speak, as a father, gently, on her forehead, amid her blonde curls, or on her cheeks, innocently, as one does to babies. Not a hint of seduction or provocation; a little gallantry, but the cheerful and benevolent gallantry that is appropriate to amiable old men.

Thus, on days when he was in a good humor, he bought the girl trifles admirably chosen to please her and embellish her; he chose fabrics for her dresses, and hats, and occupied himself with her, perhaps not entirely as a father occupies himself with his daughter, but at least in the fashion of an uncle who protects and spoils his niece.

They day when he asked her to undress for the first time, he was astounded by so much docility. Gilberte did not show the slightest hesitation. Serenely, as if she were undressing in her room to go to bed, she took off her bodice, bared her shoulders, rounded with a pure and harmonious design, the gracious and supple arms of an ancient amazon, velveted with an imperceptible down of golden silk, giving the flesh the vermilion shadows that the brush of Henner delighted in caressing. Beneath her active fingers the laces of her skirts were undone, the corset yielded, delivering a young and charming torso; two small feet slightly bruised by old fatigues emerged from a pair of mules as long as a child's hand.

When she was in her chemise, her legs bare, she had a moment of silent reflection, only betrayed by a frown that shaded her profound eyes; then a shrug of the shoulders, a slight gesture of the head that meant "let's go!" and the chemise fell, circling her feet like the skin of a swan, while, with an adorable gesture, Gilberte put her hands to her chignon, and spread the heavy golden cascades of her hair over her shoulders, all the way to her rosy heels.

That sitting gave birth to the sketch of the *Bacchante*,[17] a superb page that Paris admired at the Salon of 1876, which won the master the grand medal of honor. The public and the critics were unanimous; it was more than a great success for the academician, it was a triumph.

Before that memorable year Hermann had seen himself categorized among the ancients who were surviving their glory and sleeping on the withered laurels of their young years. People said of him: "He's finished." Well, not at all; he suddenly reappeared, younger than the youngest, with an admirable canvas that owed nothing to anyone or any school. It was beautiful and it was bold. The most advanced agreed that one could belong to the Institut and still have genius.

People searched for the key to that surprising mystery, the explanation of the miracle; there was talk of a voyage through foreign museums, new studies, of Velasquez, Michelangelo, the Flemish school...but no one thought about the pretty girl, dressed as a little queen, who came every morning, for an hour, to contemplate the master's masterpiece, and to listen, shivering with pride, to the admiration of the crowd buzzing around her.

From then on, she belonged to Hermann, body and soul. She became both his slave and his child, his thing, in sum. When the old man chattered, talking about his art, his admirations, the naïve passion that had survived in his heart the bitter disappointments and disenchantments of a long career, when he talked about the masters, the dazzling family of minds and talents maintaining its traditions of genius from Giotto to Manet, the girl listened with a religious attention, striving to comprehend, opening her intelligence to that initiation to the beautiful and the great.

---

[17] William-Adolphe Bouguereau, previously suggested as a model for Père Hermann, produced several nudes entitled *Bacchante* in the course of his long career, but the two best-known were painted in 1889 and 1894, after the present story was written; perhaps he read it.

Gradually, the seed of an ideal was born in her.

It seemed to her than in delivering her from servitude, in taking her away from the obscure abode in the Rue des Martyrs, Père Hermann had opened to her, very wide, the doors to an unknown, marvelous world, whose illumination left her dazzled. And what disdain she felt when she happened to think about her former existence, which she glimpsed in fugitive shadows, like an improbable nightmare! How differently she judged the girls among whom she had lived. That slut Irma! And her childhood! The staircases to sweep, the letters to take up to the tenants, the evenings shut away in the lodge with her surly and moaning mother, the dresses of harsh black wool, the cambric aprons, the sleeves worn away at the elbows, the repulsive labor!

And now, something like a royalty, the glory of being useful, the consciousness that art would owe a splendor to her, that she would remain an object of admiration for future ages! That magic word "art" rang in her ear like the triumphant blast of a warrior trumpet, preceding a majestic parade of heroic creatures: goddesses, ethereal fairies, dryads relaxing in the cool shade of woods, empresses with vestments sown with precious stones, trading on tiger-skins, naked courtesans cradled on crimson carpets or borne away by florid galleys.

At the Salon, in front of the *Bacchante*, she savored a delicious voluptuousness. Her eyes half-closed, her nostrils dilated as if to breathe in a perfume burning at her knees, she listened to the music of homages. The master was always praised, but sometimes there was also talk of her. A few admired her in low voices, respectfully; others, loquacious, detailed the *Bacchante* with the connoisseur composure of an anatomist. Those were her arms, her knees, her waist, her hips, her aristocratic hands, her feet like a Chinese princess, that skin beneath which one divined the quiver of a young rich sap...

Others gave their admiration a brutal form, a dressing of desire boldly expressed; and the audacious praise shook the girl with a frisson. She did not feel offended; quite the contra-

126

ry, it pleased her to hear the homage of boors, it gave her the impression of having tamed the beasts, it was like a hint of bitter odor fortifying the incense scattered around her. She would gladly have stayed there for hours, an entire day, listened to the whispering voices mingle, while, dreamily, she no longer saw herself in the *Bacchante*, nor in that reckless and delirious pose that made her akin to a drunken virgin, but even more beautiful and a thousand times different, similar by turns to each of the glorious beauties immortalized by the prestigious hands of masters.

A sovereign egotism possessed her and, in good faith, by virtue of an illusion that Hermann was glad to stimulate, she imagined herself having the right to a share in the triumph of the *Bacchante*. Had not the academician said repeatedly that he owed his success to her? Besides which, at that first Salon, she had made comparisons. Certainly, there were nymphs and faunesses in hundreds, but none offered to the mind, at the same time as the eyes, the realization of the absolute in beauty. Those faces lacked something indefinable and necessary. Those girls retained an air of stupidity, having assuredly not understood the pose, having not penetrated "into the skin of the character" as actors say. In sum, they had not "got it."

Then she had made the acquaintance of one of those girls, on Hermann's arm. Oh, in truth, they were all Irmas, neither more nor less. All sluts and idiots, hardly models, preoccupied above all with a lover, a spree, a dinner in a private room, and dresses to show off in barrière dance-halls. A fine society, truly! A pretty collection! Only two or three of them appeared capable of posing veritably and fully. And the rest! The others, worn out, exhausted, with thick waists, drooping bosoms, hollow cheeks. Not one could have posed for the *Bacchante*. And their manners! And their voices! Raucous speech emerging from a throat burned by absinthe and hollowed out by bellowed songs. Some were coughing pitifully, and certainly would not see next April. Soon addressed familiarly by those girls, Gilberte allowed them to do it, took it in good part, fearful of appearing stuck-up, but she judged them loftily and, deep down felt nothing but scorn for the troop.

That unexpected pride delighted the academician. After having feared that he might lose the girl for a time, he now began to feel tranquil. He had watched her at first, very closely, soliciting her confidences and setting traps for her, searching the words and actions of the singular creature for signs of vice a regret or a penchant. Nothing. She really belonged to him, to him and the bizarre ideal that he had caused to shine within her. She remained chaste, calm, icy, never thinking about her mother, her sisters or any friend at all, divining her soul, feeling neither a heart nor senses: a woman only for art, and in a plastic relationship. She loved nothing in the world, nothing—except that old man of sixty-five, whom she would have quit without a shadow of regret if he had suddenly renounced painting.

In the Café de La Rochefoucauld, which she had adopted as a restaurant when she came to reside in the Rue Laval, she had been assailed and tempted several times.

First there was David, a stupid fop who tried to lead her astray by offering her the fifty sous for her dinner from time to time; then there was Willine, a witty charmer, gently and seductively polite; and finally, the water-colorist Florin, who followed her obstinately through the streets for two months.

She rejected them all, but without arrogance, wittily, like a good girl. To David she responded with a few brief, curt but polite remarks to which no reply was possible; she treated Willine, whose seductive language interested her, differently; Florin was cheerfully mocked. Certainly, none of those men frightened her. While they talked to her she thought about something else, the painting commenced, the day's sitting, imminent triumphs. She could not be reproached for any affection of prudishness. She never struck the pose of an offended queen, and never pronounced the stupid phrase in which the comical hypocrisy of sluts is revealed: "What do you take me for, Monsieur?"

Soon, therefore, the colony at the La Rochefoucauld liked her, with an amity fortified by a good deal of esteem. Old Legaz had proclaimed her "a serious young woman" and that sufficed to protect the beautiful creature, who followed a dubious métier proudly and remained a virgin ignorant of modesty, from the negligence and importunities of the sidewalk. For in that milieu of cavalier and fast-living men, the girl was not frightened by words, even when pointed. Although she never joined in with conversations in which vigorous remarks were exchanged, no blush ever rose to her face. One might have thought her a shameless old man whose ears had, in certain suspect milieux, become accustomed to dirty jokes.

In the first few weeks, she listened to such things with a grave expression, and a bizarre attention, as if to engrave them on her memory. When a coarse expression struck her ear, Gilberte experienced an impression that was, so to speak, reassuring, and her scorn for men was further augmented. Yes, brutal and boorish, that was what men were. One spoke indiscreetly about his mistress, a married woman, a bore, a leech, that he was about to ditch, just like that. Others boasted of never loving; infatuations took time and were costly. Others formulated theories capable of making a clerk at the assize court feel sick.

Only one astonished her among those brazen jokers: Roland. That tall young man was nothing like the others. Gilberte began by finding distinction and charm in him, something feminine that came to delight her, a touching and polite timidity. In addition, he was less talkative, did not let himself go, and listened while showing a vague bored disdain. The girl reflected, and arrived at the supposition that the poet Roland was meditating under some sorrow; she imagined a sort of dolorous romance such as the lovers of the consumptive school produced. But was it appearance? The young man had his moments of merriment and enthusiasm; he sometimes rambled like the others—but he still remained different from the others, and his laughter rang out with a clear, frank tone that always took Glberte by surprise and made her raise her head, as if to an appeal.

So Roland quickly became a comrade. Hazard brought them closer together one evening when the café was crowded, there was only one table for the two of them—an accident that was established thereafter as a habit. Gilberte resigned herself to it.

Roland was poor; he was known to have a minor post at the Bibliothèque Nationale, the salary of which was sufficient for him to live modestly. He had published three volumes of beautiful verse, one of which had been crowned by the Académie Française. Finally, he published short stories in literary journals, delicately sculpted, which the truly literate held in high esteem. He had been seen in the café for three or four years, always alone. No mistress had ever arrived on his arm, no friend had ever shared his dinner. From time to time, he disappeared, did not appear for a month. And that was all.

Without intending to, Gilberte showed more reserve toward Roland than anyone else. Perhaps, after all, the fellow was simply a hypocrite, who had something to hide. She found him singular, disquieting, a little too similar to her. No mistress, no friend; his only preoccupations were work, reading and art. No taste for the girls; nevertheless, he spoke familiarly to the band of models, never refusing an extended pretty hand, and even sitting down sometimes beside Victorine or Bertha, but with a visible indifference, like a man who wants to act like everyone else and adopt without repugnance the habits of his chosen milieu. He never left with one of them in the evening, as the others sometimes did. Alone, among all the regulars, he retained an air of mystery that invited reserve and prudence.

After a few days, Gilberte's suspicions vanished. There was no doubt about it, Roland was sincere. One might even deem him naïve. Although he was twenty-five, he conserved enthusiastic admirations; to hear him, the girl imagined Hermann young. Yes, he was a believer, impassioned, like Hermann. With the aid of habit, the presence of the poet soon became necessary to the model; she waited for him when she arrived before him, felt impatient at certain times to see him again. In spite of the promise she had made herself to leave the café every evening immediately after nibbling her dessert, she lingered opposite the young man, forgetting the time as she listened to him. On the evenings when he arrived clad in black with his white cravat, she scowled and pulled faces like a petulant child, reproaching him for his liking for the Français or the Opéra. Then she went home sooner than usual, went up to her little apartment in the Rue Laval, annoyed and regretful, with a sensation of emptiness and absence.

He was just as pleased with that charming camaraderie. They formed a kind of little household, devoid of domesticity, stew and the prosaic. In sum, it was genteel. The girl brought grace into his poor life. Until then he seemed to have been living like a wood without birds. His amity became ingenious in delicate attentions. He often gave Gilberte trinkets of no great value, but always chosen with exquisite taste—just like Père Hermann, with forty years fewer. He gave her books, engravings, chinoiseries, old jewelry discovered in the antique shops of the Rue de Provence and the Rue Lafayette. At dinner, he did not talk about her or himself, but about a poem published that morning, a play performed the day before, about Alfred de Vigny and Victor Hugo.

Never a word of amour; only once, he thought of telling her that she was beautiful, and he succeeded in saying it well, for she was now familiar with the art of fine speech. In the same way that Père Hermann had initiated her in the admiration of red colors and divine forms, Roland revealed to her the mysteries of thought and the appeasing charm of rhyme. The old painter had purified her taste, the poet elevated her intelligence. He explained the masters in the art of writing, composed a small and select bookshelf for her, applied himself to interesting her and educating her.

It was charming. And what a fine handshake, in the evening, when they separated. They said *au revoir* in the middle of the café, in front of everyone. Roland insisted on that. It was necessary that evil tongues—the gamines at table under the staircase—could not wag. He had that delicate thought first. Gilberte was grateful to him for it, but only as a simple politeness. What could the opinion of those sluts matter to her? In what way could their gossip afflict her?

When she talked to Père Hermann about her new friend, the academician was haunted by an anxiety.

"Oh, damn it!"

Then he told her the story of the other, the beautiful chorus girl from the Théâtre Historique who had turned out so badly. He had encountered her a year after her affair with that clown from the Boulevard du Crime; well, the poor girl was unrecognizable, absolutely unrecognizable. A lump! Imagine that! After having been Ingres' *Source*, capable of becoming Venus, Omphale, Diana—who knows?—to resign herself to being nothing but Madame Clown!

Gilberte had listened to that story without understanding its pertinence. Was Roland in love with her? Was she in love with Roland? Indeed! Think about it! To be sure, if they were the only two people left on earth, the world would end very quickly.

She did not reply to the old master.

In fact, her affection for Roland remained admirably innocent. She did not think there was any harm in it, considering the poet as another Hermann, a young Hermann, a new master who permitted her to address him as *tu* and treated her somewhat like an elder brother. In any case, Roland was not thinking about her. So...

She was right, then. Roland was not in love.

One evening, after dinner, he got up and reached for his hat.

"What, you're leaving?"

"Yes."

"Where are you going?"

"To the Opéra-Comique."

"Oh..."

132

She had said "oh," with an expression of annoyance, frowning. Roland calmly put on his overcoat.

"Are you going alone?"

"Yes."

She hesitated momentarily, afraid of seeming indiscreet and fearful of a refusal, but she finally added: "Would you like to take me?"

"Certainly."

The young man had been surprised. The girl had never addressed such a request to him before. Ordinarily, they separated placidly. Perhaps the child was bored. After all, she did not have a very cheerful existence.

Ten minutes later, they set off. Gilbert was enjoying herself greatly. On Roland's arm she had a light, lively step and her silk dress rustle prettily.

After the performance, they went back along the Rue Fontaine and the Rue Breda, chatting amicably. At the door of her house Gilberte retained her friend momentarily, still having something to say to him. They talked about the play, the music they had just heard, the actresses, etc. Eventually, they bid one another adieu.

The girl had rung the doorbell. They were holding hands and, as the door opened, Roland, mechanically, without being fully aware of what he was doing, had leaned toward Gilberte to give her a kiss.

She recoiled, saying in an angry tone: "Oh! No, no!"

And she escaped abruptly, went indoors and slammed the door.

While undressing in her room she had a fit of nervous sadness; she wept.

What! Roland too? He had tried to kiss her, he had held her hand, he had drawn her toward him. So, he was a man like all the rest. A memory returned to her: Édouard, the fiacre, the road to Asnières, her tears and her humiliation on that dolorous night. Her decision was made. She would not return to the La Rochefoucauld, would never see Roland again, never.

And then? Afterwards? Certainly—she understood that now—it was impossible to live as a savage, like a solitary bear, without shaking a friendly hand from time to time, without hearing a cordial and tender word. There was still Père Hermann, of course, but that was not the same things. Where would she go tomorrow? At the Café de La Rochefoucauld they knew her little habits, they kept her corner for her, they served her well. She might have to go from brasserie to café to restaurant to estaminet for weeks to find one as convenient. And then, it was so close...

On thinking about it carefully, she recognized that she had been severe, even unjust, toward her friend. After all, what had Roland done that was so terrible? A kiss—not even that; merely the offer of a kiss. Well? When one has been friends for a long time, what's wrong with that? Père Hermann kissed her all the time...

Yes, but it wasn't the same thing.

All the same, Roland must have a fine opinion of her. On the very evening when he had been so polite, so pleasant, so kind? For, in sum, he had been charming at the theater. No, frankly, she felt that she was in the wrong, and tomorrow, she would not fail to tell him so...

Come on, let's see, what could she say to him tomorrow?

She slept for a long time, and was still thinking about it.

Roland did not hold it against her. When he saw her again he took her hand and said: "Don't worry. I won't do it again."

For the first time in her life, Gilberte felt herself blush. The blood rose to her face warmly. She was embarrassed, awkward, foolishly serious.

Roland, seeing her at odds with herself, did not say much. No allusion was made to the previous evening, absolutely as if they had not gone to the theater. They scarcely dared look at one another, and resembled two big children caught being naughty. That minuscule incident, that kiss nonchalantly requested and rejected with an extreme angry energy, caused them no longer to be the friends they had been the day before. Something had changed, was new: an indefinable but definite embarrassment.

The young man felt disposed to think it all ridiculous, but an incomprehensible timidity stopped him. Well, yes, something had changed.

If, the evening before, at the moment when he had tried to kiss the girl, she had advanced her beautiful cheek, simply, tranquilly, without malice, Roland would have gone home quite distractedly. But she had resisted, she had been annoyed. Why? Was it, then, so very nasty, what he had tried to do. Why? It was impossible to think that he had veritably offended Gilberte. A model! A model, certainly, true, but not comparable with the other models. After all, if it displeased her to be kissed, that girl, she was perfectly free...

They parted as they had met up, with the same compassed familiarity and the same controlled smiles.

That evening, for the first time, Roland came to contemplate the girl's windows.

And Gilberte, retained behind her blinds by an instinctive hope, watched him for a long time.

Roland does not understand.

Now he spends every evening at Gilberte's house. The little colony believes that they are "together." and the gamines at table under the stairway in the Café de La Rochefoucauld affirm that "It's been going on for a long time."

Bah!

Every evening, after dinner, they go up to the little room in the Rue de Laval, and Roland comes down again before midnight.

What hours! Since the first day, the chain of conversations has been broken. Long silences cause a delightful anguish to weigh upon their thoughts. Roland prostrates himself, kneeling, murmuring words that are prayers, prayers that are strophes: the exquisite, intoxicated, foolish, charming babble of first confessions. Burning tears, then delighted smiles.

Word that one pronounces just like that, unawares, for no reason, and in which there is grace and tenderness.

Mute, almost mechanical, Gilberte abandons her small marmoreal hands to the poet, which he covers with hectic kisses. While he speaks, she hardly listens, her head tilted back on the back of the armchair, her gaze lost. Not a word falls from her lips.

"What's the matter, Gilberte? What are you thinking about?"

"Nothing's the matter. I'm not thinking about anything."

"Do you love me?"

"Yes."

And that is all.

One evening, tense, intoxicated by desire, Roland took the child by the waist, tried to pull her toward him with a more ardent movement. The girl became indignant. She voiced severe, harsh, cruel, reproaches, threats to disappear forever.

Come on, it's necessary to be good, reasonable. Can they not love one another without belonging to one another? Would it not be more pleasant always to love one another thus? Why not? They will be good comrades, they will live happily. Wonderful!

Roland does not understand.

During the summer, they went on excursions, escapes to the country, through the verdure.

On Sundays, at seven o'clock in the morning, they took the railway and disembarked at a small village in Seine-et-Oise, Saint-Ouen-l'Aumône; they went upstream along the towpath, between the green waters of the river and the vast fields of ripe wheat. They had lunch between Pontoise and Auvers, at Mère Chennevières' tavern, under a shady arbor of clematis, near an orchard where chickens were pecking. The ferry took them to the Île de Vaux and left them there until the evening, free and alone among the tall ferns under the trees full of birds. When they came back, very late, laden with flowers, Gilberte did not let Roland in.

Having heard talk of the island, Père Hermann wanted to see it.

The girl took him there one weekday, without saying anything to Roland.

The island is narrow but seemed profound, so tightly clustered are the bushes. Where there is only a curtain of trees, one might think there was a forest. Grass and heather grow there without cultivation, summoned bees and wild flowers. There is no solitude more delightful, more secure, more perfumed. The isle remains mysterious to the passers-by on the bank as to the boatmen who have themselves towed between the lock at Parmain and the barrage at Conflans.

On the way back, Père Hermann said to Gilberte: "You see, my girl, it's a jewel, your islet. I understand why you like it, and Roland is definitely an intelligent fellow He knows how to choose. He could be a painter and wouldn't have chosen better. It's necessary to see. For years now the messieurs of the free expositions have been fatiguing my ears with their 'open air'. The 'open air', of course, I could do whenever I want. And it won't be long. Just now, I thought about it watching you run through the grass. It's superb, true nature, the sky, the trees, with the gleam of light on the leaves. If I'd only had a box of paints! You'll give me the pleasure of coming to pose as Eve for me in that terrestrial paradise. No later than tomorrow. The season's getting on. It'll be autumn soon. There's already a hint of rust at the tips of the branches. So much the better! Can you see an Eve there—no, but can you see?"

The painting was begun the following day.

Every morning, Gilberte and old Hermann met up at the Gare du Nord, went to Saint-Ouen-l'Aumône and ran to hide in the deepest part of the isle, in a narrow clearing sheltered by old oaks, hung with ivy and wild vines. The girl showed an admirable patience, posed her Eve attentively, without complaining about the cold or fatigue. When resting, she rolled herself up in a vast furry cloak, and stretched out on the grass in the sun. Then, at a sign from the master, she resumed the pose and maintained it with perfect docility. And the sitting dragged on, without a word being exchanged between the painter and the model, until the indecisive hour when the light changes, trembles and blurs, darkening slowly in the demi-tints of the sunset.

They always returned to Paris at about the same time, in order that Gilberte could go to meet Roland. The girl said nothing to the poet about that open air study. She let him suppose that she was going as usual to Père Hermann's studio behind the Luxembourg. Roland did not suspect anything.

One evening, though, seeing Gilberte shiver, he became anxious.

The child had a cough. At times, her voice was strangled by a dolorous oppression, ending in a fit of dry, hollow coughing that shook her entire body. Soon, the illness got worse. A mat pallor stained Gilberte's exquisite face, hollowed out dark circles around her eyelids. The frightful cough became frequent, and acute.

"It's nothing," she said, smiling.

In vain, Roland tried to retain her, to make her rest. She refused, wanting to finish the Eve, seized by a rage, encouraging the old academician to multiply the sittings.

Toward the end of September she consented to be cared for. The painting was finished.

As soon as the first afflictions of the disease, Gilberte had sensed that she had been touched by death. Oh, there was no doubt about it; that was it. A mortal cold in the chest, icy shivers, continual sweating, and a fever that became more burning and more painful every day. She was immediately resigned, measuring the months and the weeks, thinking about the first snowfalls. That was without regret, with a kind of heroism, an intoxication of devotion and sacrifice.

But before dying, she wanted to live.

She gave herself to Roland.

They have loved one another for three months.

Now Gilberte is dying. Winter and passion have exalted the suffering, hastened the end.

Lying on her big bed veiled with white muslin, the girl sometimes smiles happily. A pride reassures her and consoles her. The girl knows that she is immortal. She will have the Louvre; she will have glory.

She has had love, when she realized that she had become useless to art.

Before dying, a model caprice occurs to her. She wants Père Hermann, with a board and his old bottle of champagne. The girl will pose one last time. She insists; it has been necessary to consent.

The master came, somber, exhausted vanquished. At first, he wept.

Soon, he set to work, with a feverish precipitation.

The girl adopted an attitude, sought the pose, the desired movement, dramatic and composed, something like the head of the dead woman in Léon Cogniet's *Fille du Tintoret*.[18] She organized the disposition of the sheets, the arrangement of the lace, the dark background. Scattered flowers and large green branches cover the bed, enlivening the dying woman with a final grace, a perfume.

Père Hermann finished the study emotionlessly, his eyes dry, solely haunted by the preoccupations of the painter.

Then Roland understood. He understood what a strange, rare, double creature he had loved. A great chagrin seized him at first, but almost immediately, seeing himself forgotten in that supreme hour, he shared the ideal egotism, uniquely turned toward art, of that old man and that child.

He no longer saw anything in Gilberte but the model, the superb, fake, predestined being, the divine monster.

And it seemed to him that it was another woman who died.

---

[18] The actual title of Léon Cogniet's most famous painting, exhibited at the Salon of 1843, is called *Tintoret peignant sa fille morte* [Tintoretto painting his dead daughter].

AMOROUS PHANTOMS

To Mademoiselle...

No one, apart from the two of us, will read your charm-
ing name on this page, at the head of these little tales, which I
addressed to you this winter, when you asked me "to tell you
some stories."

I dedicate them to you very humbly, glad if you can find
among these lines you find those in which my thoughts ap-
pealed to your thoughts, and in which my hopes offered to
your noble spirit the white bouquet of betrothal.

Charles-Marie

25 May 1885.

One Minute

Down here, everything is fragile. Glory, success, fortune and pleasures are subtle smoke, carried away by the slightest breath. There is no security in a future full of traps, no immobility of memory in the past. Of the emotions of yore, few survive the initial cause. One turns round, one looks behind, at the perspective of the road travelled: nothing any longer but shadows, floating faces, profiles already half-effaced. Beyond, the void, a morose desert in which thought can no longer find a spring. And that desert was the Elysian paradise of last spring!

Forward ho!—toward the land of chimeras that one loves all the more because they do not exist, and toward which our exiled dreams fly away. We march through the dense night of our ignorance, drawn by vain hopes, dragging futile regrets at our heels. It's foolish. Life is contained in its entirety within the present minute, in the emotion that one possesses with certainty, and which slides over us with the temporary frisson of the bow over the long strings of a viola. Almost nothing, a shiver, a smile, a fleeting melody—and that's all. It's over.

The minutes are all there is.

Who remembers a year, who can specify the circumstances of a journey? One only recalls the pause, or even a line, a form, a shade that struck the mind by virtue of its brightness or its pallor. The rest is fatigue, ennui, nothingness. Only the sensation of chagrins recurs incessantly, a scar leaving more trace than a kiss. The intoxication of dead joys is buried with them forever, while nothing fills in the imperceptible furrow of tears. It seems, in sum, for the martyrdom of humankind, that in this life, in which everything is transient, dolor alone is immortal.

There are, however, exquisite minutes.

That woman glimpsed, that woman whose name, home-land, family and heart one does not know, but who neverthe-less, in passing, yielded herself in a gaze, gave herself in a gesture, in a flash and without a word—you'll never forget her, never.

You recognized her among the crowd, at the corner of a banal street, or in a dance-hall, or under the chestnut-trees of the boulevard; you don't know her at all, you haven't dared to greet her, you never see her again, and yet, she had carried away something of our thought. Your dreams and your desires follow in her wake, forever.

A second was sufficient; you possessed her entirely. Without effort, by a simple predilection of faithful memory, you could paint her, respire after years the perfume with which she was enveloped, describe the color of her eyes exactly. You still know the form of her dress, the hue of the fabric, the de-sign of the trimmings, the delicate harmony of the lace, the discreetly veiled radiance of her bracelet.

Have you heard her? Her voice sings in your ears like an unforgettable music, and her words remain a favorite melody, delightfully obsessive. As for the gaze she allowed to fall upon you, as if she were giving a sou to a pauper, you value it to the point that you would not exchange it for the complete aban-donment of herself.

And as none of that lasted, as the vision has vanished, flown away, so to speak, as soon as it appeared; as the memory is made not of hours, but of seconds—scarcely a mi-nute—you will never forget it, never.

I am enduring the nostalgia of a chimerical ambition.

On a road sheltered by large oaks, a house, a small white house covered with an elegant gable of scarlet tiles; around it a garden devoid of bushes, entirely given over to roses, with a calm background of lawns; shutters of new oak, constantly open, allowing the divination, through the windows, between the satin and lace of the curtain, the intimacy of the interior elegance. Not too high, there is a broad balcony of wrought iron, bulging like a Boule chiffonier, whose ramp half-disappears beneath Moorish drapery with long, trailing pleats. To the right and the left, to either side of the road, in the old trees, birds are singing.

I will go into that dwelling, simply by pushing the gate and the door. Having traversed narrow drawing rooms stifling under velvet, I will go straight to the hothouse, where palm-trees are languishing, and I will fall to my knees, without saying a word, at the feet of a princess who will be waiting for me without knowing me, with a book of poetry in her hand.

She will be gentle and beautiful, young and sincere, for a garment she will have a cheerful Japanese peignoir embroidered with strange flowers and silvery dragons, solely retained at the hips by a loose belt; as for the hair, blonde or brunette as she pleases—preferably blonde.

And we will love one another for the profound eternity of one minute, forgetful of humanity and nature, with chaste caresses and mute benedictions. Not a word. Amour has its apogee so long as it has nothing to say; speech is already proof of a misunderstanding.

I shall not know her name and I shall not tell her mine. I shall quit her without regret; she will allow me to draw away without retaining me, without recalling me.

The next day, wandering along the road, I will no longer find the house, carried away as if by the flick of a magic wand. An obscure forest will have grown in its place

Well, I sense that I shall never attain that good fortune, that I shall never extract that minute of supreme ecstasy from banal, miserable, cruel life, always the same.

That makes me, and often.

Many people die without having savored the infinite possession of that dear minute. Oh, the unfortunates! Oh, the paupers! Oh, the innocents! Oh, the damned, driven away from the promised land! They have not been able to calculate the immortality of an impression, or know how life can condense emotions, intoxications, dolors, ecstasies and despairs in the briefest possible measure of time.

To live an hour in an hour, what poverty! To expend one's sensibility sou by sou, stupidly to exchange for everyday down-payments a wealth that, spent all at once, would counterbalance a royal fortune; to diminish gradually, worn away, so to speak—is that living?

But to give oneself entirely, for nothing, in one minute! To exchange an instantaneous but divine emotion for years of mourning—yes, years, if necessary! To promise oneself, to deliver oneself, to annihilate oneself in an impossible desire, to attach oneself to an ideal, is to assure oneself of the epic adventure of the Athenian dreamer who, in a surge of noble passion, stole the sacrificial cup from the altar of Zeus and drained it in a single draught.

Immediately, he fell completely to dust on the sacred steps—but he had drunk the wine of the Gods!

Olympus has withdrawn to a great height, to the fire of the stars. The marble statues of goddesses and fabulous heroes have fallen, broken, into the dry beds of old rivers; the minutes that are worthy of being lived can no longer be bought for cash.

Today, the possible minute, the unique minute, costs the incurable regrets of a lifetime.

One has loved as much as one believed, as much as one could—alas! A woman has gone by, an unknown woman you will never see again, who will never be for you a friend, a wife or a lover; but her memory will remain to you, precise, living, pitiless. Perhaps she will be dead for a long time to others, while she still lives for you, in you, as on the day of the fateful vision, with the same stride, the same dress, the same singing voice.

It did not last, or hardly, but what does it matter? You have steeped your lips in the burning nectar of Olympus. Henceforth, you love that woman. Perhaps you will love another, several others, but her, you will never forget.

Never, never.

The Clown

Marius had prepared his little speech. The exordium commenced as an andante, with tender flats, over a muted bass accompaniment. It would open the symphonic demonstration broadly—*lento maestoso*—soft pedal. Afterwards, his eloquence would agitate the trills, the *pizzicati allegretti*, with a well-orchestrated sentiment in which he would have placed a little ballet of the Old Sèvres variety. Minuet for the stringed instruments alone. After a pause—*a tempo*—the characteristic phrase would advance, solemnly, in fanfare of brass and gold. Choirs of foolish virgins in the wings, choirs of little angels in the balconies; melodious voices in the indefinite distances, *dolcissimo, decrescendo*, harmonies dying away little by little with the softness of amorous plaint. The "nail" of the partition. To the soft awakening of fanfares would succeed, *plu lento*, the melancholy song of oboes celebrating the bourgeois peace of true happiness, the sonorous calm of evenings. An idyll, as fresh and simple as all idylls; no deliberate science of counterpoint or fugue, no arpeggios. Finally, on an evoked fragment of the magisterial phrase calmed by the tenderness of choirs, the oratorio would finish on such chords, elevated so high, from octave to octave, in the flight of harps—*fortissimo, appassionato*—that nothing would remain for Marius to do but offer his soul and his life to Fernande—over an organ stop!

Sunday evening had been marked for the sole performance of that masterpiece.

But just as he was about to bring down his ideal conductors' baton on an imaginary lectern, Marius could no longer find his sheet-music. The musicians, nonplussed, went away, taking their instruments with them, blowing out the little candle-flames. Nothing any longer remained but Fernande and Marius, in the dark.

Marius tried out a few notes: Mi, mi, so, me, do, re, la, so, fa, re…but his song broke off into a pitiful tremolo, underlined by Fernande's little laugh—a charming and cruel little laugh.

Having arrived home, Marius understood the necessity of adopting an attitude. What? That was the whole question. He changed obsession twenty times over. First, he wanted to die, like everyone else. Then he had the idea of a voyage round the world. Oh, to go further, much further, to the ends of the earth! He began the first verse of an ode and did not finish it. He lit ten cigarettes without smoking them, opened a book without reading any of it, and went to bed without being able to sleep.

At daybreak, he thought he understood.

There are a hundred ways of being stupid; imbeciles only have one, and in consequence, ninety-nine remain for men of intelligence. Marius, an intelligent fellow at times, had been far too anxious about what he had promised himself to say, and not at all about what he was at risk of hearing. He had striven not to be banal, like everyone else, and he had shown himself to be as stupid as anyone.

One is a big man, proud and disdainful, one affects to see nothing in life but fellows sketched by Daumier, one likes battle and has one's moments of valor, one thinks oneself strong because one has been under fire—and one becomes timid, hesitant, ridiculous and cowardly before the little blonde head that one has chosen.

Oh, if it were a matter of taking a redoubt bristling with cannon vomiting death, that would be another matter. One would have a stout heart, one would put on white gloves as if for a revue, one would speak in a familiar fashion to one's sword, dear God! And one would march boldly into the hail of bullets, flag held high, with the band playing.

But to conquer the right to place a kiss on a little hand, to confront to mocking eyes, to expose oneself to a smile! That was enough to make old captains retreat. Oh, the terror of feeling ridiculous! To be unable to find a syllable to pronounce.

To struggle awkwardly against the impotence of speech, and contain inexpressible confessions in one's heart!

Marius swore that he would not return to the combat.

Alas, he thought, *since I have to renounce moving her, I shall try to make her laugh. She has such pretty teeth!*

From that day on, he enclosed his thought in a jargon.

He fashioned his speech in accordance with the boulevardier wit of Paris, the worse wit there is and the most brilliant, the spirit of Chamfort and Gavroche, of the Duc de Richelieu, of Joseph Prudhomme and Madame de Staël. A laugh in which was summarized the sum of ferocity permitted to men of good company, a tumult of formidable and puerile expressions and false judgments; a tongue made of words stamped by the die of biting sarcasm, English terms, Arabic locutions, countersense, nonsense, stupidities, gunshots, redundant formulae, noisy gaieties, and which, bounding, howling, colliding with precise ideas, serious thoughts and solid theories, slaved away regardless, crushing skulls of multicolored paper, flattening and springing up again in tightrope-dancer capers, evoking the vision of a masquerade of hectic pierrots released into an American ballet performed during a earthquake.

Marius repeated these lines of Coppée:

Weary of the pedants of Salamanca,
And the school of black steps
I want to be an acrobat
And live with strolling players.[19]

And, renouncing becoming a husband, the friend or the lapdog of the beloved woman, he resigned himself to becoming her clown.

When he saw her again, he told her stories.

---

[19] The lines are from François Coppée's poem "Le Jongleur" [The Juggler] (1869).

"There was once a prefect named Romieu. The emperor, whom he amused, invited him to one of his hunts in Compiègne. One day, the prefect reflected that nothing could be more monotonous, for such a powerful sovereign, than always shooting grouse and pheasants. He advised the master of the hunt to have a few flocks of parrots released before the emperor's guns. At the first beating, three hundred lovebirds and five hundred cockatoos were launched in the presence of the master. Napoléon III, slightly astonished at first, took aim at one of the birds, fired and killed it. As he leaned over to pick it up, the parrot gathered all its strength and, with a supreme effort, died crying: *Vive l'empereur*!"

Fernande laughed, and Marius admired her pretty teeth.

Gradually, he slipped into customary irony, made himself a skeptic, hung around his neck the sky whistle of Mephistopheles and made use of it to whistle everything, indistinctly. Without descending as far as cock-and-bull stories, he ventured compromising intimacies with vagabond puns. The notion of justice was gradually effaced in him along with the sentiment of respect. His former sensibilities, corroded by mockery as if by acids, died a lamentable death, devoid of tears. "How cheerful he is!" exclaimed passers-by. "What enthusiasm! What good humor!" Oh, that was a happy man! Existence has been clement, pleasant, facile and smiling for that Marius! How amusing he was!

Good people, there are pagodas in Asia that resemble my friend Marius somewhat. The traveler goes into them, and salutes, dazzled, the high portal where the ivory panels are maintained in circles of gold; then he passes under vaults sustained by porphyry columns, muffled by bright velvets extended over the mosaics; then there is a lapis room, a covered garden in which spring water agitates the perfume of flowers in marble pools; then, the august sanctuary, of blinding luxury—and on the altar, almost nothing, a frightful little deformed Buddha in black jade.

Marius, the cheerful Marius, bore within him, behind the splendors of his determined whimsy, the lugubrious idol of his impossible amour.

Sometimes, however, in his solitudes, the frightened clown, no longer daring to look his life in the face, took a deep breath as he put on his mask, and experienced, in sum, the vile nostalgia of the boards. Regrets gripped him.

It would, however, be good to love, to love wholeheartedly! One would have a pleasant existence, honest and peaceful, a pure, solid, immortal happiness. And the detail of the ambitious future, more seductive than the future itself! For him, work, triumph, talent—one has talent when one is in love—the religious concern to make her happy. For her, a little house in which she would command as queen, a little garden in the depths of an old faubourg, near the river. And the serene hours of the evening, in the firmly closed drawing room, under the lamp, between the hearth where the fire was allowed to go out and the piano left closed; the large armchair on which she would relax, lulled by conversation, while he would fall to his knees, with a new emotion every evening and sweeter desires...

Let's go! Hup, Paillasse! Let's go, clown, you're dreaming again! On your feet! Powder your face, put on your rouge—put lots of it on, so that your tears, if necessary, can lose themselves in your grimaces. Be a caricature, my lad.

And now, on stage. Throw yourself about. Look out! Beware of breaking your neck. If all goes well, if you don't fall off your trapeze, inert and bloody in the sawdust, you can go on the quest—and perhaps your Fernande will drop a sou into the felt hat that you usually juggle at the end of your sticks, like a huge bat.

Under the Commune

I had encountered her a few months before the war, in the town house in the Avenue de Friedland where Arsène Houssaye then hosted such marvelous Venetian fêtes.[20] It was on the night of a ball, at the back of the Moorish drawing room, near the large divan that she filled with her skirts. Behind her black satin mask, I divined that she was pretty. The indefinable undulation of lines revealed a young, supple, slender body created for profound caresses and idle abandonments. None of her movements was designed in banal gestures. From her nape, with tawny hues, which supported a golden chignon traversed by a long blonde tortoiseshell pin, to her impatient and pert feet, arched in black mules, one sensed the smooth, chaste, almost divine figure the testimony of which an artist admires religiously in pure antique beauties.

She was wearing a uniquely cut dress, one of those satin sheaths plastered to the hips, which the elegant ladies of the Third Republic were later to adopt, but which, in that era of hypocritical luxury, could pass for a rare audacity of feminine coquetry. No ribbons, no lace, no jewelry. The fabric adhered faithfully to the amorous form, and, toward the knees, was lost in a floating train enlivens by the brightness of white undershirts. A veil of Venetian lace compressed her blonde tresses, from which rose a singular perfume, timid and heady, which one might have thought blonde too. Her right hand, gloved in kidskin the color of mourning, was swinging a large jet-black

---

[20] The writer Arsène Houssaye constructed a Moorish house at no. 37 Avenue de Friedland, where he hosted famous bacchanals, which the author's father might have attended. It was demolished in the late 1850s in the course of Baron Haussmann's remodeling of Paris; the chronology of the present story is therefore dubious.

fan, each of whose two outer branches bore a black diamond, in a rhythmic movement measured by the distant echo of waltzes.

No one was speaking to her; she seemed a stranger in that joyful crowd, which was laying the formal etiquette of aristocratic society to rest in a racket that was simultaneously vulgar and refined. Her large bizarre eyes, as green and intoxicating as living absinthe, were coolly contemplating the crowd of gentlemen, senators and bedecked officers whose were filing slowly beneath the chandeliers. From the divan where she was lying, huddled, so to speak, in the attitude of a she-cat, she was considering at leisure the entire cortege of the fête, the marble staircase illuminated by odorous candles, the loggia whose glass walls sheltered palm-trees and laurier-roses, the high somber galleries that the Flemish tapestries rendered solemn, the little Japanese boudoir, with its cheerful flickering gleams, its panels of transparent lacquer, crazy lanterns, and silk drapes where fabulous chimeras galloped through golden, crimson and azure landscapes, amid bizarre flowers and dazzling suns.

When the time came for the valets to set up the little supper-tables in the hall, she stood up, traversed the Moorish salon, went down the majestic stairway, keeping to the center of the steps, and disappeared.

The following day, in the Bois, I recognized her immediately. It was quite unnecessary for me to have seen her face. She betrayed herself immediately by the feline grace that was particular to her and which I have not found since in any other woman. The woman I was following under the acacias near the Pavillon de Madrid could not be anyone but her. There was the same slow and undulating stride, the same cut and color of costume, the same eyes like liquid topaz. In the sway of her supple figure, the rounded movement of the arms and the inclination of the neck, I grasped her in her entirety again with her black charm, her mysterious nocturnal indolence.

I soon knew her name, her residence, and that she lived alone in a villa in Auteuil, but that was all I knew. I was unable to discover, and never found out, whether she was unmarried, married or a widow.

I wrote to her—in vain.

She soon deserted the Bois, keeping her shutters firmly closed at the hour when I passed beneath her windows on horseback.

Was I in love with her? I dare not say so, or deny it. She preoccupied me, that's all. No effort would have been costly to get closer to her, but I did not suffer from my solitude. That tranquil little romance, sweet and melancholy, added to my natural good humor something tender and caressant that sometimes resembled happiness. Then I found the pleasure of being able to love again like a schoolboy, futilely, stupidly, simply, without a hidden agenda, without desire...

Come on, come on; I think, all the same, that I loved her...

The war came; it was necessary to be a soldier, like everyone else.

Maréchal Leboeuf sent me to Limoges; I never knew why. The Comte de Palikao sent me to Roche-sur-Yon. General Le Flô finally recalled me to Paris and gave me my captain's stripes, decanting me into a newly-formed squadron.

On the second of December, as I was traversing the Plateau de Tremblay at a rapid trot, a German bullet hit me full in the chest and threw me unconscious into the dirt. I only woke up the next day, in the field-hospital at Valentino: a long room equipped with little white beds in which other vanquished were lying, physicians in military uniform with Red Cross armbands, women in black dresses protected by broad white aprons—volunteer field-nurses. I distinguished all that confusedly, the serious women, the pale wounded, the uniforms. But soon I no longer saw anything but her, the lady from Auteuil, standing next to my bed and looking at me with her habitual fixed and profound gaze.

It was her!

Oh, I had already forgotten the war, the fatigue, the perils, the anger. A corner of the past filed with light. There was the Moorish drawing room in the Avenue de Friedland, the solitary pathways of the Bois, the garden of Auteuil, my dear little end-of-summer romance...

As I was about to speak she lifted a finger to her lips as a sign of silence, and, behind a white hand, I contemplated her first smile—a discreet, sad, scarcely-designed smile, like the smile of la Gioconda.

It was thus that, for three months, I was able to pay court to her—oh, a respectful court, very timid. It is sometimes precious to have received a gunshot in the chest.

When I left the field-hospital, it was at the beginning of the Commune. Delescluze entered the Hôtel de Ville, Grousset was installed in Jules Favre's study. A tragedy was commencing. But the sun had returned, there were buds on the chestnut-trees in the Tuileries, thousands of sparrows were returning, and then we recovered the marvelous white bread that is never whiter than in the aftermath of a siege.

Under the oaks of the old imperial park, I now met the lady in black almost every day. Not talkative, the lady. In spite of my questions, I learned nothing of her life—nothing, nothing, nothing. I only observed her prudent behavior, her haste to flee from me as soon as a stroller appeared at the entrance to the pathway, then often deserted. One might have thought that a surveillance weighed upon her and controlled her life. She had been obliged to abandon her villa in Auteuil, visited by Prussian shells, and had returned temporarily to an apartment in the Rue d'Alger, where she never consented to receive me, in spite of my insistent pleas.

However, she gradually softened, and in the evening, toward the fourth hour, and the moment veiled by demi-tints when "the regret of the setting sun leaves a softer adieu", we had a long, silent embrace. It was always at the corner of the last clump of bushes, in the darkened verdure, near Barye's lioness. I took her two gloved hands in my trembling hands, and I said "Until tomorrow," in a whisper. We remained thus, face to face, without a word, listening vaguely to the cannon-fire rumbling in the distance, toward Mont Valérien, toward Vanves and toward Bezons.

Who was that woman, then? Where did she come from? Why was she lingering in that poor Paris, then deserted? And if she lived alone, why not permit me to visit her?

I asked her that one evening.

"Are you afraid of me, then?" I said to her.

"Afraid? Me?"

Then she stood up, quitting me, and pronounced, in a strange tone: "You'll see whether I'm afraid."

That evening, when I got home after dinner, a lackey handed me a note:

Tomorrow, two o'clock, at my house in Auteuil.

L.

Auteuil, that was assuredly ironic, or perhaps to put me off. Who knows?

For a week, the batteries of Mont Valérien had been devastating Auteuil. The federates, expelled by the shells, had abandoned the sector and were retrenched behind barricades. The same evening, Dombrowski had been wounded there while inspecting his posts. The troops of the line were advancing slowly toward the rampart, in serpentine trenches. The quarter had been completely abandoned since the first days of the civil war.

In those conditions, to go to Auteuil was folly.

I was in Auteuil, in spite of the barricades of the Quai de Bily and the machine-gun fire sweeping the Point-du-Jour. I hugged the walls, seeking the protecting of corners, hastening my steps, contemplated with amazement by the federates at the barricades, who thought they ought to send me a few futile gunshots. Finally, I arrived in the Rue Boileau, outside the villa.

Poor villa! The gate was smashed, twisted by the victorious action of cannonballs. Shredded shutters hung down from the windows; an enormous breach opened in the roof allowed the sight of a gaping black hole. Meager grass was growing in the pavement of the driveway. The garden was devastated. I can still see a lilac branch decapitated by a bullet, swaying in the breeze...

Having climbed the perron, whose slabs had been jostled by a cannonball, I pushed the door nearest to the steps and went into a small bright drawing room.

The lady in black was waiting for me, huddled in an armchair, still with the same troubling allure.

As I fell at her feet, a volley of machine-gun fire struck the lawn, and the ricochet of a musket-shot expired on the carpet.

"Am I afraid?" she said.

And I saw her first smile reflourish again, the smile from the field-hospital.

I dared to say her name—I will not dare to write it—and seized her beloved hands. What I said to her in those hours of battle, in that frightful torment in which we were hidden, what exquisite, sublime and passionate words fell from her lips, to what profound indescribable ecstasies we belonged under that frail roof shaken by the war—why reveal them? The avowed memory evaporates and only leaves in the depths of hearts an old, often bitter, perfume. I retain within me, like a miser, the still-living testimony of those dead intoxications.

She gave herself, a thousand times more tender than she had ever been severe. The mystery in which she normally enclosed herself seemed to have accorded her a truce in that lost corner, more deserted than the immense desert. No one could perceive or encounter us there. When we met up there, every day, it was after traversing bleak solitudes, empty streets on which our light steps resounded in the sonorous repose of the cannon-fire. No passers-by. Not one soldier.

The danger? Oh, we scarcely thought about that. She never talked to me about it. Soon domesticated, we took possession of the garden, the poor garden all the prettier because it grew by the grace of God. What moments we spent, kneeling in the grass, without hearing the whistle of bullets in the branches!

Finally!

How far away it is, already! It will soon be fifteen years.

On the twenty-second of May, the day after the re-entry of the troops, she wrote to me:

There is no longer a corner in which we can hide our amour.

Adieu, my love.

L.

I never saw her again.

She has returned to her mystery.

The Role

It was Père Kernouan who told me this story, last summer, out there in Quiberon, under the hangar of the Amieux sardine-cannery, one evening in August. The only spectators of the drama, in the Breton peninsula, were the old mariner Kernouan and Mère Le Cardec, a worthy octogenarian who fattened pigs at Port Haliguen.

"In those days, a woman celebrated for her talent and beauty, who was particularly illustrious in tragedy on the major stages of Paris and abroad, was suffering ennui in Paris."

"Was it Sarah Bernhardt?"

"No, it wasn't Sarah Bernhardt. So, the illustrious tragedienne was suffering from ennui, as one can in Paris when one possesses a fine town house, horses, diamonds, worshipers perpetually bowing down, and a loving husband."

"What did you say?"

"I said, 'a loving husband.'"

"That's what I thought. Go on."[21]

"Eaten away by spleen, completely at a loss, as Kernouan said, the artiste had a whim to play a role, a fine big role written expressly for her by a true poet, on her advice, and in which all the resources of her enormous talent would be cleverly utilized. To that end, she cast her eyes upon the illustrious author of...I can't name him. If you wish, and to render the narration easier, we can call him Ernest. You'll recognize

---

[21] The point of this insertion is that the narrator's interlocutor does not seem to have believed the assertion that the actress is not Sarah Bernhardt, although this detail, if true, would prove it; the divine Sarah had married Jacques Damala in 1882, who was anything but loving. Some readers might have suspected that "Rébecca" was more likely to be Sarah Bernhardt.

him easily anyway, when you know that he isn't yet fifty, that his blond hair is abundant, that he counts numerous successes in journalism, books and the theater, that he always wears an overcoat even in the hottest days of summer, and that he talks in pidgin."

"Pidgin?"

"Yes; I mean that, religiously careful of form when he writes, he doesn't take the trouble to formulate anything when he speaks. His conversation resembles the result of a telegraph transmission.

"So, the beautiful tragedienne addressed herself to the celebrated Ernest and the author, flattered and seduced, immediately replied: 'A role…haven't one…written nothing for two years. Am brutalized by Paris…need solitude, meditation…when solitude found, will have role…hope for great success.'

"'But my dear friend, can't you retire to the country for a few months, or the seaside, and out there…?'

"'Impossible…hotel life mind-numbing…have tried, can't. Would be too free, have desire to go to café, casino, beach, theater, dance-hall. Wouldn't write anything at all.'

"'What can we do, then?'

"'Come with me…watch over me…take care not to let me go out. Supervise household, kitchen, servants. Let's rent chalet, villa, house, doesn't matter, but no hotel. Sea-baths will do us good. Agreed?'

'All right, agreed,' said the beautiful actress. 'I'll find a peaceful little beach, and we can leave in a week. Anyway, nothing retains me in Paris; I'll be glad to get a little fresh air. Oh, my dear friend, what a fine collaboration we'll have out there.'

"Indeed, a week or ten days after that conversation, the author and his future interpreter disembarked in Quiberon and took up residence in a pretty house situated on the headland to the east, between the town and Port Haliguen. It took a good week for the installation to be complete, for although the celebrated Ernest had contented himself with a summary baggage, the tragedienne, as was her custom, was followed by thirty crates as vast as Swiss chalets, each containing five or six dresses. Furthermore, she had take care to bring everything necessary for painting, sculpture and making marmalade."

"You're sure that it wasn't Sarah Bernhardt?"

"So I was told, and I believe it. Do as I do.

"So, the two collaborators were installed. The tragedienne occupied the entire ground floor, the dramaturge took possession of the first floor. The dining room was arranged in a conservatory attached to the villa, which overlooked the sea. No distractions: no theater, no casino. No café-concert. Only walks. No neighbors. The passers-by were mariners, fishermen from the port, the sardine-packers of Belle-Île and Concarneau, employees in the canning factory, and customs men. Nothing therefore prevented the two friends from devoting themselves entirely to their work."

"The author was delighted, and his satisfaction was translated daily in proclamations such as: 'Good, the Ocean, very good. Sea breeze...blue horizon...roar of breakers...grandiose infinity...fresh lobster...lulled by rumor of waves...inspiration...peace of mind...delightful winkles...'

"The tragedienne adapted as if by magic to that calm existence. It's astonishing how much is needed for a woman to be satisfied and how little is sufficient for her to be happy. She was going to have her role, a role made for her. Not only was she assured of her success, but she was counting on the fact that Rébecca, her rival of the day, would not have any role at all. Indiscretions of the wings had informed her that her author, the fortunate author she had abducted from Paris, had been vaguely planning to write a role for Rébecca. Given that, her success would be augmented by a victory, for in Ernest's play there was only one great female role.

"The celebrated tragedienne did everything possible to encourage her author. Knowing that he was very appreciative of Rébecca's talent, she was able, thanks to the admirable flexibility that is the foundation of her talent, to do violence to her own nature, to assimilate the means, the intonations and the gestures of her rival, and showed herself to be superior even in that imitation.

"On the other hand, she pushed back the bounds of complaisance, as if to please her poet. The latter having said to her one day: 'Caporal tobacco bad, heavy…used to Latakia from Smyrna…no Latakia here…very disagreeable,' she telegraphed an agency in the Boulevard des Italiens, and the next day, the author had an enormous crate of his favorite tobacco.

"One day—or rather, one evening—Ernest manifested other demands. He complained of his first-floor apartment, talked about air currents, an intolerable south-westerly wind that shook is shutters and threw perturbation into his dreams. In brief, the tragedienne offered to trade the apartment that she had initially furnished for herself for his. The dramaturge protested, affirming that he would leave rather than inconvenience his friend thus. But he did not stop moaning, and as night fell a few hours later, the sky was full of stars and the air full of perfumes, he said beautiful things to the artiste that remained beautiful in spite of the fashion in which they were said; he was pressing, tender, persuasive, knelt down, struck his breast, talked of eternal fidelity and unalterable affection.

"That evening, the great tragedienne was on edge. In the tribunal of a woman, it is attraction or merit that pleads your case, but it is opportunity that wins it. The actress remembered that God gave woman a tongue in order to speak and eyes in order to respond. She responded with her eyes.

"It was only the following day that she thought about her husband, and was very proud of having given herself, in her own eyes, a new proof of her independence, For a woman, independence is the right to change what she has elsewhere, with the best will in the world, for the right of choice.

"That incident gave a new activity to their collaboration, henceforth extended infinitely. The tragedienne no longer thought about Rébecca without a shrug of the shoulders. The author renounced strolling and fishing entirely. They had cheerful furniture and bright drapes sent from Paris. The third act not proceeding as desired, they decided to rewrite it and also to rewrite the fourth, for the reason that there was no urgency and the two collaborators were only thinking of prolonging their sojourn in Brittany for as long as possible.

"The tragedienne sometimes exclaimed, after long eloquent silences: 'I've never been so happy!'

"To which Ernest replied: "Me too…never as happy…ideal has taken a form…dream of my entire life attained…blue sky touched with finger…we'll never quit one another…never.'

"After two months of that delightful existence the drama was finished. There was a solemn reading. It was on that occasion that the old captain Kernouan, whom the two collaborators had met during their walks, was invited to the villa for the first time. Ernest had said: 'Kernouan isn't literate…primitive entire, abrupt, not corrupted by the criticism of Gustave Planche…will give his opinion frankly, like a true public.'

"And Kernouan witnessed the reading. It was a beautiful evening. Mère Le Cardec, who had entered the artiste's service as cook, retained the most profound memory of it. She still talks with emotion about the big scene in the fifth act, in which the young female lead rediscovers her mother's cross, which is indispensable to her to open the casket containing the proofs of her noble birth.[22] It seems to her that she can still hear, like on ophicleide in which the mistral is blowing, the imposing voice of the celebrated Ernest, who, for that evening alone renounced talking like a Hughes apparatus.[23]

"Old Kernouan was captivated. He only remarked to the author, when consulted, that he might have abused the word 'notwithstanding,' a nice word, he said, but which it as necessary to use in moderation.

---

[22] "Her mother's cross" was a phrase used repeatedly by the *feuilletoniste* Paul Féval to satirize the hoariest of all melodramatic clichés and the tawdriest of all denouement devices; its citation here proves that the story is pure fiction.

[23] The printing telegraph system invented by David Hughes (1831-1900) became standard throughout Europe in the 1860s.

"The great tragedienne was transported.

"Only the illustrious Ernest displayed a reserved attitude in which they saw the modesty that befits true merit. He defended himself, refusing the praise. 'You think so...good play, then? So much the better...a hundred performances...premium...will write to Peragallo's successor to ask for considerable advance.'[24]

"For a long time after the old mariner's departure, the two friends, leaning on the balcony of their villa, chatted about the drama, the emotions of the première, the jealousies of the dear comrades. The actress made plans for the costumes that she was going to order from the great tailors in Vienna and London. It was agreed that they would take the next train in order to read to play to the actors, to distribute the roles and begin the rehearsals.

"The pallors of dawn were beginning to brighten the sky above the rocks of Saint-Gildas-de-Rhuys when they thought about going to sleep.

"The following day, at lunch, while finishing a lobster tail, the dramaturge spoke. 'Reflected well, this morning...that role, not what you need...will write another for you next year.'

"'What are you saying?'

"'Not within your means, that role. Too...how shall I put it...? In sum, not right for it. Would certainly be my opinion...going to give the role to Rébecca.'

"'To Rébecca? But that's odious!'

"'No, not odious. Your fault, anyway. Have always reminded me of Rébecca, talked like Rébecca, walked like Rébecca...influenced me...will give role to Rébecca...what an effect...can see the première.'

"The great tragedienne went into an indescribable fury, cried treason, swore vengeance, to have the play whistled, to

---

[24] "Peragallo" is presumably Léonce Peragallo, who was an agent attached to the Societé des Auteurs et Compositeurs Dramatiques during the 1860s.

retire to a convent—to the Grande-Chartreuse!—to throw herself in the sea. Then she calmed down, recalled the happy days and the all-too-brief nights, the famous evening when Ernest had complained so much about the north-west wind.

"The author remained implacable and, cutting short the heart-rending farewell scene, leapt aboard the train and soon disembarked in Paris, where Rébecca received him like the Messiah.

"After his departure, the great tragedienne fell ill. On the evening that followed Ernest's departure, she caught a chill.

"Old Le Cardec informed Kernouan, who called a local curé known for practicing medicine illegally.

"The venerable ecclesiastic came, was unable to recognize that the patient was afflicted by the commencement of bronchitis, and treated her for an enlargement of the liver. In the same way that he was mistaken about the nature of the illness, however, he was mistaken about the nature of the regime to follow, and prescribed against the enlargement of the liver exactly the remedies that were needed to reckon with bronchitis—with the result that, in a short time, the great tragedienne had recovered completely, thanks to the redoubtable incompetent, whom she has been obstinate ever since in comparing, for science and skill, with Dr. Ricord.[25]

"The celebrated Ernest's drama was staged with an immense success. Rébecca played the principal role valiantly. The play is to be put on again this winter.

"The great tragedienne has not yet forgiven him, and probably never will forgive, for a woman only forgives an infidelity when she is sure that it is not a preference."

---

[25] The physician Philippe Ricord (1800-1889), Napoléon III's personal physician and an expert on venereal diseases.

The Museum of Sovereigns

There was once, in the Breton village of Plouharnel, a little girl named Bérengère, whose parents were prosperous cultivators.

As the child was polite, refined and intelligent, and at the age of thirteen she already played the piano like the celebrated violinist Paganini, her parents resolved to give her an education less in conformity with her situation as a Breton village girl than the brilliant social status to which she seemed irresistibly avowed. One morning, therefore, the mother took the child to the nuns of Saint-Gildas-de-Thuys and left her there, instructions those pious women to treat her in the same way as a demoiselle from Nantes or Vannes.

The environment was admirably chosen. In fact, not only did the nuns of Saint-Gildas devote themselves to penitence, fasting and mortifications, but they also rented out furnished rooms in their monastery, and sold colonial foodstuffs and pharmaceuticals.

That combination is perhaps not in conformity with the austere rule that governs the order, and one might wonder, on seeing the Vannes coach stop outside the cloister, whether the passengers who descend therefrom are coming for the sea-bathing, to receive music lessons to buy a pound of large pears or convert to the true faith, but the people of the town nevertheless take advantage of that state of affairs.

The young boarders entrusted to the convent encounter city-dwellers there, and can thus easily assimilate the usages of society; when they have concluded their studies, they possess, in addition to the lessons taught in the usual establishments, positive information regarding wholesale and retail grocery and a superficial knowledge of the pharmaceutical codex. They are equipped to govern a household, conquer paradise, fake brown sugar and apply leeches. What bachelor has not dreamed of a wife cut to that pattern?

In the convent, young Bérengère developed at leisure and became a very sage young woman, in accordance with the Scriptures. Religion is the only form of romanticism that befits certain feminine souls, and the only dose that they are able to support. Bérengère's education was exclusively provincial; at eighteen she knew that the battle of Tolbiac had been won by Clovis, that the pope was named Leo, that France was avidly awaiting the advent of the Comte de Paris, that the Danube has its source in the garden of a German magistrate and that Tierra del Fuego is a long way from Saint Nazaire; she had learned to sew, embroider and play scales for five hours in succession without eating or drinking.

Of the world she had perceived nothing. Her longest walks had been limited by the cliffs of Saint-Gildas, the coast of Port-Navalo, the Île de Gavr'inis, the Château de Sucionio and the village of Arzeau, where Lesage was born. Only once had she been taken as far as Vannes, and had come back quite dazed, her head full of what she had seen: the courtyard of the Hôtel de France, with its bustle of travelers and its noise of horses, the market where the great winged bonnets of the young women of Auray fluttered like white butterflies, the old tower where Monsieur de Closmadeuc[26] had installed his curious megalithic museum, the comings and goings of the harbor—all the buzz and petty luxury of the town, unaccustomed for her.

That glimpse of a town, however, that new glimpse, which, in a young man, would have broadened the domain of is ideas, had no result in Bérengère but to enlarge the circle of sensations. She emerged from that banal adventure more impressionable and more nervous, and conceived a mysterious terror of the worldly life for which she knew that she was destined. She thought fearfully that, having barely emerged from

---

[26] The surgeon and archeologist Gustave de Closmadeuc (1828-1918).

the convent, she was to be married to her cousin, established as a money-changer in Paris, in the Rue Vivienne, and that Paris would doubtless be more redoubtable and noisier than the chief town of Morbihan.

Things worked out in accordance with her fears. A week had not gone by since Bérengère had emerge from the convent when the cousin, Armand Lantibois, arrived in the peninsula, had the banns published, and, when the legal delay had elapsed and the marriage had been celebrated, took his wife to Paris. The marriage had naturally been concluded under the endowment regime, for, in those delightful times, parents wanted to deliver to a husband the body, health, happiness and existence of a young woman, but not her money.

It was an abrupt emotion for the young woman raised in the peace of a disdained coastal resort to find herself suddenly transported, without any transition, to the heart of the Bourse district, into a narrow shop traversed every day by busy men shouting numbers, quoting share-prices, dictating orders and talking rapidly in strident voices.

How much ennui she suffered it would be difficult to say.

The words pronounced around her—liquidation at two sous, closing price, term, yield, first quote, final quote, three per cent—did not appear to her to have any meaning. It was as if she were living in a lunatic asylum or a fairy tale.

Only one thing interested her in that troubling milieu, and that was gold. She had never seen gold coins in the convent or in Plouharnel, where she had only possessed copper coins, large sous of the kind only found on the coast, with typical patches of verdigris. And now she possessed beautiful louis d'or, new ones with gleams of red flame, others with a lovely yellow patina that reminded her of marigolds in the meadows. It was her great distraction to play with écus, florins, napoleons, old fredericks, and she devoted herself to it as to a unique resource.

Lantibois was not a poet, one of those men who plant a ladder on a star and climb up it playing the violin; he was a practical and serious fellow who, having passed the age when one marries in order to establish oneself, had perhaps married in order to re-establish himself. Possessed by his business affairs, kept out of the house for a large part of the day, he only had a little time to devote to the comforting joys of the conjugal hearth.

With the aim of distracting his young wife, and probably also to obtain a constant surveillance of his clerks, he had installed the unfortunate Bérengère behind a counter defended by an iron grille, and the poor young woman spent hours there, continually absorbed in the contemplation of the little yellow medallions that she loved to caress at length and cause to jump in the copper bowls.

One day, Madame Lantibois did not come down to the shop and for nearly three weeks the clerks did not see her. She had brought into the world a child of the male sex, who was immediately sent to a nurse in a village in Touraine, where the money-changer owned a property.

Back on her feet, Bérengère resumed her place behind the counter and her monotonous existence. Lantibois was increasingly absent, absorbed as he was by his financial operations.

After eighteen months the child came back. That was a day of celebration for the family. When he returned home, Lantibois covered his heir with caresses but, as he lifted him up in his arms to contemplate him at leisure, he stopped abruptly, his eyes wide open and his expression anxious.

"Well!"

"What is it?"

"Look at the child carefully. You don't notice anything?"

"No."

"Well, it's astonishing how that child resembles the Emperor of Austria!"

It was true.

The Lantibois baby offered an exact, striking, telling portrait of the sovereign who had accumulated, as if to play with them, the crowns of Austria, Hungary, Croatia, Bohemia, Bosnia, etc., etc.

Lantibois was not in the least delighted by that discovery. He wondered whether, two years ago, His Majesty Franz Josef might have visited France incognito, and the most outrageous suspicions hung over the virtue of Madame Lantibois.

In despair, the money-changer even tried to poison himself by swallowing Monsieur Andrieux's photographic developing fluid. He was successfully saved, thanks to an energetic antidote, and all his doubts were dispelled by assuring him that His Majesty Franz Josef had not left Austria since the meeting of the Three Emperors.

Time and toil completed calming the poor husband down, but he was not completely reassured when, three months later, Madame Lantibois gave birth to a daughter who resembled Pius IX like two drops of water. This time, no doubt could subsist, since it was publicly notorious that Pius IX, by his own admission, had spent his final years in a prison cell.

It was necessary to reconcile himself to it, for Madame Lantibois was not disarmed. Every year saw the money-changer's family augmented, and every child bore a striking resemblance to a sovereign of Europe or the New World.

In addition to the first-born son who resembled the Emperor of Austria and the daughter who resembled Pius IX, she had eight more children, six boys and two girls. The boys resembled Leopold II, Christian IV, Oscar of Sweden, the Emperor of Brazil, Tsar Alexander III and the Queen of England. The daughters resembled Queen Isabella and the King of Holland.

Yesterday, while passing through the Rue Vivienne, I went in to shake Lantibois' hand and pay my respects to Bérengère.

It was seven o'clock. The soup was about to be served. The children were arranged around the table for dinner. One might have thought it a small-scale Congress.

The Baby Portrait

His name as Jacques, hers was Jeanne. On the day of their marriage he was twenty-five and she was nineteen. They adored one another.

The divine *concetti* of Shakespeare's lovers were reborn on their ignorant lips.

When they went for a walk on Sunday along the river-bank at Meudon or in the forest of Chaville, through the peace of the woods and the rumor of nests, frightening the spring birds with their kisses all along the snowy hawthorn hedges, one might have thought that they were two legendary lovers escaped from some ancient ballad. The quiver of the branches above their heads resembled wing-beats.

They walked in an ecstasy, he protective and gentle, surrendering his soul to an enamored loquacity, she wonderstruck and docile, all her faith taking refuge in that tenderness.

During the week they worked hard. Jacques departed at dawn for the workshop where he slaved away valiantly amid the din of hammers and the stifling atmosphere of the forge. Jeanne remained at home, spending hours composing lovely little hats, masterpieces of bonnets to which she gave the light grace peculiar to the slender fingers of Parisiennes. In the evening, when he returned, Jacques took Jeanne's blonde head in his large hands and blinded her with two good kisses on the eyelids.

After a year, nothing was lacking in their terrestrial paradise. A little angel had come to bring the blessings of heaven.

It was necessary to see that young household celebrating him. He's so well-behaved, Monsieur; he looks so intelligent, Madame. In sum, a little cherub! Can you imagine that after six months he already had a fashion of looking at Papa that was not that of an ordinary child? It was that of a grown-up. Jeanne sustained that the little one resembled his father like

169

two drops of water; it wasn't difficult to see, one only had to look at the nose and the eyes. Jacques protested. For one thing, all babies look alike. Later, they would see. However, it seemed to him that the kid looked more like his mother. That was the idea he had.

Hence, interminable quarrels. It was charming. The little one grew up amid that joy. We would find it very hard to say whether he resembled Papa or Maman, but the fact is that he was superb. Jeanne was proud of him. She had a fashion of saying "My son," that was quite majestic. Jacques smiled as he watched the little fellow walk.

One day, it was decided that they would take the boy to a photographer in order to have a fine portrait taken. They would pay the price, but they wanted something good. Baby posed with a risible gravity. He had been seated on a cushion in the depths of an armchair, in his best clothes and bareheaded. The objective lens of the camera had seemed imposing to him, but during the operation that had made him look at a pretty picture. Thus, attentive and alert, he was very droll.

The portrait was framed in passe-partout painted with flowers and hung over the mantelpiece in the little family's bedroom. They took relatives and neighbors to admire it.

One evening, as Jeanne was going to bed, Baby coughed. The following morning, he coughed more forcefully, and Jeanne noticed that he was a little pale. They heated tisanes, but the child did not stop coughing. Jeanne was going mad. Jacques was somber. The paupers' physician could do nothing. Croup had seized the unfortunate child, who died, stifled, after a week of the mute, dejected suffering that small children have. Jacques and Jeanne wept all night over the blue and icy body of their stolen little angel. Black-clad men came who took Baby and nailed him in a coffin to take him to the cemetery. Having returned to their home after the burial, Jacques and Jeanne resumed weeping without being able to say a word.

From that day on, the household felt its links with the past breaking. A heavy silence reigned over the house. There was no longer any trace of the gaiety of old. They no longer kissed one another in the evening.

In any case, Jacques often came back late, which irritated Jeanne. Does one come home at such an hour? To make her wait two or three hours with dinner on the stove, I ask you! Does he take her for a servant? Necessary to say so right away; one would know where one stood then. And during that time, Monsieur went off to the wine-merchant's with his friends. His friends! One could say more about them! Something distinguished!

Jacques could not have been more amiable. Firstly, it was necessary not to put herself on the footing of treating her like a brute. Possible that some did, but not him. Did she think it amused him to come home to such a hovel to a woman who never had a pleasant word in her mouth? Oh, yes, it was cheerful, the house! If only he had unknown. Anyway, it couldn't go on; he had had it up to here. It was like a rusty old saw. Madame was impatient! Had she become a princess now? It annoyed him, in sum.

One night, after an altercation more animated than the previous ones, the household reached the point of drama. At a rather keen invective from Jeanne, Jacques marched toward her, his face red with anger, his hand raised.

Jeanne went as white as a corpse, but did not flinch. There was a moment of suspension and challenge; then the wife spoke:

"Look, Jacques, I've had enough of this life. Today, you're a little frightened, but tomorrow you'll beat me. I prefer to finish it immediately; let's separate."

"Let's separate, let's finish it forever. You see, Jeanne, I'm not bad, and you're a good little wife, but we can't live together. It's impossible; it's become unbearable. Take everything you want from here and go back to your mother. As well now as later. If, after that, you have need of me, you know where to find me."

They were now talking without anger. One might have thought that their decision to separate had calmed them down, liberated them.

Jacques sat down in his corner, following his wife with his eyes as she came and went through there dwelling. Jeanne had opened a large chest into which she threw, pell-mell, her modes dresses, her underclothes, her bonnets, and the objects to which she attached some value. Not a word, not a gesture. They were thinking.

At one moment, Jacques saw his wife advance toward the mantelpiece and detach the portrait of the dead baby from the wall.

"Just a minute!" he said. "That's mine. I'm keeping it. Do me the pleasure of putting it back."

"What! You want to take that from me!"

It was no longer Jeanne; it was a Gorgon. One second had sufficed to turn her into one of the Eumenides. She was even paler than at the moment when she had seen the blacksmith's large hand raised over her. Then, abruptly, her attitude changed. Her eyes filled with tears; she became humble, pleading.

"No, I beg you, let me take it away. Let me have it, Jacques. There's only been one thing good in my life, and it was the baby. I'm his mother. I bore him, I nursed him, I cared for him. I kissed him, and that was good. Poor little darling, who's dead. He was so good. When I woke up in the morning, I went quietly to watch him sleeping in his little bed. He was all pink, I couldn't hear him breathing. His little round leg stuck out of the covers. Oh, Baby, who's gone! Jacques, you'll let me have the portrait, won't you. We fight, we agonize, but we're not monsters. It's mine, the portrait. You remember, when it was taken, Baby was looking at a picture. Look—you might think that he's looking at me.

Jacques wept.

He leaned over the portrait and examined it without saying a word. His head was almost touching Jeanne's; their hair was touching. Jeanne wanted to go on pleading, but the blacksmith closed her mouth gently.

"If I don't give it to you, what will you do?"

"I won't go."

"Well, I'm keeping it!"

And as she stood there, astonished, he drew her into his arms, tenderly, as of old, and he murmured in her ear:

"Stay. Forgive. Forget. Love me. We'll keep one another."

It is four years since all that happened.

Today, there are two portraits in Jeanne's room, over the mantelpiece.

Vision

You don't believe in ghosts? You're wrong.

Certainly, revenants are not the fantastic apparitions of old, surging forth on the stroke of midnight, in the vicinity of cemeteries, to petrify some belated villager with terror. Phantoms have improved with time; they have marched with progress, and, if they still penetrate into the homes of the living without being announced, at least they retain in society the irreproachable manners of true gentlemen.

I knew one of them—only one—whose assiduities absorbed me for six months. Can I say that I regret his departure? No. But all in all, I have to render him this justice: that he was a phantom of good faith and spirit.

This is what happened.

A few years ago, on a calm winter evening, I was working by my fireside on I no longer remember what lyric poem—I was suffering slightly—when I distinctly hear tapping on my window. At first I thought it was the stupidity of some nocturnal bird beating my shutters with its wings, but the noise recurred at regular intervals—tap, tap, tap. I looked up, vaguely anxious, not too anxious to go see what it was. Know that I live in a fourth floor apartment with neither a balcony nor a terrace, in a quiet neighborhood, rather deserted. But the tapping was repeated, more rapidly, with a nervous impatience. I went to the window and opened it wide, with a single thrust.

Outside my window, suspended in the void, stationary, was a long white form. It was a tragic moment. A glance was exchanged between the apparition and me, one of the glances that the two adversaries in a duel with pistols exchanged before the combat: an anguish and a challenge; the fear of death and the desperate resolution to seem brave.

How long did it last? A minute? An eternity? At any rate, in spite of my stupor, I experienced a kind of relief when the specter addressed to me, in a scarcely distinct voice in which I thought I observed a slight British accent, the simple words: "May one come in?"

Too emotional to respond, I nodded my head and stood side before my visitor, with a hospitable gesture.

The specter glided into my room, quietly and politely, with the discreet salutation of a guest. I indicated an armchair to him, where he appeared to sit down, while he stammered a few words of banal apology: "I'm doubtless importunate...very sorry to disturb you at this hour...believe that...no, I'm truly confused..."

One might have thought that he was an elector soliciting a letter of recommendation from his député.

I examined him. The phantom belonged to the strong sex and seemed to be about thirty-five years of age. Contrary to legend, he did not present himself enveloped in a shroud, but fully-dressed. Dressed, you understand...which is to say that in his costume, which was not a costume but merely a transparent vapor, I made out a modern design, complete with waistcoat. The impression of the ensemble, physiognomy and vestment, was favorable. There was no doubt about it, I found myself in the presence of the shade of a very well brought-up fellow.

When we were both seated, he enveloped me with a determined gaze and said: "Let's get to the point. You don't recognize me?"

I had recovered a little calm, and it was in an assured voice that I was able to respond: "Not at all, my dear Monsieur."

He shrugged his shoulders.

"I expected that," he continued. "Oh, you've certainly remained the knave of old! No matter. Your denials won't do you any good. Furthermore, I can confound you with a word. Do you remember Le Morne Rouge?"

Le Morne Rouge? Yes, I remembered Le Morne Rouge. It's out there, in Martinique: a superb mountain behind Saint-

Pierre, with a fer-de-lance in every bush. Had I encountered this revenant alive? I searched, and searched. Nothing.

He went on: "Ah! You're hesitating. You're caught, eh? Well, listen. Yes, I'm poor William Perkins, whose fiancée you stole, my poor little Millia. The day you left in your frigate, she died. I swore to avenge her. Work and poverty retained me in the Antilles, prevented me from following you. Since yesterday evening, I've been dead. I'm free. It's the two of us now. To be sure, I can't kill you, but I can poison your life. Henceforth, I'll no longer quit you. Every evening, you'll see me at your side, and you'll hear me say: "Louis Vermont, remember Le Morne Rouge!"

Now I felt perfectly self-controlled. I stood up, like a host determined not to continue a conversation, and I said: "My dear Monsieur, we are, at this moment, the victims of a misunderstanding. You've mistaken the floor. I have visited Martinique and I'm not unaware of Le Morne Rouge, but I don't have any memory of the demoiselle Millia of whose misfortune you have been kind enough to inform me."

The phantom stood up as if to take his leave. "You persist in denying it!" he exclaimed. "So be it. But you have been warned; henceforth, I shall attach myself to your every step."

It was my turn to shrug my shoulders. "My dear specter," I said, "You're making progress. You're scarcely defunct and you already have the ideas of the other world. By my dear chap, we've lost the superstition of the fantastic. To employ an expression foreign to the *Dialogues of the Dead*, but which renders my thought precisely: that no longer cuts any ice with us. If, in spite of my advice, you want to visit me again, you'd be wrong to inconvenience yourself. I receive every Monday, but don't flatter yourself that you can make me suffer; I'm a child of the nineteenth century, and I don't believe in the supernatural."

"Louis Vermont," retorted the specter, "remember Le Morne Rouge!"

I opened the window. The specter withdrew, after ironic and brief congratulations.

The next day, when I woke up, I thought I had dreamed a story by Edgar Poe.

*

At about three o'clock, at the Chambre des Députés, as I was chatting with the honorable Paul Sandrique[27] in the Salon de la Paix, I saw the shade of William Perkins emerging from the wall, visible to me alone. He slipped between the delegate of the Aisne and me, looking at me and sniggering, and, without my interlocutor being able to hear a syllable, talking to me about Le Morne Rouge. At first that displeased me, but I quickly got accustomed to it. In any case, without passing for a lunatic, it was impossible for me to allow my disturbance to be detected.

In the evening, William Perkins came to join me at the Théâtre des Variétés, sitting next to me in an empty seat. I was amiable and told him the story of the first two acts, which he had missed. Afterwards, he went with me to visit Henri Gervex,[28] who was giving tea to his friends, and as he was still talking to me again about the Antilles at two o'clock in the morning, outside my door, I deigned to enlighten him further.

"My name is Charles-Marie de Larmejane, not Louis Vermont. I only went to Martinique with a hydrographic objective. Millia is unknown to me, and I've conserved the worst memories of Le Morne Rouge."

The phantom turned his back on me, sniggering.

I was sincere. William Perkins soon recognized that he was not scaring me. I began to give him a warm welcome. As soon as he appearance, I held out my hand to him.

"It's you, old chap? How are you?"

He remained grave, fixed in his sempiternal evocation of the Antilles, and calling me Louis Vermont all day long.

---

[27] The left-wing député Paul Sandrique (1845-1892) was best-known for being Léon Gambetta's secretary in the early 1870s.

[28] The painter Henri Gervex (1852-1929) fond of "mythological" paintings that licensed the depiction of nudes.

"Patience!" he sniggered. "One day I'll succeed in making you bleed."

"I said: "By the way, Perkins, I'm not going out this evening. Shall I see you?" or: "I'm going to the Bal des Artistes. Don't forget to pick me up afterwards. We can chat about Le Morne Rouge."

Nothing discouraged him.

One day, I went to pay court to Blanche, who had come back from a singing tour in Egypt—you know, Blanche, the one who loved candy so much that we nicknamed her Blanche de Pastille.

It was during the time she was living in her pretty villa in Maisons-Lafitte, where Jules Claretie found his décor for *Le Prince Zillah*. As it was my first visit, she wanted to show me her little park, her poultry-yard and the greenhouses, and even a little warren in which there were no rabbits.

It was a pleasant stroll. We ambled slowly under the trees, often stopping to look at the same flower, the same shrub, or the same patch of blue sky cut out by the branches. The birds saluted us with agile little trills, the roses wore smiles, the large poppies leaned over in reverences. With the aid of the imagination, it was lovely.

Bang! William Perkins touched me on the shoulder and showed me his malevolent smile. Louis Vermont, Le Morne Rouge. He was stubborn. Impossible to make him understand his lack of tact. No means of calling him to account.

Doubtless he divined my annoyance, for his insistence increased. I found him, no longer on my right but on my left, between Blanchette and me, in such a fashion that I could hardly see Blanchette any longer, and when I strove to pick up the thread of my madrigal, broken by that macabre intervention, the ill-bred phantom brought me back to his tiresome Le Morne Rouge, to the snakes out there, to the despairing Millia.

And then something atrocious happened.

Suddenly, Blanche stopped, her gaze fixed on the ground. Horrible tracks were imprinted in the sand, the tracks of bare feet. William Perkins, doubtless weary of floating between heaven and earth, or ill-intentioned, was marching between us, matching strides with us. Blanche looked uncomprehendingly, interrogated me with a glance, and saw me so pale that, abruptly divining something frightful, she fainted, uttering a cry of terror.

I carried her, inanimate, to the house, still pursued by the sniggers of the odious Perkins.

"Louis Vermont, remember!"

Scarcely had I returned to the house than I handed poor Blanche over to the care of a chambermaid, and went back down to the park, where my phantom was laughing to the point of tears.

"Damn it!" I cried, going up to him. "I've had enough. This matter has to be settled.. This life can't go on!"

The wretched specter was still laughing.

"Come on," I said, "I'll be calm. As long as you were content to come to find me at the theater, in the Chambre or at my hairdresser's, I didn't say anything. I even found it amusing to have a revenant for a friend, even though—this isn't a reproach—your conversation truly isn't sufficiently varied. But now, this can't go on. If you're determined to prevent me paying court to that prima donna, who must have brought back ultra-oriental ideas from Cairo, I'm determined to give you notice!"

The shade replied: "I told you that I was going to make you weep!" Remember, Lois Vermont…!"

I did not let him finish. "For six months I've been telling you day and night that my name isn't Louis Vermont…"

"As if I don't recognize you!"

"But I assure you…"

Another shrug of the shoulders. "Futile to pretend," said Perkins. "I can paint you from memory. Look, you have a little black mark on your right arm, between the wrist and the elbow…"

I had already rolled up my sleeve, and showed the phantom an arm exempt from any unusual mark.

Immediately, the physiognomy of the late Perkins was transformed. He looked at my arm very closely, several times, and, immediately afterwards, in the tone of a profoundly humiliated revenant, he exclaimed: "Oh, Monsieur! What an error! I don't know where to put myself...never such a blunder...yes, indeed, now that I look at you closely...such a resemblance! It's the nose. Oh, damn it, what must you think of me?" And he continued, increasingly vexed: "Look, I'll offer you my apologies, in the newspapers...I believed that I was in the right...would you like me to find the young lady and explain it to her?"

"No! No!"

Introduce Perkins to Blanche! A disaster!

"But I want to repair..."

I consoled the late Perkins, who disappeared forever.

Since then, I haven't seen the revenant again...but I never saw Blanche again either.

Bah!

The Tamer

The grooms have pushed the great varnished and gilded vehicle, closed with large panels and bronze handles, into the ring. Behind the panels there is a rumor, heavy footfalls, quivering breath, something savage and sly that is detectable, and which imposes an anxiety on the crowd. The orchestra, above the coupé, falls silent. On the tiers, the men become serious and attentive; the women, slightly pale, savor the caress of a frisson.

The panels fall away in the hands of lackeys, the grilles are doubled, rising under the action of hooks—and in the dazzle of the chandeliers, the huge russet lions emerge, bored but majestic, dejected by an aristocratic sorrow, like captive kings. There are six: three male lions and three lionesses. Five were born in the cages of Hamburg Zoo, where the commerce in wild beasts is negotiated; they have been subject all their lives to the enervation of slavery, the humiliation of cracked whips, the spleen of cages.

The last, whose mane seems black, comes from the profound forests of the Atlas; he is superb, enormous, formidable. He has possessed the desert, terrified the tribes, drunk the rosy blood of gazelles, held beneath his claws the broken heads of hunters, has afforded mercy to the life of herdsmen. The regret of lost splendors burns in his coppery eyes; and before the bourgeois and the talkative women perched on the circus benches, before that mannered civilization that worldly life stifles and withers, he thinks of the immense solitude of mysterious woods, frightened herds running in the plain, the nights of Africa, the inviolate cavern made of giant blocks of stone.

He has been named Sultan, and rightly. He has the epic cruelty of pachas; already, three tamers have expired under his claws. In the cage, he alone dares to roar while prowling.

The other beasts make themselves small at his approach; he looks at them as a Caesar must have looked at his brothers' bastards.

A man appears at the entrance to the ring, as handsome as a young god. It is Eric; he is the tamer. He alone, henceforth, is the lion. Eric is twenty-five, with the stature of a hero, the courage of a gladiator, the strength of a Titan, the athletic graces of a Discobolus.

When he descends into the arena, in the midst of the mute fear of the public, the men are jealous of him, the women watch him. A Muscovite princess, a cousin of tsars, adores him and follows him from capital to capital, glad to contemplate him, in the evenings, at odds with the wild animals. Think about it! To see that beloved head, perfumed every night by kisses, confided to the horrible maw of wild beasts, and to think that under the effort of a single thrust of those teeth...that's enough to spice up the love-making of a great lady.

Eric's costume is the true costume of acrobats: silk leotard and black velvet jerkin widely cleft at the neck; a crimson satin belt at the waist, white sandals with soles rubbed with resin, which grip the floorboards of the cage.

He traverses the ring and, standing before the little iron door, he salutes the public slowly, with a statuesque gesture. Sultan has howled! The lions of Hamburg run along the bars, trembling, bounding to the summit of the cage, crawling with the movements of fleeing cats. The silence is such that one can hear Eric's curt words, snapped at the beasts like orders to little dogs. "Hup, Sakla!... Jump, Nero!..."

The spectators shiver, unable to take their eyes off the cage where the felines are crawling and the man alone gives the impression of roaring. Eric is truly superb now.

But Sultan is motionless. He alone remains crouched in a corner, anxious, menacing, with the attitudes of a hunter. It is, however, necessary that he "work." Eric takes his time, makes sure of the stock of the whip in his right hand, and, with a firm tread, marches toward the black lion.

In the first row of the seats, the Russian watches, on her feet. She will soon be thirty years old, but one would hardly grant her sixteen. Blonde, thin, frail and unhealthy in appearance. A pretty, suffering flower. However, she alone seems unafraid. Habit, perhaps. She knows the session by heart, completely regulated in all its steps; Eric's movements are foreseen as well as the leaps of the wild beasts. She watches the spectacle as one listens to old music, always interesting but devoid of surprises.

An anxiety wrinkles her forehead when Eric raises his whip at the black lion, which parries the blow with a movement of its paw—an enormous paw, armed with hooks. But that only lasts the duration of a lightning-flash. The beast has yielded. Sultan is exasperated, but simultaneously humiliated. The brave tamer senses that he is the great victor. If all goes well, perhaps he will dare to present the lion with the barrier and the hoop. No he doesn't dare. Sultan is displaying a disquieting slyness. One might think that he has decided, that he is resolved to put an end to it.

Look out! This is the most dangerous moment. Eric goes to gaze at the lion at close range; then he drops his whip and, disarmed, almost naked, he blows into the horrible muzzle of the beast...

It's done! Sultan's roar has made the hall tremble. Eric smiles. He walks backwards to the iron door, holding the monsters in respect. The door opens slightly, and closes again. The tamer is in the ring. Bravo!

The Russian has not taken her eyes off him—but now she trembles, as if a rush of blood has risen to her face, because Eric has only saluted one person in the crowd: a tall brunette woman with a the profile of a Jewess, who is gazing at him with shining eyes.

What a scene!

The Russian has not wanted to give him the time to dress. She has stopped him in passage in the stables, as the grooms are taking the cage away, and she is holding him in the corner of a stall, talking to him excitedly in a low voice.

Eric smiles, and then shrugs his shoulders. What? A brunette woman? What brunette woman? He hasn't even seen her. It's fiction! Come on, let's see...

But the Russian is annoyed. She has seen. She can't be made to believe. She has seen, that's all!

While she is speaking she nervously agitates the stout whip that she has stolen from Eric's fingers with a mechanical, hypocritical gesture, without appearing to do so. And as the tamer persists in his denial, she strikes him in the face, brutally.

She is a lioness in her turn. Her face inflamed, excited, she is transformed. She is not longer the little morsel of a woman of while ago; she is a Cossack, a kind of savage, something wild.

Eric recoils, frightened, and tries to go to his dressing-room, but the whip reaches him again, raised by a little iron hand. He cannot go up, he cannot flee. Only one retreat remains to him: The cage.

He leaps into it with one bound. It is Sultan; it is death. Too bad! Anything rather than that Russian woman.

The lions surround him, roaring, menacing. Sultan is crawling.

"Oh, the coward!" cries the Russian.

And she is right.

The Telephone

"Hello! Hello!"

"Hello!"

And I pay my court.

I have finally discovered a lover that no suspicion brushes, a docile woman, flexible to my whim, and of whom I shall not weary. When I desire her—and according to my voluntary caprice—she is blonde, or brunette, or red-haired, or perfumed with powder; without it being necessary for me to say a word, she dresses as I wish, sometimes as a dainty Parisienne of whom clinging satin reveals the noble purity of forms, sometimes as a princess, sometimes as a beautiful actress. She consents to take on, at need, the face of some woman that I have only perceived from afar, but whom I desire. When, gripped by an impossible ambition, my dream flies far, far away, into blue lands of virgin forests enlivened by the bizarre plumage of birds of paradise and the agility of young monkeys; when my mind haunts African shores, blue havens, the exquisite distances of the Bosphorus or Yokohama, she transforms herself at the whim of my desire, becoming the enervating Creole of Havana, the copper-colored Chinese woman intoxicated by languor and opium, the chaste and immodest beloved, the veiled Mooress who profound dark eyes alone are glimpsed between the smile of the mask.

In brief, she is my mistress—or my slave.

"Hello! Hello!"

"Hello!"

And submissive! At the first summons, she hastens. If the conversation doesn't amuse me, if I'm in a bad mood or I have a headache, I abandon her, I quit her. I pick up my hat and go. She doesn't get annoyed, no protests, no puling faces. It's sufficient for me to alert her by a triple signal of pearly bells, conforming to regulation. Sometimes, she calls me, but always with absolute disinterest. A friend is asking for me, and she offers herself as an intermediary.

We chat most often at night, because, for part of the day she rests. Her service at the central telephone exchange is thus regulated. If I happen to return home late to my bachelor apartment, to which I only climb up reluctantly—nature abhors a void—I run to the plaque and the vibrations commence. Thanks to her, every evening, a woman's voice wishes my good night, sleep well and pleasant dreams, concluding my day with a little charm and grace. Her "Bonsoir, my friend," often makes me forget the miseries and distresses of quotidian existence. Witty and cheerful, she laughs merrily, like a child, which enables me to divine pretty teeth and fine lips. And it does me good to hear her laughter, when my head feels brutalized by work or my heart drowned in spleen.

"Hello! Hello!"
"Hello!"
"Is that you?"
"Yes! Bonjour! Bonjour!"
I remember delightedly the day of confessions.

I had just been talking to my notary and, when the conversation was finished, she had forgotten to break the connection. Hearing her laughing and chatting to her young friends, I called her back, and persisted with my madrigals of the day before. I was going through one of those morose hours that favor sympathy; instead of repeating everyday stupidities, I became earnest, seriously earnest, with a conviction that I could not explain subsequently, and I allowed to fall into the Graham Bell instrument a desire to weep retained since the previous evening.

It was exquisite. I had the aplomb to be plaintive, to talk to her about my loneliness, the stupid void of my bachelor life. She revealed herself as benevolent as good bread, gave me advice like an elder sister, took kindness so far as to scold me. Then I heard her sob her confidences. She lived alone too, and sadly. No more Papa or Maman, no lovers, and no friends apart from her comrades at the exchange. Oh, life wasn't cheerful!

I proposed to her squarely that we combine our two solitudes in an intimacy. What a blunder!

"What do you take me for, Monsieur?"

"For me!"

She cut off the current dead, and when, determined to make her accept my apologies, I cried "Hello! Hello!" she had had herself replaced by an old gentleman who replied "Hello! Hello!" in a voice broken by forty years of Swiss absinthe.

During the day, I was able to beg her pardon. She took pity on me. I swore never to do it again—never, never. And as a vague tenderness dazed my with its vertigo, I dared. Oh, the duration of a lightning-flash.

The vibrant plaque, astonished, repeated the sound of a kiss that ran quivering through the wires and ended up in the ears of my conquest—and that sonorous kiss prevailed, victoriously; another kiss responded, gentle, gentle, as gentle as a breath. And crack! The connection was interrupted, alas!

"Hello! Hello!"

"Hello!"

I once went a week without hearing her. Some other young woman replaced her, of whom I did not dare ask anything. What was happening? Had my mistress been sacked? Had she been exiled from the central exchange to a local exchange? How could I find out? The slightest question might compromise her. Besides which, I did not know—I still do not know—her name.

One night, the bell woke me up. *Évohé!* It was her ring.

"Hello! Hello!"

"Hello!"

She explained her long absence: a bout of bronchitis, a vile bronchitis that had nailed her to her bed for a week. Poor little puss! I recommended tincture of iodine to her and hot infusions. Her convalescence furnished me with a thousand pretexts for communication. Twenty times a day, I asked after her health. It's getting better? Good. Talk to you soon.

And that electric idyll will soon have lasted for two years. Contrary to custom, we have no children, but that's explicable. Well, the wire...

We love one another like that, and believe me, we're happy. That love will last. I have the right to grow old, and she can become ugly, for we'll never separate. I shall always see her with eyes resolved to admire her, and if her hair turns white and her teeth fall out, I won't know.

As for me, I can go bald, become obese, one-armed, stooped or gouty with impunity, without ceasing to be loved.

"Hello! Hello!"

"Hello!"

The Rock Lobster

She was as blonde as an August crop, but, by virtue of a coquettish duplicity, not judging herself sufficiently blonde as yet, she covered her tresses and the curls on her nape with a fine powder the color of Messina tobacco, from which rose up, in a little gilded cloud, perfumes of an indefinable tenderness, something like subtle essences of Chypre. Her slim bosom, with pure and tempting lines, palpitated under the softly draped crease of a ruby corsage, contained by a thin crescent of diamonds. Her delicate visage, certainly dreamed by Latour and divined by Watteau, drew its light from two from two large ravishing and perverse eyes whose glances, like blue kisses, made starlight shine, and her small mouth, like a crimson carnation, uncovered at capricious moments thirty-two pearls of a marvelous orient. Her hands—the little nervous hands of a Hungarian pianist—floated over object that they seems to touch like the white wings of turtle-doves. And in the ideal China that haunts the nostalgia of poets, one would not have discovered, even in the idle princesses of Tau-Tai, feet more improbable than hers.

Her name was Cécile.

Alas, over the cradles of the best-fêted little girls, a bad fairy sometimes appears, more malevolent than an itch, and mingles with the promises of good fairy godmothers a present charged with sly tricks. On the spring day when Cécile was baptized, which archangels granted her all the seductions, a marine demon came in without being invited, and cast over the innocent baby these simple words:

"You will love rock lobster in mayonnaise sauce passionately, and that blind love will doom you!"

It is not enough to love mayonnaise sauce; it is also necessary to know how to prepare it. You take the yolk of a fresh egg and you tip it into the bottom of a bowl—some amateurs mistakenly crush it in a soup-dish—you take hold delicately of the crystal phial in which the liquid gold of the oil is drowsing, and you put it in gently, very gently, drop by drop. While pouring you stir regularly with a little spoon—the heretics of the dish go so far as to make use of a fork—and you beat it energetically, relentlessly without weakness. The fingers that beat ought to manifest the continuous rapidity of the flywheel of a steam engine, and can get carried away if necessary. The hand that has to pour maintains an impassive calm, a majestic and serene coolness. One second of forgetfulness and all is lost; the shiny combination immediately takes on a perfectly repulsive marshy aspect. Everything is spoiled. The best thing then is to start over: you take the yolk of a fresh egg and you tip it, etc. etc.

The author of the *Cuisinière bourgeoise* has forgotten to mention the essential conditions for the elaboration of a god mayonnaise. A glacial atmosphere is necessary. It is important, in order to succeed, to place oneself in an air current, at the summit of a belfry or in the vicinity of Monsieur Caro. To attempt to produce a mayonnaise in the crater of Mount Vesuvius, a corridor of the Folies Bergère or alongside député Langlois[29] would constitute an ultra-temeritous enterprise.

In addition, it is as well to be two—not three, but two. When there are three, there is one who does nothing. With two, the sauce comes together marvelously. One holds the little spoon; the other distributes the drops of oil exactly. But when the sauce is finished, rivalries burst forth; the hand that has poured tries to usurp the glory of the hand that has beaten, and at the psychological moment that the vinegar is added, it is possible to quarrel with one's oldest friend.

For a mayonnaise is prepared between friends; hence one must choose one's society. I would not have any dread with

---

[29] The radical firebrand Amédée-Jérôme Langlois (1819-1902). The previous contrasting reference is presumably The Christian philosopher Elme-Marie Caro (1826-1887)

collaborators like Berton or Lina Munte,[30] but I would expect continually to see the oil of Provence lost in dangerous liaisons if I happened to venture an enterprise of that sort with Daubray or Sarah Bernhardt.

In brief, to succeed in a mayonnaise it requires:

A fresh egg-yolk;

A bowl;

A little spoon;

Oil;

A sympathetic collaborator;

And *sang-froid*.

One evening, when Abel had come honestly to share Cécile's meal, he perceived, sprawled on a silver platter supported by the Gothic dresser in the dining room, an enormous rock lobster, a kind of rugged and vermilion marine monster which one might have thought to have been chosen to feed a garrison.

As he tried to reassure himself by considering that table, where only two places were set facing one another in an intimate fashion, Cécile came in, readjusting amid the lace of her neck the crescent of her diamond-studded brooch. Her normal happy smile was transformed into a sulky pout. Abel though about a lost bracelet, a faded ribbon, or some chagrin of a spoiled overgrown child annoyed by her milliner or her lap-dog.

Infernal gods! The catastrophe was worse! A distracted cook had spoiled the sauced destined for the gourmet's favorite dish. Instead of a harmonious mayonnaise she had served a sickening mixture, a marinade frightful to the naked eye. The dinner was ruined.

---

[30] Lina Munte remains famous for having been the first actress to play the lead in Oscar Wilde's notorious *Salome*. The reference coupled with her might be to the novelist and playwright Caroline Berton

Abel protested. What is simpler than making a sauce? And without permitting any objection, he took off his gloves, chose from the dresser a large bowl of old Rouennaise faience, requested an egg-yolk—very fresh—and set to work. From the first swirls of the little spoon, however, he recognized that his good intentions would remain vain; either by virtue of lack of culinary experience or the return of the disturbance brought about by the contemplation of Cécile's large eyes, he called for help. He was just in time. The oil, spread capriciously, was threatening to transform the mayonnaise into soup.

Cécile intervened. Her white hand seized the old Madrileno oil-dripper with the double tube, and poured.

But what is held in destiny!

While gazing at that delicate little hand, in which the blood designed thin azure lines, and admiring that aristocratic grip braced by the attachment of a frail wrist charged with bracelets and drowned in the lace of the sleeve, he sensed vertigo rising from his heart to his head, temptations putting a folly of kisses into his lips.

Soon, he dared. And Cécile, alarmed at first, had difficulty refraining from compromising the sauce. In spite of her indignant plaints, in spite of the emotion that caused a troubling frisson to pass through her adorable person, she kept her hand extended and clenched, the wrist firm.

The little spoon was still swirling.

Glad, without remorse in the crime, Abel became bolder. His kiss brushed the child's fingers, caressed the nascence of the arm, where his moustache trailed a silky softness. She, attentive and heroic, considered the mixture.

Momentarily, suspiciously, she leaned over, and the voluntary scullion, closing his eyes, descended, lips open like two red wings, amid the blonde hair steeped in odorous powder.

The little spoon stopped, the Madrileno oil-dripper nonchalantly resumed a place at hazard among the crystal of the place-setting.

A few exquisite words were exchanged in low voices, and when they both raised their eyes, as if emerging from an ecstasy, Cécile showed Abel, on the silver platter, the huge rock lobster that was listening to them, and blushing.

Betrothal

Irène is thirty years old; she has remained a spinster. A mysterious regret has emptied her soul, perhaps the rancor of an offended hope. Her lip is bitter, her eyes mocking; she laughs in a nervous fashion, abruptly cut off by the apprehension of a sob. Ghosts haunt her, sad ghosts draped in mourning, and it sometimes seems to her that she is living in a necropolis. Nothing any longer exists for her that is alive, nothing that might be the future, nothing that might be tomorrow. She awaits with serenity the end of it all, feeling as if she were the widow of someone who is not dead, martyr to an oath that no one has asked of her and which she has not pronounced before anyone. She has loved; dolor, which kills petty sentiments, eternalizes grand passions; and a woman's heart is so made that it only retains a trace of that which has left a scar there. Hence, a bleak sadness, ever heavier; for it is on women especially that the years weigh, all the more so if they are empty.

No anger against life, no jealousy of the happiness of others. The individuals that adversity renders malevolent were malevolent from the start; their perversity was lying in wait for an opportunity. Irène is good, and has remained good throughout her proofs. She often weeps, but the tears of others double her chagrin. Like all creatures that suffer an inconsolable regret, she knows the divine art of consolations. To those whose are in doubt she talks about hope—she who no longer has any of her own. And to distract a foreign ennui, to give wings to black birds leaning over the foreheads of friends, she finds nervous, noisy, macabre gaieties in which an immense incredulity gasps. Her visage is not so much a visage as a mask; her speech is not so much the vestment as the disguise of her thought; her smile is a décor devoid of illumination; and in the contemplation of that mocking sphinx, one thinks of those theater curtains decorated with harlequinades, which descend, rigid and joyful, over the denouement of a tragedy.

She adores her mother—Maman—with the ambition to die first. Only two friends, Marie and Marguerite, know the price of her tears and the measure of her renunciation. A taste for society gives her a means of fleeing, and grips her with the furtive temptation to disguise herself in order not to be recognized. She lives thus, on the pleasures, emotions, impressions and hopes of others, waiting submissively.

The phrase that she pronounces most frequently is: "I'm so sorry..."

Pierre is thirty years old, ten of which have been futile. The emptiness of things weighs upon him. He has defended liberty and has been put in prison; he has made war and has seen that it is butchery; he has sought heroes and has only found men. Weary of the terrestrial, slightly sickened and slightly pained, he has taken refuge in the immaterial. He loves ideas—not many, but some: art, fatherland, rhythm, sacrifice. Because of that, people say of him: "He's a dreamer." The unfortunates riveted to the ground are naturally mistrustful of bizarre individuals who have rendezvous in the Milky Way and maintain long relationships with the stars. Frequenting the stars is suspect. What completes Pierre is that he is something of a demagogue—an infamy that he shares with Hugo, Garibaldi, Bakunin, Zorilla and Kossuth. Rumor has it that he has constructed barricades and, as he is an adversary of the death penalty he is sometimes qualified as a blood-drinker. He speaks of martyrs with respect. Fundamentally, politics scarcely excites him. He still believes entirely in the Republic, but not at all in republicans. To console himself, he seeks rhymes and founds his joy on the perfection of scansion.

He has traveled, and the world seems small to him. What! At the ends of the earth already! But yes. He has seen virgin forests, blue, black, yellow and pink lands, great rivers, verdant isles flung over the Ocean like stripped bouquets, insurmountable summits—and he has come back sadly, to find no one at home.

Pierre also wears a mask of artificial frivolity, which he parades in the renewed cares of days. He has Irène's resigned falsity, and the same cruel pleasure. However, he does not endure as she does the regret of a vanished hope. The women he has encountered are those who forget and are forgotten. None has survived in his presence; they have passed with the rustle of a silk dress, quickly or slowly, but with a tread so light that no trace remains of them. To begin with he regretted those furtive flights, desirous of retaining one of those creatures—the best or the worst, provided that she stayed. It is so profoundly heart-breaking living alone that one arrives at comprehending the old women surrounded by cats and birds. Everything living populates; the dregs of abandonment consist of only being surrounded by things.

When one is not loved by anyone, one loves everyone, with a banal affection summarized in blind sympathy. One adopts a few rare preferred individuals and distributes the small change of one's heart to the rest. It is ruining oneself without enriching anyone. Bah! From then on, one is soon categorized. Passers-by shrug their shoulders and your handshake becomes valueless. One lives disdained among the indifferent, and one requests petty revenges of irony.

Pierre lives thus, isolated, wondering every day whether it might not end soon, savoring the joys, the emotions and the hopes of others—and waiting.

The phrase that he pronounces most frequently is: "What's the point?"

And, the thirtieth year having come, those two individuals, similarly struck for different reasons, chanced to encounter one another on the highway, at a time when they were heading toward old age as toward an inevitable victor from whom one hopes for better conditions...

Is there, after marriages of amour, of business, of rationality and of convenience, the marriage of resignation, of mutual assurance against future abandonment, destined to repair, to the extent that it can be, the abyss hollowed out by the disillusionments of yesteryear?

Is it the case that Irène and Pierre, one having toured calvaries, the other having gone around the world, are no better armed against ennui and the burden of life together than little schoolgirls and young sub-prefects married in the haste of skimped unions?

Is it that there will no longer be time to create a good, egotistical and narrow existence? Time might have prepared the betrothal, pity announced the affection; and they might have married in order to console one another reciprocally, or even to weep together.

Is not having someone with whom to weep, already not living alone?

Faded Love-Letters

It is surprising how the past evaporates! One thinks that writings remain, one trusts in the permanence of the real, one hopes for memories in testimonies—but when, after ten years, one sadly opens on old casket, the nothingness of things chills you; one understands that the reliquary was a coffin, that nothing remains of that which endures. The most reliable witnesses forget. The confided secret volatilizes and disappears in the wind of the passing years. One has wept without having suffered; the heart has grown old without having lived. In going back to the abolished epochs, one experiences the sensation of a pilgrimage through a cemetery, of gravity, a kind of respect for that which is no more, of skin-deep sadness. The impression settles and flies away, like a bird that has paused. Then, nothing more. Quotidian monotony grips you again, tames you, and you resume living solely in the present, like a beast.

Yesterday evening, I opened the little ebony box with old silver decorations in which, since I thought I divined my youth, I have buried in fits of instinctive religion letters of sincere appearance, desired scraps, bouquets of violets fallen from corsages—the frippery of bachelor bohemia; trivia momentarily cherished, sweet nonsensicalities, stupidities that made me smile. I ought to have emptied the box into the fire closing my eyes. No. I wanted to read, to attempt a cruel proof, to seek the extinct luster of ribbons, the lost scent of flowers, to know whether my follies at the age of twenty merited a regret....

Two days without seeing you, wicked boy! Maman is sad. Father is annoyed and says that your vile politics will land you in prison. For myself, I'm unhappy to the point of writing to you secretly, which isn't good.

See you soon, Monsieur!

Paulette

My cousin Paule! She was nice. She was eighteen and I was twenty. When small we had played at "husband and wife"—with conviction. Oh, an admirable conviction! We had baptized dolls together. Later, having grown up a little, she had persisted. I had neglected her for the Bibliothèque Sainte-Geneviève, for the mobs of Bellevue or a frightful little literary journal the published my first verses. On winter evenings I went to sit down beside her and played interminable card games with the old uncle, for which I pretended to be passionate. Paule crocheted me pretty silk pouches lined with bright chamois leather into which I stuffed the blond clumps of my Maryland tobacco. During the war she sent amulets to the camp for me blessed by Our Lady of Victories. That was kind.

Now, Paule is the wife of a notary and the mother of two bookish messieurs. And all that was fifteen years ago.

Alas, yes, Paulette, fifteen years already.

Goin to work this evning. Come fech me at ten.

Lison.

A funny girl, all the same! Not malevolent, not knowing, not at all perverse. A bit stupid. I remember a fishing trip during which she slyly returned to the Oise all the small fish I pulled out of the river, out of the goodness of her heart. She was a little dressmaker encountered one morning in the quincunxes of the Pépinière, where she was crumbling brioches for the birds. Surrounded by a flock of white pigeons, she had seemed so pretty that I had immediately offered her my heart, lightly rhymed, in lines of eight beats. She had replied "yes" in order not to hurt me. Six months of intimacy with the turtledoves of the Luxembourg. One day, she left me, in order to avoid a chagrin to my friend Michel, who liked birds more than me. Thus she passed through life, doing good. *Transit bene faciendo.*

A funny girl, all the same.

Don't forget my lilac branch for the third act. Bring it to me in cotton.

A thousand grimaces.

Suzanne.

And to think that she still plays ingénues! She'll keep the employment all her life, and toward her sixtieth year, will still be making use of grimaces by the thousand, to the aristocratic habitués of her Tuesdays. Oh, where ingenuousness nests! At sixteen she was supported by a bald protector who was able by the transmission of his nominal titles to cause the irreparable outrage of the years to be forgotten. To that deluded old man she annexed a poet, two cavalry officers and a suburban medical student. I had been adopted as a florist, for the third act, the ballroom scene. Seven hundred francs' worth of white lilacs in fifty days—and at least five francs' worth of cotton. I only regret the five francs worth of cotton.

My dear Léopold, don't forget my lilac branch for the third act. Bring it to me in cotton.

A thousand grimaces.

Suzanne.

Her last letter. I kept it, even though my name isn't Léopold.

What could she have done with all that white lilac? I found out later that there were ten of us furnishing the adornment of the third act every evening. A chambermaid sold the superfluous bouquets the next day.

And to think that she still plays ingénues!

…Above all, bring me a Louis terrine, the Bontoux pie-dish, a small punnet of peaches and too much jam.

Séraphine.

She probably died of indigestion. She charmed me with the capacity of her stomach. A gulf! We met one another at the buffet in Avignon, and, on seeing her swallow, with a vertiginous rapidity, a meal for fifty, I was penetrated by admiration. On arriving in Paris I ran to open an account for her at Duval the butchers. She loved me as she loved roast beef, in the English style. No common tastes. In literature, she understood Brillat-Savarin and Monselet. In history she professed scorn for Sparta a superstitious veneration of Lucullus. All that was not without a certain gastronomic poetry. In her aperitive dreams, she willingly returned to ancient times, to the fabulous feasts of the aedile Marcius, with Gallic wild boar in Trojan sauce, stuffed with nightingales' tongues, served on porphyry tables. She would have liked to taste the perfumed wines of Mount Massicus and Cos, to bite into the gilded grapes of Mount Esquiline, to savor the moray eels on which Domitian nourished slaves. We parted because of an incompatibility of menus. She adored veal and I was never able to tolerate it...

She probably died of indigestion.

Don't come this evening. I'm dining with my aunt.
Jeanne.

She often dined with her aunt.

But so what? As she rightly said, I had no right to make her neglect her family duties. Her duties...she didn't talk about them much, her duties. The statue of Austerity, neither more or less. Gazes like Raphael's, but affections like Fragonard's. Violence and resignation mingled. An exemplary assiduity at low mass as at high. Escapes to the confessional from which she returned with her soul relieved and her mind troubled. She was one of those women who, in church, believes that she is self-controlled because she is observed, and meditative because she is silent.

The woman never went home except on someone's arm: hence the utility of confessors. I would have tried in vain to retain Jeanne when her spiritual director was expecting her, but that venerable ecclesiastic could not have retained her for one minute longer if I was expecting her. She was truly pious, and truly tender. I had a rival, but it was God.

Amours, delights and orgies.

All the same, she very often dined with her aunt.

Everything is burned. The empty box is burning in its turn, for I want it to die with the vain relics it contained. Sad flames rise up in the fireplace, and the bouquets become grass burning with a little dry crackle of straw. The ribbons writhe in the fire, and the minuscule shoe of the Neapolitan dancer, of which I made a match-holder, splits, cracking dolorously. The hearth darkens, the flames die down, further and further, contracting into a little blue light. Then, nothing but gray ash, melancholy in appearance, which I stir with little thrusts of the tongs, coldly, without a tear.

That is my entire past, that dust. That was once fever, excitement, intoxication, the unhealthy and fatal merriment of energies poorly expended. I'm certain of losing nothing in annihilating those frivolous souvenirs. Better than that, I'm glad, rejuvenated since that execution.

What would I regret? Those amours resembled amour much as perfume is reminiscent of flowers. I'm weary. I'm alone. The nullity of frivolities sickens me, and I breathe, with a soul henceforth new, the pure and holy, proud and noble, lofty and sacred grand passion that ensures the infinite in the eternal!

MY INTERMENT

Mr. F. O'S., a French writer, on his way through Cairo, has just been the hero of a terrible adventure.

On Monday morning, the waiter in attendance at the Nile Hotel, on entering his room, found Mr. F. O'S lying on the bed, quite cold and lifeless.

The waiter immediately informed Mr. Fridman, the proprietor of the hotel, who, after having procured a death certificate from a doctor, communicated with Monsieur le Marquis de Reverseaux,[31] the French Consul General, who ordered seals to be affixed to the luggage of the deceased gentleman.

The next day, according to French custom, the body of Mr. F. O'S. was laid out and put in a coffin to be taken to the cemetery.

While engaged in lifting the bier on to the hearse however, the porters were startled by a peculiar noise that seemed to proceed from the coffin.

They opened the lid at once, and, to the profound emotion of all those present, Mr. F. O'S, was found with his eyes wide open and his arms trembling convulsively.

Soon completely reanimated, the cataleptic was able to return to his apartment and to take some nourishment. A few hours later, Mr. F. O'S. was so completely returned to health that he received without fatigue the visitors who called to congratulate him on his marvelous escape from the horrors of a premature burial.

---

[31] The career diplomat Frédéric Guéau, Marquis de Reverseaux de Rovray, was the French consul-general in Egypt in the early 1890s.

That same evening, Mr. F. O'S. attended a dinner at the French Consulate, at which he was the object of general interest.

The Egyptian Star
20 November 1891.[32]

My first impressions of the sepulcher date from early Monday morning, at the moment when I was woken up by the valet de chambre and the guide that I had hired the previous evening for an excursion by road to Elizeh and the isle of Roudeh. In spite of the terrible emotions of those twenty-eight hours of agony, my impressions have remained engraved in my memory with a marvelous precision; every minute, every second and every fraction of a second brought me a new anguish, the terror of which did not disperse my initial terrors.

It is not my prerogative to follow the physicians, Messieurs Horton and Volgretz, in their research, nor in their study of the circumstances that might have determined that long catalepsy. I shall only say that I found myself the previous day in perfect health, and that I had not experienced the slightest illness since my last attack of bronchitis, which was about three years ago, and had lasted no longer than two or three weeks. For the same of completeness, I recall that in the aftermath of that malady, my physician had judged me to be slightly neurasthenic—which is to say, prone to nervous ailments. I note that diagnosis even though no particular affliction has since confirmed it.

In sum, I want to declare that it is gratuitously, without any confidence on my part, that Messieurs Horton and Volgretz have suggested "that I had doubtless been subject to recent chagrins to which I was unable to link the effects of my

---

[32] The original version of the story is preceded by a duplicate text in English and French, the French text pretending to be translated from the English, although the English is clearly a slightly inapt translation from the French. I have provided my own, marginally improved, translation of the French text.

physical condition." I had, in fact, experienced, not recently but fifteen months previously,[33] an immense chagrin that no consolation can appease, but that profound dolor certainly had no effect on my physical condition, even in the exceedingly acute period of the initial affliction. Furthermore, those gentlemen were unaware of it. What is certain is that I was marvelously well the day before.

For two weeks I had no longer been undertaking long excursions on foot, limiting myself to moderate strolls, visits to the citadel, to the Al Azhar mosque, to Boulaq and along the Nile; five or six kilometers a day, never more. The day before the sinister event, a Sunday, I was not fatigued. Having got up at about six o'clock, I worked, and made a neat copy of my travel journal, until nine o'clock, Afterwards I walked very slowly as far as the Arab cemetery, passing by the mouled, where I expected to meet the guide Ali.

At midday, instead of returning to the Mouski, I had lunch at the table d'hôte of the Shepherd Hotel, in the hope of running into a young Russian, Monsieur Herzen, with whom I had sent a week in Alexandria and who had notified me of his arrival in Cairo for that day. I did not see him there. At two o'clock I returned to the Nile Hotel, where I occupied myself until dusk developing prints from my most recent photographic plates. I dined with a good appetite. At nine o'clock I went to bed. I read there for quite a long time, about thirty or forty pages of the poetry of Leopardi, in the Italian text. I think I went to sleep at about eleven o'clock.

Monday

Abrupt awakening. Someone is knocking on my door, and it's scarcely daylight. I recognize the guide's voice:
"Ana ya, Sisi, ana."[34]

---

[33] The author's father had died in August 1890.

[34] The author adds a footnote giving a French translation; an equivalent English translation is: "It's me, sir, me!"

I try to reply. Impossible. My jaw feels heavy, the teeth clenched. I try to get up, but the desperate efforts in which I exhaust myself do not even lift the thin sheet that covers me. At that moment the sensation that dominates me is that of an indescribable stupor, an imbecilic astonishment. Then, reasoning returns; I'm dreaming; I'm having a nightmare, for sure. Nightmares deliver you to emotions of this terrifying sort; one thinks one is lying down unmoving at the bottom of a well or precipitated from the top of a tower. Evidently, I'm experiencing one of those abominable dreams.

However, someone knocks again, and shouts more loudly:

"Ana ya, Sidi!"

Then nothing more. I remain immobile in the gloom and the silence. Then a noise of footsteps, which draw away, resounding, in the corridor. The noise decreases and fades away on the steps of the staircase.

One minute, two minutes, three minutes go by, while I begin to suspect a paralysis. That's a frightful anxiety. Yes: a sudden attack of paralysis. In any case, no pain, not the slightest sensation. I can't even feel the contact of the sheet on my skin. It's as if I've been petrified during the night—and yet it seems to me that I've never been as robust. Each of my surges, my efforts—efforts with no result, which don't displace my sheet by a millimeter—costs me energies capable of shaking the heaviest burdens. I could lift up enormous stones, crushing weights. But nothing…nothing. Am I going to remain in this wretched inertia for long?

This is what I can perceive now: approximately half of the sheet that covers me and, beyond that, the foot of my bed; the mantelpiece just as I've seen it for a fortnight, with its square mirror framed by a thin golden ring; the clock, whose face I can't make out well enough to distinguish the time; my cork helmet covered with white fabric, on top of a little marble receptacle; cravats, gloves, my purse and a book. Alongside the chimney-breast, the armchair on which I threw my clothes yesterday evening. Up above, the ceiling and the hem of my bed-canopy. Down below, the section of carpet stopping beneath the armchair…impossible to extend my gaze beyond that. It as if the eye is fixed in the orbit. It's only by means of the reflection I can see in the mirror that I perceive the corner of my table laden with papers, on which I can make out a large developing tray, which I was using earlier....

That's all.

Have I gone deaf? No sound reaches my ears, although I have hearing of a rare sensitivity. What time is it, then, at which no sound can be heard in this busy hotel? And now I observe that I cannot any longer hear the familiar noises produced incessantly within me: my breath, the echo of my heartbeat.

Has my heart stopped beating, then? I listen: nothing.

No, I'm not deaf. The rumble of a carriage down below, quite far away. Then someone walking up the stairs, along the corridor; they stop outside my door and knock.

"Mossyer Mossyer!" It's the valet de chambre, a German, like most of the servants in the hotel.

"Mossyer!"

Unable to respond! There are two of them; they're talking behind the door, but in low voices, so I can't grasp a word of their dialogue. Another rap on the door. Then a kick. They'll break down the door; they'll come in; they'll run to fetch a doctor. But no. They go away, and I fall back into the depths of my anguish. How long will I be abandoned like this, without help?

Someone comes back. And my door opens. The manager of the hotel, Monsieur Fridman, comes in first; I perceive behind him the valet Guillaume and the guide Ali. Monsieur Fridman must have been woken up in view of the urgency, because he's clad in Moorish fashion. The three men surround my bed and contemplate me with amazement mingled with fear. The manager calls to me three times, and then, abruptly, uncovers me, and all three lace their hands on my bare skin. I can see their gestures, but the touches are absolutely insensible to me.

I hear these words:

"Impossible!"

"Is fery unfortunate!"

"Ohi! Ohi!"

"The doctor! Fetch the doctor! Ali, go fetch Dr. Volgretz."

And Ali decamps while the servant groans: "Vill be too late! Ze poor man is kaput!"

Dead! A few moments go by during which I have no precise consciousness of anything. Confusedly, I see Monsieur Fridman lean over toward my chest and apply his ear to it, above the heart. And when he straightens up, his face expresses a naïve fear, the egotistical fear that absorbs a man confronted by death in the preoccupation of his own end. The valet pronounces that I'm as cold as ice, already rigid.

Dead! The commotion that I experienced on hearing that word was extraordinarily violent. My intelligence vacillated, rolling as far as the confines of madness. It was like a vertigo, the complete sudden electric concussion of a stunning blow in the back of the neck.

And it seems to me now that I have woken up in death itself, and have really ceased to exist. Yes, I have traversed two or three seconds, more or less, of complete darkness. Is it, however, during that brief interval that life has quit me? It's so strange to think, and so brutal and so frightful, that I remain incapable of regret. My memory instantaneously evokes what George IV said on his deathbed: "Is that all death is?"

Dead! My mortal envelope has ceased to be. It has lost the movement and the warmth of life. Henceforth, I am a soul. That which was me, the visible me, the carnal me, the miserable and vain me that had enjoyed and suffered, will soon rot, dissolve on contact with the earth, and beneath the drool of the filthy worm, will be annihilated in putrescence. Then my bones will whiten, and crumble to dist.

It's unspeakable! I've looked death in the face twenty times; I've confronted it under the fire of battle, on the sea, in the mysterious contingency of duels, and, without fearing it any more than is required, I thought of it as the most frightful crisis with which humans are menaced. In reality, it's nothing. It's just "that," as King George said. A nameless concussion, as prompt as a lightning strike, and then, almost immediately, an awakening in immense peace, in finite liberty. The afterlife, I'm there! The great mystery, I know it! Eternity, I'm entering into it.

Pure essence! I don't feel the hands that are palpating my cadaver at all. Life, the will, sentiment, have abandoned me, and yet, I exist. I am my own dream. Nothing that surrounds me escapes me, neither words not gestures not sounds nor the dazzle of the bright Oriental sunlight that is now traversing my curtains and falling in golden flames on my dead flesh…

Monsieur Fridman seems very upset by my abrupt disappearance, and he is taking measures to conceal the afflicting news from his boarders.

"Not a word of this to the travelers," he orders. "If anyone asks you for this gentleman, you say…you say that he's left the hotel, that he's left Cairo, that he received a telegram obliging him to return home. Do you hear?"

"Ja, ja, mossyer!"

"As long as that imbecile Ali doesn't talk…"

Silence.

The valet de chambre approaches the armchair and mechanically starts arranging my spare clothes. When he picks up my trousers he undoubtedly thinks them a trifle heavy, for he starts searching the pockets curiously. He takes out a handkerchief, a bunch of keys, a little pouch of Latakia, my Colt pistol, which he opens to see whether it is loaded and from which he removes the cartridge. Monsieur Fridman inspects the mantelpiece, visits my portfolio, which contains a portrait and my ticket from Alexandria to Port Said. He arranges them, blows away a little dust, and says to Guillaume: "It's necessary to secure all this. Does he owe much? Oh, no…he settled the latest bill yesterday morning.

"Are you going to notivy his vamily?"

The manager shrugs his shoulders without replaying.

Footsteps in the corridor. The door opens. It's Dr. Volgretz. He comes in, very surprised by what Ali had said.

"What? This poor gentleman?"

He approaches, feels me.

"Dead?" asked Fridman.

"For some time. The rigidity is complete. He must have died at about midnight."

"But of what? My God. of what?"

"Oh!" says Volgretz, with a vague gesture. "He wasn't ill? He didn't complain of anything yesterday evening?"

"Nothing. He went out, he ate well. It's extraordinary that one can go just like that!"

"Perhaps an attack of apoplexy, the rupture of a blood vessel. How do I know?"

"You can't recognize..."

"What do you expect? Without carrying out an autopsy..."

Perplexed, Monsieur Fridman seeks advice.

"What do I have to do?"

"He's a Frenchman?"

"You I think so..."

He goes to my table, picks up a few letters with French postmarks and shows the envelopes to the doctor. "Here, look..."

"Well, it's necessary to inform the consulate; they will do the necessary. Do you know his name and age?"

"Yes, in the register."

"It becomes a simple formality. One the consul is informed, you won't have to occupy yourself with anything else. It's his affair. In the meantime close the shutters and draw the curtains. It will soon get very hot in the room, and the decomposition... For greater security, you could send up a jar of disinfectant—calcium chloride, phenol, it doesn't matter—then lock the door and leave the chimney wide open. The dead man doesn't know anyone in Cairo?"

"I don't know."

"Tell me..."

He draws the manager into the corridor and doesn't re-appear. Shortly afterwards, Fridman returns.

"Go downstairs, Guillaume."

These incidents have taken scarcely half an hour. Furthermore, the face of the clock is now perfectly visible. I read one minute to seven. Pay attention! That's the click of the mechanism releasing the graduated wheel of the chimes; the mechanism grates, and the seven strokes of the bell ring out.

So, even though only existing in a purely immaterial fashion, I've conserved the senses of sight and hearing intact. I can see and hear. I can hear without ears and see without eyes. Touch is lacking, since my flesh can be touched without quivering.

So not everything is dead in death?

Eight o'clock. My memory is running through a sequence of memories, various, often obscure and sometimes contradictory, which inflict strange and sudden dementias of their own accord. I'm mistaken. I hesitate, doubtful, as if I were still alive, and my memories are dominated, as in life, by essentially egotistical preoccupations. I'm thinking about myself, what I was, my past now closed forever, about what will subsist of me. I think, vaingloriously of Horace's *Non omnis moriar.*[35]

A lugubrious confrontation of my years with my years!

The dispersal of things that have belonged to me suggests my first sadness. I see my gourbi again, my dear little house to the north of the Mediterranean, on the edge of the pinewood. I see my red study, with my books, my trinkets, my weapons, my geographical collections. What will become of all that? Who will succeed me in that hermitage where it would have been so good to die? Who will pick my roses next spring; who will eat my fruits the following autumn, the grapes of my vine extended in a vault over the terrace, the peaches in my grounds? How will the news of my death reach

---

[35] "I shall not wholly die."

that little village, and who will be the first to penetrate into my dwelling?

My thought—which is to say, all that remains of me—haunts my lovely and cherished retreat, but not in the free and voluntary fashion of a soul freed from all terrestrial bonds. It remains in Cairo, one the second floor of the Nile Hotel, as if, appointed to guard my cadaver, it's forbidden to leave it. I remain leaning over myself, riveted to what as the man that I have ceased to be. Only my imagination takes flight, crosses space and the seas, disembarks at Sanary, climbs the cliff covered with almond trees, reaches the threshold of my cherished abode. The visible, the evident, is circumscribed to the sector embraced by the sight that I no longer have. I still perceive, still and only, the sheet the cover me, and, beyond the foot of my bed, the mantelpiece, the mirror, the clock, and my clothes on an armchair beside the chimney-breast. Up above, the vault and the hem of my bed-canopy; down below, the section of carpet stopping under the armchair. Beyond that, nothing...

Nine o'clock. It's insensate that purely human sensations persist in me.

I'm wondering what the hotelier will do with my luggage: my clothes, my bag, my photographic apparatus, my maps, my Winchester carbine that had brought down such beautiful pink ibises during my strolls along the Nile. Perhaps the consul will order that everything be sent home. But to whom?

Truly, I'm ashamed to be entering into eternity thinking about such wretched trivia.

Regret comes to me regarding works idly abandoned, other works prepared by long reveries, of which I haven't written a line Naturally—I am made that way—the last conception holds sway over all the others in urgency and importance. I deplore less the abortion of my manuscripts avowed to an inevitable destruction, save perhaps for those that are in an editor's hands; I am neglecting my novel *Le Matelot*, three-quarters finished, my Florentine drama in verse, and others. What afflicts me, what seems to be dolorous and regrettable to the highest degree, it that I haven't written the bizarre and original novel with which my brain has been torturing itself for three months, since my arrival on Egyptian soil: the novel, as grave as a historic testimony, which would have fixed the Orient of our day, with its mores, its decadence, its sun, its dirt and all its people, from the pacha to the fellah.

Under my window I can hear Yacoub, the old blind beggar who has a monopoly on access to the garden, where he holds the travelers to ransom every day, and to whom I gave a little twenty-para coin every morning. No one can tell me how old that unfortunate is, and he does not know himself, perhaps ninety, perhaps more. I've never encountered anyone so old, so broken and so fleshless, to the point that it's a surprise to see him again every morning, sitting in the sun, crouched in his pitiful rags, extended over his hairy skin like torn bandages over a Boulaq mummy.

Yesterday, after receiving my alms, he thanked me by saying; "*Allah Kerieu, Sennet enta taib.*"[36]

How could I imagine, on listening to that hopeful voice falling from that deformed mouth, that I was living the final day of my final year, that I had no more than twenty-four hours to live and would not see the next sunrise?

Ten o'clock. Well, yes, I can see it now, the sun, in spite of the shutters and curtains. I'm no longer alive, but I'm still earthbound. Hence, a surprise and a delight.

What a strange speech Dr. Volgretz has pronounced! According to his judgment, I ceased to exist, not at the early hour when Ali came to knock on my door, but a long time before, in the middle of the night, while fast asleep. Oh, the gentle slide, without any shock, without panic, without clamors, without consciousness, into the liberation of the spirit. Oh, the insensible passage from the real to oblivion, from the known

---

[36] According to the author's note, "God is good! May your days be fortunate!"

to the mysterious, from the finite to infinity. And what good luck, doubtless unmerited, to have been able to die like that, shielded from death-throes.

A noise of footsteps in the corridor. Voices. I know: it's the young Austrian couple who occupy the apartment at the rear. Yesterday, during dinner, they asked me for information about Joseph's Divan and the Citadel well. They're probably going there.

More footfalls. Someone stops at my door, and opens it. It's Guillaume. He's bringing a earthenware vase, the prescribed disinfectant, which he places on the carpet, between my bed and the fireplace. Then he goes to leave, and with a habitual gesture he picks up my shoes, forgotten behind the door, brings them in, and puts them under a chair, as usual...

More footsteps. Here come Fridman and Volgretz, and Monsieur Horton, and a man whose name I don't know, but whom I remember having seen before at the Consulate.

"Has the death been certified?" asked the gentleman.

"No," Monsieur Fridman replies. "I sent notification to the Moudhir, but the physician hasn't arrived yet."

"But then...?"

Dr. Volgretz, this morning, has..."

The two physicians approach, palpate my cadaver, and examine it rapidly. I see their hands going back and forth. They exchange a few words in English during that inquest. I only understand the word "heart," repeated three times. Finally, Horton continues in French: "Complete absence of respiration."

"Of circulation."

"Of contractibility."

"Hippocratic face..."

"Of, that's not peremptory. The Hippocratic face often only announces the imminent approach of death, and the phenomenon sometimes disappears with death itself."

"In addition, complete rigidity..."

"Yes, yes...any trace of stria?"

"No. In any case, stria hardy ever appear in cases of peaceful death, like this one. They're produced by a certain laboring of the epidermis, violent distensions, for example..."

"The eyes?"

"Soft...flaccid..."

"As for the relaxation of the sphincters..."

Horton introduces his index finger between my lips and my jaw, under the right cheek, in order to assure himself that the sphincter of the lips is inert, with no resilience.

In the meantime, Guillaume opens the curtains and pushes back the shutters.

"And no putrefaction"

"Not the slightest."

It's Volgretz who is speaking. He adds, indicating the receptacle placed on the carpet: "I took care to recommend..."

Aided by the hotel manager, the monsieur from the Consulate has carried my table to beneath a window, and I don't miss any of their actions.

It's a matter of consulting my papers, to discover my identity documents.

A glance at my traveling journal, time to ascertain that it contains no information. Then the last letters received, but they only bear my name and inform me of intimate facts. My permission to visit the prison of Tourah. Finally, in my black shagreen briefcase, my passport. This time, it's complete: name, age, profession, qualities, domicile. There too is the firman that Ali Mubarak Pasha, the Minister of Public Education,[37] sent me in order to facilitate my free passage through the governorates of Kosei and Al Arish, which bears the signature and seal of the Khedive Mehmet Tewfik.

That document, of recent date, dissipates the investigator's hesitations.

My identity details are copied therein.

"And of what did he die?"

---

[37] Ali Pasha Mubarak (1823-1893) was the Egyptian Minister of Education and Public Works when the story was dated.

Messieurs Horton and Volgretz look at one another, non-plussed. But their good faith doesn't weaken. Clearly, they declare themselves unable to respond on that point with certainty.

"But it's necessary to be perfectly certain...."

"Of what?"

"Of the natural character of the decease. There might have been a murder by means whose traces would have escaped an overly hasty examination. The hypothesis of a poisoning for example..."

"Oh, as for that...!" And Dr. Horton concludes his protest with a formal gesture.

"First of all," he explains, "it results from Monsieur Fridman's declarations that the deceased took his last meal here, in common with twenty other travelers or residents of the Nile Hotel, who have not experienced any malaise. But it's sufficient to consider the cadaver. Such a rapid poisoning would inevitably have produced characteristic symptoms. The bed would conserve traces of abundant salivation, particular defecations; the skin would offer visible pink or livid patches, the marks of military eruptions or blisters. The death-throes would have given rise to movements, spasms of the tendons and convulsions that the rigidity would have conserved for us. Finally, the mouth would exhale one of the odors peculiar to poisons—which is to say, an odor of soda in the case of alkaline toxicity, an odor of sugar or ink if a mineral poison had been employed. The epigastrum and the abdomen would show a marked swelling. Here, nothing similar. The bedclothes are orderly. The body is intact and odorless. One would think him a man asleep rather than dead."

"A contusion!"

"Impossible."

"What, then?"

Horton has recourse to his English origin. "In my country," he concludes, "when we have to certify a decease in analogous conditions, we employ the formula: 'Death by divine visitation.'"

The monsieur smiles. "That's convenient. In France we're more meticulous. The last word is spoken at the Morgue."

"In sum," concludes Volgretz, "one final observation: in case of a suspicion of poisoning, a physician has a duty to look around for some trace of poison. There is none in this room. Nothing, neither liquid, nor powder."

At that moment, Fridman announces in a low voice: "Ah, here's the Moudhir's physician."

He is a little old man, busy and neat, brisk and smiling, who bows gracefully, neck and spine, putting a hand on his fez.

"Where is he?"

He approaches, examines, palpates, observes.

"The last prescriptions?"

"What prescriptions?"

"The last prescriptions of the physician. Who was the physician who was treating him?"

They inform him. There was no malady. It's a case of sudden death.

"Ah!" The voice becomes suddenly grave. He strikes a reflective pose, strokes the white mane of his beard, asks for further information. He's visibly searching, trying to grasp a cause of death."

"Apoplexy?"

"Never!" protests Horton. "Look at him. There's no sign of an apoplexy. The neck is of medium length, the head of normal volume, the general conformation regular and devoid of obesity. Furthermore, in the conditions in which we find him, it's not probable that the deceased has suffered a more or less considerable stasis in the cerebral vessels, which would have favored their rupture and the production of a hemorrhage."

"Aneurism!"

"More likely. I could believe in an internal aneurism that developed in the splenetic cavities, for example, in the abdomen or the torso. You know how difficult an internal aneurism is to diagnose. The man might have been afflicted by an aneurismal tumor for some years without suspecting it. Perhaps, too, he had an aortic aneurism, a dilatation of the artery at the level of its curvature. Valsava's treatment might have saved him, or bleeding, absolute rest, a strict diet. Instead of that, the sick man travels, walks, doesn't have himself bled, eats the invariably somewhat hot and spicy nourishment of hotels. It wouldn't take any more to precipitate the denouement."

"Then, according to you…?"

"My word, yes. Your opinion, my dear?"

"Absolutely the same," conforms Volgretz.

The Moudhir's physician recovers is good humor. He observes that I've just benefited from a regular consultation. "But a trifle late," he adds, finally.

It is therefore settled that I have succumbed from a rupture of an internal aneurismal tumor, a rupture determined by my fatigues and my excesses at table during the last three months. I am, however, certain of having lost eight pounds since my departure from Marseille.

The coroner scribbles on a piece of paper that he has taken from his pocket.

"What was the time of death?"

"In truth…"

They don't know. Fridman intervenes. The law requires a delay of twenty-four hours between death and inhumation. Is there any means of fixing the death yesterday?

Impossible. The Moudhir's physician is very sorry, but it's impossible.

"You're in error. The inhumation does not have to take place at least twenty-four hours after the death but at least twenty-four hours after the verification of the death. That's quite different. The verification having taken place today, at eleven o'clock, the interment will be tomorrow, at eleven o'clock. Truly very sorry…"

Eleven o'clock. My interment!

If I were not inert flesh, if I had conserved the slightest sensibility, that word would have gripped me like the unexpected bite of an icy chill.

My interment! Where will that be, my interment? Where are Christians taken here? Will I be taken to the great Arab necropolis under the citadel, to rot in the implacable sun, among the white stone tombs from which two square pilasters rise?

Now eternity begins to frighten me. There is a living me superior to my dead me, who is still subject to the surrounding action of life.

Life? Do I really no longer possess it? I still enjoy—for it really is an enjoyment—seeing and hearing people, even these funereal men, experiencing sound and light. Yes, even lying on this mortuary bed, it is delightful and radiant to me, life! I'm savoring it and reveling in it. My semi-naked body is receiving the radiation that's falling from that window, and it's so good, that heat that I can't feel! Oh, don't draw the curtain, doctor, don't draw the curtain! Open the widows, so that I can hear life singing! With the wind from the desert, distant music is passing through the great eucalyptus trees in the garden, the distant voices of women, the arpeggios of flutes, the chords of harps. Those noises, those voices, those vibrations, those gleams of light, those harmonies, that universal and eternal joy, I shall lose tomorrow in the tomb; for I have the frightful certainty that my soul will not separate absolutely from my body. It is absent from it, not distanced. It will remain my companion in the night of the tomb, forever and ever, in that glacial and corrupt night...

Yes, eternity frightens me.

He has finished, the monsieur from the Consulate, and the prompt success of his mission satisfies him. Now he is addressing his recommendations to Monsieur Fridman.

"You must light two candles here and sent someone up to maintain vigil over the body. That's the custom in France.

"It will be done."

They all go out.

219

A vertigo seizes me. I don't know any more.

A universal human error! Error, and not doubt. Doubt implies a hesitation, between hypotheses or before certainties. A man doesn't doubt, when he meditates on the beyond, he errs. As may illusions as intelligences! I remembered just now the astonished remark of George IV; perhaps it's not as strange as it seems at first glance. That prince, a drunk and a thief, cruel and monstrously lustful, might have believed himself avowed to a vengeful and expiatory agony. And, when death took him with a clement hand, he marveled, exclaiming: "Is that all it is?" In the same way, the Lord Protector, doubting at the last moment the legitimacy of his justice, murmured between two gasps: "I'm saved!"

But what about the others? So many others! Frederick V, shivering with vertigo and yielding fearfully, swearing that there is no blood on his hands. Elizabeth, offering her crown for one more minute of agony. Byron sighing: "Now is the time to go to sleep." Walter Scott, doubtless experiencing what I thought I was experiencing just now, an inexpressible liberty, an entire liberty of spirit, and pronouncing that illuminated speech: "I feel that I'm becoming myself again." Goethe calls loudly for more light, like Mirabeau, like the last Napoléon. Lamennais consoles his friends with the promise of their future reunion. Henry VIII howls at the monks. Madame de Staël invokes God, her father and liberty. Washington approves: "It's all right!" and Charles II instructs someone to feed his little bitch Nelly.

No one senses the mystery in advance. No one has glimpsed it. That instant of death has given rise to innumerable superstitions. As for me, who has scorned the fabulous inventions of religions and has only accorded an artistic curiosity to the ingenious systems of philosophy and science, I contemplate infinity with a disdain mingled with disgust. The afterlife is ignoble. That eternal imprisonment of the mind in the horror of the tomb, so that is what it is reserved for us all to suffer; that is what human imaginations, in the most profound of their cowardices, at the summit of their audacities, have not even suspected. It was too simple. We are too superior to what is. It is perhaps only foreseen by savages.

We have done well to invent paradises and infernos. Paradises exalt, infernos. Dante has invoked nothing as flatly disgusting, nothing as naively horrible as that eternity of the idea in the sewer and in darkness. What an abode and what a destiny for a soul!

Oh, if I could only speak! If I could escape death—not for a long time, like Lazarus, for a new lease of life, but only for a quarter of an hour, for a few minutes, the time to pour out to humankind all the certainties of oblivion! Not in view of my glory, not finally to ensure the perpetuity of my memory among human beings, but in order that they might finally know that Jesus lied, that Mohammed lied, the Buddha lied, that infinity is summarized in a few feet of earth under the incessant and mute testimony of the immortal soul! The abode of the sidereal clouds recounted by Manu to the pariahs of the Ganges, the radiant Elysium of Greek mythology with its majestic gods and adorable goddesses, the Latin Olympus dazzling with sumptuousness and glory, the sensual dream of Mohammed through the impossible desire of humans, the Christian paradise with its justices its benedictions, its calm enchantments, ending in reality in lugubrious burial, with no limit, with the vile slavery of the idea, in sempiternal blindness: all the anguish of spirits confined in that putrescence!

Noon. The twelve strokes of the clock have, I believe, reawakened my soul, recalled my impatient thought, which was already preceding me to the tomb. Or is it that noise, that suspicious noise that is filtering hypocritically from the corridor through my door—something like a very soft grinding? I can't hear very well because of the rumors with which the house is full, violently dominated by the bell for lunch. People are talking beneath my windows in the garden; the guests at the table d'hôte are chatting while swilling pale absinthes before the meal. But the singular grating continues and my door opens.

221

Oh, gently, so gently, as if under the calculated push of a prudent and anxious hand. It turns on its hinges with a regular, very slow movement. Slowly…very slowly…

A head slips through the gap, nothing but a head, the body remaining leaning over the threshold, the feet lingering in the corridor. A bistre visage with a looked nose, a glabrous chin, swollen with heavy fat, with little sparkling eyes beneath thick eyelids. Perhaps a Levantine Jew, coiffed by a fez surrounded by a dirty ribbon.

His eyes look at me, or, rather, search for me in the gloom, finally perceiving me. Then the visitor comes in, at a rapid, silent pace, gliding over the floor. With the same slowness he closes the door to the junction of the catch, and bolts it. A distance of about three meters separates us. I distinguish the man: about forty years old, short and thickset stature, an impression of strength and solidity, poor garments. Where has he come from? What does he want with me? What has he come to do here? Why has he been allowed to come up? Why isn't my door forbidden?

A few seconds go by without the intruder changing his posture, except that he leans his repulsive face toward the corridor, his ear pricked. Good. He advances and, his two hands placed at the foot of the bed—enormous hands, the hands of a butcher or a cut-throat—he looks at me. Then he turns round and goes to the mantelpiece. Oh, the wretch!

My purse. He takes three Egyptian pounds of a hundred piastres and other coins, which he puts in his pocket after counting them with his gaze. Filthy thief! Trivia still tempt him: cravats, gloves, a pocket-knife, my Colt. Then I see him head for the table, where he reaches for my watch. But a noise reaches him from outside and he puts it down abruptly. Soon reassured, he nevertheless refrains from touching it. The thief's cowardice interferes with his temptation. To steal that item, easy to recognize, difficult to sell, and for which the hotel staff would be sure to search…

I can no longer distinguish the scoundrel, but I can hear him. He searches, he fumbles. For a moment I perceive him in the mirror, examining my carbine, of a model that he is doubt-less seeing for the first time. And abruptly, he appears very close to me, two inches from my face!

I'm afraid. It's hideous, the face of that robber of the dead, hideous and ferocious, the muzzle of a hyena. If I had encountered him yesterday, in the open air, in some out-of-the-way street of the Masr-el-Fostat, I would probably only have experienced a vague repulsion, but here, in this silence and this solitude, his apparition scares me.

Emotion troubles me to the extent of conceiving an attempt at cannibalism on my dead flesh. The two evil eyes dart their blazing pupils at me. The two hands descend upon me. I see them without my body trembling, but for a long time. Already they have disappeared under the sheet, which agitates obscurely. What? Why?

The man straightens up again, holding my ring between his thumb and index finger, which he has just removed, stolen, torn away—how would I know?—from the ring-finger of my left hand. He weighs it, estimating it, makes the amethyst shine, and makes it disappear into a fold of his belt.

His gaze now inspects every corner of the room, in search of a final prey. I lose sight of him while he passes to the right of the bed, where his foot collides with some invisible object; he appears to me again close to the door, in the attitude of his entrance, his atrocious face leaning out into the corridor, his ear cocked. His hands open a silent passage. It's like the gliding of a shadow. The door closes again, grating softly. Oh, softly, so softly!

I'm alone.

Lacunae. An intermittent weakness suspends my faculties of reflection and observation. At the very moment when I apply myself, or interest myself in the manifestations of my immaterial state, interrupting disturbances break the tenuous thread of the idea. Instants of absolute oblivion, the duration of which I calculate by consulting the clock, in vague resurrections of a sort, demi-slumbers.

Without that clock, I would lose the notion of time.

Two o'clock. An assault of the past: something comparable to a vehement tempest blowing storms through my mind, or an upheaval of the depths of my memory. Images, thousands of images, escorted by thousands and thousands of other images, wander in disorder over the immensity of my psychic horizon. That against the backcloth of a dawn such as one can only contemplate from the summit of a mountain, with infinite prolongations of darkness dissolving in the distance in pure light. From the somber foreground to the paling extremity of that perspective, the distance is immeasurable. A world.

Perhaps a symbol, that vision of the beyond. It is vast, diverse, tormented, enlarging, gradually darkened, like my life, which it resembles.

Here, similarly, there is candor at first, the ineffable candor of a spring dawn illuminating calm extents, where all the promises and all the dreams of infancy palpitate in the matinal freshness.

A very bright and lively steppe, rising in a gentle slope toward regions where the light, losing its white glare, seems woven of virgin gold, and caresses immense fields of flowers. Faces traverse that expanse: a child guided by grown-up ancestors; then the same child, already grown, advances—while around him, nature also grows as he passes, setting traps, saddened by dusks, bristling with barriers, cut by ditches and precipices. Individuals that I have known accompany that ephebe—forgotten individuals, exiled or long in the grave. It's my life unfurling...

The images hasten. They rush, wildly, in the fulgurant crimson of battles, and I distinguish furtive episodes through the gaps in the smoke: a plain covered with canons, with regiments trudging toward villages in flames, the highway of Villiers-sur-Marne, a corner of the Place des Vosges, the bunker of bastion 54—a panorama of Paris by night, in the redness of conflagration.

New faces rise up, the visages of women, the complexions of young women, laughing faces and severe pouts, smiles and masks, tragic eyes and scattered hair, caprices that were sins, amours that were joys, passions as dolorous as martyrdoms: the cortege of my amorous Bohemia following my twenty years with a light tread. There are some I can't name who dart long gazes of adieu at me in which a tear glitters; others extend white arms toward me that appeal to me. Some go away, leaning on the shoulder of another lover.

Clouds, a hurricane of clouds, veil that corner of space, where I suffered for such a long time. The shadow, at first scarcely blurred, becomes heavier, mutates into a desolate sunset without gaps in the firmament, devoid of stars. Airs of sadness howl beneath, lugubriously...

Now there are entire countries filing past, new horizons, corners of houses and porticoes of temples, naves of cathedrals and galleries of palaces...a street in London, the column in Trafalgar Square, the docks of Folkestone, a small garden on the Isle of Wight; the Vivier in The Hague, the great courtyard of the Binnenhof, the beach at Scheveningen, Utrecht, the polders, the steamboat at the Moerdyek, the cabin I lived in on the isle of Marken; Brussels, a corner of the woods at Groenendael, Antwerp, Tréguier, the cemetery of Spa, the Meuse at Huy, my cell in the prison of Petits-Carmes; a large square that is the Place de la Signorina in Florence, a corridor in the Pitti Palace and the Ponte Vecchio, the glacier of the Via Tornabuoni, the road to Pisa; a quay encumbered by carts and porters, the parvis of the Doge's Palace, the old port at Genoa; the hall of the Estates General at the Château de Blois; the Heritage palace in Saint Petersburg; the fortress of Elsinore; the port of Kiel; a landscape in Colombia near Santa Fe, the Rue du Gouvernement in Colon, the entry of the *Présidente-Oliveira* to harbor at Joliette, the cliff of La Hève with the little path that descends toward Sainte-Adresse...

Then a sequence of plains, infinite terrains, distances populated by gigantic monuments, snowy mountains, pyramids and obelisks, a crazy file-past that stops abruptly to allow me to contemplate at leisure the statues of Maréchal Moncey in the center of the Place Clichy. People are coming and going over that square in different costumes, but they all show me the same face, which is mine. But night descends heavily over my vision of lost life, and I can no longer distinguish any-thing...nothing except my mortuary chamber, the sheet on the bed, the canopy, the mantelpiece, the armchair, a thin ray of sunlight...

Three o'clock. Monsieur Fridman comes in followed by an individual in European dress coiffed with a fez. It's the dragoman from the consulate who has come to take possession of my luggage: a rather long formality that consists of deposit-ing in the depths of my large trunk and my valise a considera-ble number of small packages, carefully bound with string, over which seals of red wax are set. From the responses of Monsieur Fridman, I learn that all the other formalities are complete. The last is fixed for tomorrow, and precisely eleven o'clock in the morning.

A second witness is required to sign the legal attestation of the placement of the seals.

"Shall I send up a waiter?"

"Hmm...I'd prefer someone who wasn't a member of your staff."

"I have it...would you like Dr. Volgretz?"

"Perfect!"

Electric bell. Arrival of Guillaume, utterly distraught; he thought for a moment that it was the dead man ringing, and that gave him quite a jolt. He is laughing at it now, but his cheeks are livid. He goes back downstairs, and shortly after-wards, Volgretz appears

Having provided the signature, he is astonished.

"It's marvelous...not the slightest sign of decomposi-tion...that's because the precautions have been well taken..."

They are about to withdraw when the manager, doubtless obedient to a scruple of propriety, or simply to put an end to a sad spectacle, pulls up my sheet in such a manner as to cover my face completely.

What I experience then is inexpressible. That veil imprisons me in a vague white light and immediately hides from me everything that I could see during the morning. That entirely physical phenomenon does not deceive me for a second.

Suddenly, the truth appears to me: the atrocious, frightful, demonic verity.

I'm alive!

My energy succumbed just now. On understanding that I'm not dead, but only in a state of apparent death, a lethargy, a catalepsy, I suddenly fainted. That proof of my resurrection has given me exactly the same commotion that I experienced on hearing my death established. I've woken up in complete darkness. What time is it? Where am I? What have they done to me?

A suspicion comes to me, a suspicion of unbearable horror; I think that I'm in the coffin, taken away, buried. The tomb already! While I was unconscious, the events have been accomplished. Oh! Oh...!

No. Voices are chattering. Resonant footfalls, and—benediction! The clock chimes...

Midnight. Yes, it really is the clock, to the shrill sound of which I've become accustomed. I'm still in the Nile Hotel, in my room. The hours have marched on during my prostration. Let's see, how long have I been in this state? It's very hard for me to calculate, because calculation and reflection are strangely difficult for me, even painful, with a particular kind of pain that I can't define, which has nothing human about it and isn't localized. Ordinarily, when one is suffering, the illness, oppression, contraction and anguish affect one or other of our organs, the heard, the heart, the epigastrum, the intestine, the larynx. In my case, nothing similar. My suffering is nowhere; I can't sense it, but it's unspeakable. It's...it's...I can't find the words. Even the ideas don't come, nor points of comparison

227

with anything known. Perhaps it can't be compared to anything. It can't be conceived or recounted. It's abominable in its impossibility!

Boom! Yes, I'm still at the hotel. The entry door has just slammed shut in its frame, after having let in some belated traveler. And I hear the stairway being climbed, two whispering voices. The young Austrian couple have gone past my room, the husband muttering words that I didn't grasp, the woman stifling foolish laughter, giggling laughter...

Is it possible?

Curse the stupidity of the physician! That brute who was astonished not to find me in a state of decomposition...[38]

Terrible memories come back to me.

Of François de Civille, the captain of a company of men-at-arms in the service of king Charles IX, who, during the siege of Rouen, was buried alive three times and saved, thanks to quasi-miraculous circumstances...

I see again a painting in the Musée Wiertz in Brussels, a strange and terrible picture: a man has been nailed into the coffin alive during the haste of a cholera epidemic; he wakes in the crypt of a chapel in which he has been deposited among other coffins; and the painting shows him, mad with horror, at the moment when he breaks through the lid of his bier...

In the last century, a cemetery existed in the place occupied today by the square and the fountain of the Innocents, near Les Halles. The National Convention closed the cemetery

---

[38] Author's note: "Messieurs Horton and Voltgretz are urgently begged to excuse the fact that this story might contain elements disobliging for both of them. I have ceded to a firm determination not to hold back any of my impressions. I also recognize, quite willingly, that they brought an irreproachable professional conscience to their observations. Furthermore, what is astonishing about their being able to mistake my condition, since I was able to mistake it myself?"

and ordered that the bones buried there should be transported to the catacombs. The execution of that measure was confided to Dr. Thouret, the brother of the convention-member Thouret who was guillotined in 1795. The transfer lasted a long time, the evacuation of the charnel-house only being completed toward the beginning of the Empire. When he wrote his report, Thouret declared that, in according to the evidence of the disposition of the bones in the coffins, he was certain that a considerable number of individuals had been buried alive there.

A considerable number: very nearly five per cent!

What a night! What an interminable night!

The hours resound distinctly in the silence. I can hear the clock on my mantelpiece chiming, and I can also hear others through the walls. That prolongs the chimes and forms a singular carillon in which all the sounds of the scale mingle or succeed one another. A distant chime alerts me first, a chime that seems to come from the floor below, from the room situated below mine. That vibration of bronze through the joists and the carpet is transformed, one might think it discolored. It gives the idea of a note played on a piano swathed in cotton wool. Almost immediately, my clock responds, and it has not finished before two offers accompany it dully and are the signal for a kind of hum in perfect accord. I can hear others joining in. Finally, there is one that sounds after all the others, a long time afterwards, with the aged, cracked voice of an agonizing machine. I listen to those strokes of the bell with delight, as the sole slightly living clamor that still reaches me. I cling on to it, and when the last clock gasps out its cracked stammer down below, an extraordinary sadness grips me, the despair of a lost child.

In the interval of the chimes, between the half-hours and the hours, between the hours and the half-hours, I wait for them to sound with a stupid anxiety.

The rumble of a cart makes the house vibrate and the glass in the windows quivers. A prolonged whistle-blast rips the air. The ripple of a fountain…where the devil is that fountain, flowing at this hour?

I marvel at having conserved as much sang-froid in such a terrible situation. Ought I to applaud myself for it? No. In reality, that relative quietude is made of a stubborn hope. Get away! A hope? An absolute confidence in the salutary denouement of my nightmare…

A nightmare? What if it were only a nightmare? What if this night, instead of being this very night, were still the other night, yesterday night, from which I shall son wake up quite well, without any memory of my dream?

No… And yet…? But what does it matter…?

It's impossible that I won't wake up! The phenomena of catalepsy are limited in duration. One goes to sleep. Fine. One seems to be dead. So be it. One offers all the appearances of insensibility, of rigidity, of iciness. So be it again. But one wakes up.

When?

Volgretz was already quite surprised by my condition when he signed the legal document. How surprised will he be tomorrow? And how can it be imagined that he won't oppose…?

Get away.

This is what I'm experiencing at this moment:

An overwhelming mental fatigue. More fatigue than fear. A single locution would translate my lassitude exactly, but I hesitate to employ it, so inappropriate is it: *I want to go to sleep*. Yes, that's it. And yet, that's not it, since the spontaneous passage from wakefulness to sleep is an essentially physical phenomenon. Only the organs succumb; the mind doesn't go to sleep: hence the continual dreams, of which we remain ignorant for the most part, for the memory rarely conserves them on awakening, and never without some degree of confusion and obscurity.

Now, I no longer exist physically. Even though I only have the appearance of death, my being has been provisionally annihilated. The vital functions—warmth, circulation, heartbeat and pulse—are completely suspended therein. What is it then, within me, that wants to go to sleep? And yet, that need to sleep numbs me. Veritable efforts are indispensable to me if I apply myself to any meditation whatsoever. The ideas are effaced. I have the illusion of an engulfment in fog.

Here and there, flashes of lucidity, memories— intelligent and complete ideas. But rare...

Four o'clock. The repercussion of the chimes again, from echo to echo.

Have I been asleep? Have I had a few minutes of a slumber peculiar to my condition, an unnamable repose that perhaps no one in the world before me has savored? What is certain is that an entire abolition of my intellectual sensibility has furtively drawn me from my anguish and paraded me through regions of dream in which I saw this:

On the road from Ollioules to Sainte-Anne d'Evenos I was walking with my dog Deck, who was trotting ahead of me, nose to the ground, tail hoisted. At a bend in the Gorges, near a rock pierced at its summit by a hole that frames a patch of clue sky, Deck growled to warn me of a danger, and I saw a man of gigantic stature approaching, carrying an enormous bundle of roots. The man put down his bundle; then he disappeared into the ground without my being at all astonished. I untied the bundle, and a dog emerged from it identical to my Deck: the same yellow color, the same tail sticking up, the same white patch on the breast, the same gait, the same amiability. At first that gave me pleasure. I had only had one little Deck, from now on I shall have two...

We've quit the Gorges and have climbed up to the ruins of the château. There I gave a snack to my two Decks, who ate at the same time without fighting over the morsels of my bread, and showed an equal passion for sugar...

On returning home, I became very anxious, because it was impossible for me to distinguish my dog from the dog from the bundle. They both seemed to love me as much and to have done so for a long time. They both knew every corner of my house. I thought I'd be able to recognize my dog by calling him by his name, but when I shouted "Deck!" they both came running toward me wagging their tails and jumping up with the same movement to lick my face. I thought I was going mad...

After having wept with chagrin and fear between my two yellow dogs, who were both licking me, one to my right and the other to my left, I had the idea of summoning the giant of the Ollioules road. He hastened to emerge between two rose-bushes. I told him to take his dog away. He took him and went back underground with him. Scarcely had he disappeared than I recalled him. He never came back. And that gave me a great deal of trouble, because I wasn't sure whether he had taken away his own dog, the one from the bundle. A presentiment warned me that he had taken away Deck and left me the other, and I was very unhappy about that, because I no longer dared love my dog.

I was at that point in the nightmare when I heard four o'clock chime.

At this moment there is an insect in the wood of my bed whose labor is producing an unbearable scratching behind my head: some worm, some borer hollowing out a tunnel in the vein in order to deposit its eggs therein. I can hear the grinding of the little drill quite distinctly, and, at moments, a kind of fall of fine dust sliding down the panel. It would be impossible for me to explain how interested I am in the action of that animal. The slightest groan of the wood reverberates in the utmost depths of my thought, and when the borer pauses I continue to hear it, more feebly, like an echo.

Inexplicable shivers traverse the silence. There's a loose floorboard, a step on the staircase that creaks, a doorframe that is lifting itself up. It requires no more than that to determine curiosities in me, anxieties and the applications of a particular acuity and an invariable dolorous susceptibility.

The wind is engulfed in the chimney, left wide open, and is sometimes formidably modulated, as if in an enormous flute. Vehement gusts of air bellow strident scales there, which die down afterwards and die away in plaints of an inexpressible softness. One might think that a universal resurrection has spread through space the twenty-times secular cries of the desert and that, out there, the great sphinx of pink granite is waking up and roaring. That nothingness, that silence and this funereal night are full of voices and lives, and my hope is made of the echo of those voices in my anguish.

Five o'clock. A bright light. My door has opened, and the light of a lamp filters through the sheet extended over my eyes.

Someone is speaking. I recognize Guillaume's accent.

"Chently! Turn chently!"

But these recommendations do not prevent the impact of something heavy against the wall of the corridor. Shadows pass back and forth over my veil, dividing and masking the light. There are several men in my room or on the threshold of my room. Someone queries, another responds.

"Where?"

"This way?"

"No, one can't turn it any longer..."

Woe is me! It's the coffin!

I've fainted for the third or fourth time, perhaps the fifth. It's impossible to calculate how many times fear has abolished my strength; and then I am, for a time that seems infinitely prolonged, completely unable to measure the duration of the faint. The awakening is surrounded by ignorance, and a kind of flavorsome doubt that dissipates slowly, like early morning mist at the first light of dawn. First there's the impression of a natural, customary awakening, the awakening of a man drawn from sleep by a noise whose echo is still vibrating in his ears, but of which he cannot take exact account. Has someone knocked? Has someone rung? Was there some kind of gunshot? Superimposed on that stupor is a numbness of the intelligence, a veil over the memory, a mental obliteration, a suspension of clear sight and observation. I don't know where I am or what is happening to me, and that unconsciousness is good, very good, very agreeable.

Memory comes back to me with difficulty, almost painfully; and every recall astonishes me equally as a novelty. Recently cured madmen must experience something analogous at the moment of their first return to reason, and perhaps also ponies shut up for a long time in mines, which are dazzled when they are returned to the surface. Yes, I have the impression of an abrupt confrontation with light after a sojourn of unappreciable duration in the depths of shadow and madness. My mind's eye blinks before excessively blinding light and only discerns colors and contours later, after having become accustomed to it. I can scarcely translate that state other than by the same words that the lugubrious tocsin sounded in me:

"Cairo... Yes... No... Ali... The Mouski...? Dr. Horton... The Jewish thief... The clocks chiming all through the house... What house...? Yes, let's see, what house...? Hotel... Cairo... Room 31... Guillaume... The porters...

That evocation of the porters has determined the complete awakening. At a stroke, in a fraction of a second, all the incidents of recent hours have surged forth in my brain, with their successive circumstances, their details, the scenes contemplated, the voices heard, in the unfurling of a fugitive panorama. And the last image that has struck me, at the summit of that laborious ascent toward the real, is expressed by the word "coffin."

Yes, they've brought the coffin. There are afflicting transports to make in the darkness, before sunrise. And I recall the lights glimpsed, the words pronounced, the terrifying sound of the bier deposited on the carpet, and that five o'clock had just chimed.

It must be a long time after that now, and I'm glad to think that, during my faint, no change has taken place in my position. I'm still lying on my bed, covered with the sheet that Fridman threw over my face a while ago. The tick-tock of the clock is reaching me distinctly now, and I wonder with a ridiculous anxiety by virtue of what phenomenon I was able to cease hearing it. A vague white light filters through the fabric by which I'm still veiled. Nothing is moving around me.

From that moment on, I admit to a profound disturbance of my mental faculties, That isn't equivalent to saying that I was, for a more or less prolonged time, veritably afflicted by madness. I simply want to explain that I ceased to note purely mental impressions within me; that I belonged meekly and entirely to external influences. In a word, my imagination paused temporarily. I continued to grasp and to understand what was happening around me, but I'm unable to answer for what I appreciated and judged. Perhaps I only retained the faculties of conceiving, and not forgetting; fear had killed in me the ability to deplore or regret. I was still penetrated but I was no longer thinking.

From that instant dates my fall into a similar animal condition that I attribute to this cause: that I abdicated all hope of salvation.

The inhumation appeared to me to be inevitable. I had forgotten the unique chance to which I had previously clung: a new intervention by Dr. Volgretz, who, increasingly surprised by my state of conservation, sensing a case of lethargy, might take the initiative if calling for a suspension of the obsequies. Of that I was no longer thinking, my mind having lost the faculty of calculating a hope. It is probable that that state of psychological coma implies an almost complete abolition of intelligence. I cannot do better than to compare it to what a beast imprisoned in some tenebrous ditch would experience—I mean a brute beast, one of those degraded animals that we judge and believe to be deprived of all instinct, like the catoblepas of which Flaubert speaks in the *Tentation de Saint Antoine*, which devours its own feet without perceiving it, and before which the hermit cries: "It's stupidity attracts me!" Yes, such an animal, plunged in the horror of a premature tomb, would not be thinking any more than I was thinking at that moment. There would be the same somber acceptance of ineluctable annihilation, the same grim resignation, the same renunciation of any escape.

Among the external manifestations, I noted: the hoof-beats of a troop of donkeys passing by outside under the garden wall; the intermittent grinding of the borer in the wood of my bed; whispering voices in the corridors and on the staircase of the hotel. The large entrance door opening to the Mouski had been opened wide, and I heard a large vehicle rolling, probably an omnibus.

The daylight is augmenting...

Seven o'clock. Fridman introduces men to my room whose language I don't understand. A sudden light informs me that the curtain and shutters have been opened; then, abruptly, a hand removes the sheet extended over my face, and I can contemplate the objects around me again.

Not for long.

Long enough to perceive two individuals, one old and one young. The young one is tall, thin and ugly; the old one old, short, fat, with a face that isn't bad. But behind him, through his legs, I perceive the horrible thing lying on the carpet. The coffin! The coffin! The gaping coffin, of which a ray of sunlight illuminates the frightful form and the frightful ocher color. I can see it! I can see that box into which I'm about to disappear forever, where the most atrocious agony is lying in wait for me. It is there, in the bottom of it, that life will return to me, warmth and sensibility; it's there that, after a derisory resurrection, I shall die of hunger or asphyxia. And I can't tear my gaze away from it...

Ah!

It's over. I can no longer see. What are they doing to me? The sheet has been replaced over my head once again, but no longer softly, loosely, as before. It binds me, it blinds my open eyes. Oh! Oh! I don't want that. I'm not dead! I...oh!

An extraordinary sensation of flying or falling. Voices complaining around me, hoarse breathing, brief and rapid words. Scarcely any light, a white light, a dubious, almost paradoxical, white light, giving the idea of a dark flame. Then a stop...

I've got it! I've heard the heavy plank fall over me, which terrible hands are now fixing over my face which such a racket that I'm fainting again, on the threshold of the night from which I shall never emerge...never...never...!

I can heard Yacoub, the old beggar. I can hear him close by... Where am I, then? Already? They've taken me down... Footsteps surround me, and the formal, clear nearby noises of the street. The time! It's the time! Think about a cry, a cry! A single cry!

This is what happened at that moment:

I suddenly sensed something like lava ignite beneath my forehead and precipitate with an electric instantaneity all the way to my heels: an ardent and sudden fire. At the same time, I sensed the walls of my bier against my elbows and my toes. It was then that I cried out.

I thought I had uttered a resounding clamor, but I perceived that no one could hear me, that they were continuing to carry me away. I rendered perfect account of the fact that I was being hoisted into the vehicle.

At my second cry I heard the voice that said, very loudly: "Stop!"

I shouted again, several more times, and I didn't stoop shouting until the moment when the bier was uncovered—an operation that required a minute, at the most.

When I saw the light again through the shroud, I was seized by a tremor that only died down after a quarter of an hour of rest in the office of the hotel, on the porter's bed.

I shall have nothing to add to this story when I have said that, three or four hours later, all physical malaise had disappeared.

Conclusion

While lavishing the cares upon me that were to lead to my prompt recovery, Dr. Horton insinuated, laughing, that my dramatic adventure would become fortunate for a man of letters, and that I would surely not hesitate to recount it.

Perhaps he was right. I say "perhaps" because I'm not entirely sure. What I can affirm, however, is not having brought any haste to it. Before entertaining the public with an incident already divulged by the press and which really only offers an interest to me, I wanted to take account of the utility of such a narration. Is it important for the reader to know these impressions of the afterlife? Why? In what measure?

Out of egotistical curiosity, I have studied the question of premature burials, and I have arrived at this indisputable discovery: that my adventure is banal. My impressions remain personal; my case is, alas, much more common than is believed.

A long and conscientious examination permits me to affirm—contrary to the opinion of a small number of physicians—that we are all at risk of being buried alive.

To summarize, in brief:

No physician can pronounce with certainty as to whether a death is apparent or real. After all the progress of which modern science is so proud, we are still at the stage at which our physicians are impotent to distinguish a dead man from a living one.

Except for one circumstance, one single case that we shall indicate shortly, no difference exists between real death and apparent death.

None!

One of the scientists who has studied this terrible question most extensively, Julia de Fontenelle, declares the fact in the following terms:

"In order fully to demonstrate the definitive cessation of the functions whose ensemble constitutes life, rather than the suspension that only gives rise to a apparent death, there are several signs that, taken in isolation, are uncertain, and which, in sum, only offer probabilities. These principal signs are: 1. the absence of respiration and circulation; 2. the absence of contractibility and sentiment; 3. chilling of the body and the

Hippocratic face; 4. cold sweat over the entire body; 5. livid patches and stria; 6. the relaxation of the sphincters; 7. the softness and flaccidity of the eyes; 8. the flattening of the parts of the body on which the cadaver rests. 9. cadaveric stiffness or rigidity.

"These signs taken in isolation cannot indicate a real death; in combination, they only indicate a death-like state.

"Putrefaction is the only sign of real death, for putrefaction cannot be established under the influence of life, since it brings with it the entire frightful cortege of destruction. It is therefore evident that it is the certain and irrevocable sign of death."[39]

Now, in the present state of our legislation on inhumations, given the required delays—at least in France, Belgium and Germany—is that sign, the only certain sign of real death, putrefaction, always acquired?

No.

Thus, real death is often not established. It cannot be. And any inhumation carried out in those conditions, in the absence of that single certain sign, might deliver a living person to the horrors of the tomb.

It is to respond to that poignant preoccupation and call the attention of public opinion to that peril, the mere idea of which is abominable, that these lines have been published.

The question is not new. Moses seems to have been the first to have occupied himself with it; his law ordered judges and chiefs not to allow the dead to be buried until the third day. The Romans then imposed a delay of seven days and, in spite of that lapse of time, in spite of the precautions taken to recall the dead to life, Pliny cites several cases of resurrection on the pyre: Celinus Tuberus, the consul Acilius Aviola, the praetor Lucius Lamia.

---

[39] This passage presumably comes from Eugène Julia de Fontenelle's contribution to *Médecine légale, théorique et pratique* (1837), which one might expect to have been somewhat out of date by 1892.

In the same epoch, Plutarch names sixteen of his contemporaries buried alive. And, only to cite the principal historians of premature burial, let us recall that Saint Augustine, Baronius, Bacon, Apuleius, Bruhier, Pineau, Simon Goulard, Barnard, Charles, Rigaudeau, Urisson, Père Calmet, Ramulphe, Don Luc d'Achery, Abbé Messson, Andre Vesalius, Barthez, Fossati, Durande, Louis, Chantourelle, Amatus Lusitanus, Falconer, Tascheron, Chaussier and Winslow (we are offering names borrowed from all scholarly epochs) have seen with their own eyes men buried alive.

Almost all of them attribute these cases of apparent death to the following afflictions: asphyxia, hysteria, lethargy, syncope, catalepsy, chorea (St. Vitus' Dance), epilepsy, ecstasy or tetanus. But, they say, apparent death can be determined by other causes absolutely unknown.

Shall we yield to the temptation to evoke examples from those, so terrifying and so numerous, that medical chronicles have transmitted to us? It is necessary, since those examples have not served their purpose, for want of being assembled.

Dr. Winslow, whom we have just cited, having been buried once, was buried a second time. When he died, after ninety-one years, he instructed his pupils to incinerate him—which they did after a delay of a week.

Abbé Prévost, the author of *Manon Lescaut*, is declared dead by the physicians. As they are about to proceed with the autopsy, he wakes up under the surgeon's scalpel, and lives for another seventeen years.

Cardinal Espinosa seizes with his hand the instrument that is about to open his abdomen, and survives for fifteen years.

Dr. Le Guern observes during his career a hundred and eighteen cases of premature burial, and concludes an average of thirty-seven a year for France. We deem his estimate inferior to the reality.

In 1841, the gamekeeper of a village in the Charente-Inférieure is declared dead. Vigil is kept over him by an old woman who goes to sleep, leaving a candle burning that sets fire to the funerary bed. The dead man wakes up at the contact of the flame, takes flight, recovers, marries within the year and becomes the father of eight children.

The same year, an inhabitant of Cognac dies. The physician observes the absence of warmth and a pulse. Veins incised in both arms do not yield a single drop of blood. He is buried. But the unexplained death seems suspect. Public rumor denounces a poisoning; the law orders an exhumation. The cadaver is found in the depths of the tomb turned over, covered in blood, the limbs contracted. The man had been buried alive.

In 1850 Henri Wealver, vicar of Richley in Yorkshire, wakes up in his shroud after forty-eight hours of lethargy, just as he is being placed in the bier.[40]

In Madrid, the Marquise de Lasso dies two weeks before being due to give birth. Several months later, when the family tomb is opened, the child is found on the mother's right arm. She had delivered it herself in the crypt.

Dr. Durande has interrogated an orderly at the hospital of Cassel who, reported to have died after a medical examination, remained nailed in a coffin for a week. The unfortunate man had not lost consciousness for a single instant.

Monsieur Dourre, a merchant, dies in a convent of Jacobins at Perpignan, succumbing to an adynamic fever. He wakes up in the cemetery, is liberated, and lives for a further thirty-six years.

The Prince de L***, who lives in Florence, has had the frightful dolor of discovering that his father had been buried alive. When, ten years later, he opened the crypt in order to introduce his mother's coffin, he found the skeleton on the

---

[40] Like several of the other references in this concluding section, this one is untraceable; given that one or two of the correctable names are grossly misrendered (e.g. Le Guern is rendered "Lequeent"), the typesetter presumably had difficulty reading the author's handwriting.

floor outside the bier. The unfortunate man had died knocking on the doors of his tomb.

A young physician of Calvados is resuscitated after a vigil had been maintained over his pseudo-cadaver for five days by his wife.

Dr. Lenormand knew in Châlons-sur-Saône a maidservant named Marie, nicknamed Cheat-Death, whom the physicians had declared defunct. One of her friends intervened, alleging that he had seen her in that state before. With great difficulty, Lenormand obtained a delay of a week from the municipality. On the seventh day Marie was resuscitated, and immediately went back to work.

In the church of the Recollects of Saint-Nizier de Marcigny a devotee stood up after the evening service and ran to tell the curé that she had heard clamors in the crypt where the dead are deposited. The curé shrugged his shoulders, believing that the devotee was hallucinating. Get away! Do people come back to life? The next day, the woman insisted. Then they went down below the choir, and found there, outside his bier, the cadaver of a recollect buried a week before. The unfortunate had died of fright and hunger, after having devoured his wrists and forearms.

Père Lecler recounts the story of his aunt suddenly dying and being buried in Orléans. She was buried with a valuable ring on her finger. A domestic opened the grave in order to steal the ring. The dead woman woke up, lived for ten years and gave birth to two children.

The adventure of François de Civille, mentioned in the course of the story is certainly the most extraordinary imaginable. Three times in a year he was buried alive and miraculously saved. Thereafter he signed documents "Captain Civille, three times dead and three times resuscitated by the grace of God." That is nothing. Bouhier reported that that predestined individual was born in the tomb; his pregnant mother died while her husband was away, only returning six days after the interment. He ordered that the tomb be opened, carried out a Caesarian section on the dead woman and took his son out of the sepulcher alive.

Dr. Bénard of the Faculté de Paris witnessed, in the cemetery of Réole, the exhumation of a Franciscan bruised three days before. The man was found alive in the tomb and only died six months later. He had not lost consciousness.

Dr. Louis, a Parisian physician in the time of Louis XVI and one of the inventors of the guillotine, tells a dramatic story that we shall summarize briefly: In a village in Morvan, a young peasant woman dies suddenly. The aged relative with whom she lives is confined to be by chagrin and dolor, and asks for a monk to watch over the cadaver. A young Trappist installs himself beside the funereal bed. The dead woman is admirably beautiful, so beautiful in spite of her pallor that the Trappist yields to a diabolical temptation. He profanes that sacred flesh and violates the cadaver. While he consummates his abominable crime, however, he senses the exquisite warmth and life of the young woman reborn beneath his quivering limbs. An indescribable terror takes possession of him, chases him out of the dwelling soiled by his crime and brings him back to the convent after a night spent wandering through the meadows. The next day, Morvan cries miracle. The dead woman is resuscitated. Enquiries are made about the monk; he has fled. A few months later, the young woman gives birth to a fatherless boy. Who has conceived the child? A god? A demon? An angel? The rumor of the miracle spreads. Then the Trappist returns, confesses his crime, throws his robe into the brambles by the roadside and marries the peasant woman. One would think it an improbable romance if the facts were not attested by a serious scholar.

Dr. Hatteras has consigned the declarations of one of his friends, whose death was scientifically established and who, for twenty-four hours, heard everything that was said around him, all the surrounding noises, including the blows of the hammer on the nails sunk into his bier, and only showed signs of life after the commencement of the inhumation.

The *Dictionnaire de médecine* reports that between 1842 and 1850 ninety-four cases were observed. Thirty-five persons emerged from natural lethargy; thirteen were reawakened by the excitation of desperate cares; seven owed their salvation to the coffin being dropped; nine were afflicted by the pins with which their shroud was attached, and the rest were saved by fortuitous accidents.

Nearly a hundred in eight years!

Medicine cannot establish the statistic of the unfortunates who only woke up in the sepulcher.

We could multiply these citations, Thousands of them encumber specialist treatises of medicine. Let us limit ourselves to adding that, in the last year, we have found in newspapers published in Paris alone, thirty-one cases of premature burial, twenty in France and eleven abroad.

The average number of people buried alive is, in fact, greater here than anywhere else, and there is no reason to be astonished by that when one considers the lightness with which our medical examiners carry out their functions.

Generally, a medical examiner seems to be sent less to certify a death than to investigate whether the parents, domestics and friends of the deceased might be a gang of poisoners. His only preoccupation is whether there has been a crime and, in consequence, whether it is necessary to notify the police. When the cadaver is presented to him he scarcely looks at it. It is extraordinarily rare for him to touch it.

"Show me the most recent prescriptions," he will say. By scanning them he studies the progress of the malady and, if nothing excited his anxiety, he rapidly signs the permission for burial. Is he subject dead or alive? It hardly matters. He will be buried at a certain hour, in some corner of some cemetery.

One can affirm without exaggeration that there is not one medical examiner who, in ten years of exercising his functions, has not sent at least one living person to the grave.

Could that functionary, by a serious examination, truly establish real death or diagnose apparent death? Almost all scientists will reply "No; except in the case of putrefaction, that is impossible."

Three physicians respond affirmatively. They are Burdach, Cadet de Gassicourt and Bouchut.

Let us take the theory of the last-named, the most complete and the most laboriously formulated. There, according to Bouchut, are the certain signs of death:

1. The absence of heartbeats in the pericardial region during five minutes.

2. The discoloration of the depths of the eye, seen in the ophthalmascope, which is the effect of the vacuity of the capillary network;

3. The disappearance of the pupil of the optic nerve;

4. The disappearance of the central arteries of the retina;

5. The interruption of the sanguine columns of the retinal veins;

6. The lack of action of atropine on the iris.

On the first point, Bouchut is already in contradiction with Casper, who, in his *Traité de medicine légale*, sustains that death can only be established after a pericardial ausculation of at least ten minutes, which is double the time demanded by Bouchut.

We do not intend to discuss here whether the perception of a heartbeat after five or ten minutes is sufficient to establish the state of apparent death, but we believe that we can affirm that the human ear can only detect those beats in lethargy or catalepsy with the aid of a very powerful microphone that had not yet been invented. On the day when our coroners possess those microphones and make use of them according to the formula, we might perhaps be slightly reassured.

As for the experiments too be carried out on the eye of the subject, they necessitate a serious medical kit and apparatus that our medical examiners have never carried.

Cadet de Gassicourt holds cadaveric rigidity to be absolutely conclusive.

At what moment?

Cadaveric rigidity, caused by the coagulation of syntonine, appears between one and seven hours after death, is general after eighteen or twenty-four hours and lasts between thirty-six and forty-eight hours at the most. In cases of violent death without preliminary enfeeblement, it is belated and lasts longer; it is the contrary after debilitating maladies. Thus, according to whether the physician charged with the establishment arrives sooner or later, he will or will not find the reputedly certain sign of cadaveric rigidity.

Furthermore, Cadet de Gassicourt, Burdach and Bouchut are only in accord on one point, to wit, that of all the signs distinguishing real from apparent death, putrefaction is still the most convincing.

The conclusion is evident. We ought, following the example of the English, to possess depositories where cadavers wait until that sign, the only indisputable one, the only irrefutable one, permits their inhumation.

If that measure is not decreed soon, we all risk entering into the sepulcher alive.

SF & FANTASY

Adolphe Alhaiza. *Cybele*

Alphonse Allais. *The Adventures of Captain Cap*

Henri Allorge. *The Great Cataclysm*

Guy d'Armen. *Doc Ardan: The City of Gold and Lepers; The Troglodytes of Mount Everest/The Giants of Black Lake; The Abominable Snowman*

G.-J. Arnaud. *The Ice Company*

André Arnyvelde. *The Ark; The Mutilated Bacchus*

Charles Asselineau. *The Double Life*

Henri Austruy. *The Eupantophone; The Olotelepan; The Petitpaon Era*

Barillet-Lagargousse. *The Final War*

Cyprien Bérard. *The Vampire Lord Ruthwen*

S. Henry Berthoud. *Martyrs of Science*

Aloysius Bertrand. *Gaspard de la Nuit*

Richard Bessière. *The Gardens of the Apocalypse; The Masters of Silence*

Chevalier de Béthune. *The World of Mercury*

Albert Bleunard. *Ever Smaller*

Félix Bodin. *The Novel of the Future*

Pierre Boitard. *Journey to the Sun*

Louis Boussenard. *Monsieur Synthesis*

Alphonse Brown. *City of Glass; The Conquest of the Air*

Émile Calvet. *In a Thousand Years*

André Caroff. *The Terror of Madame Atomos; Miss Atomos; The Return of Madame Atomos; The Mistake of Madame Atomos; The Monsters of Madame Atomos; The Revenge of Madame Atomos; The Resurrection of Madame Atomos; The Mark of Madame Atomos; The Spheres of Madame Atomos; The Wrath of Madame Atomos* (w/M. & Sylvie Stéphan)

Félicien Champsaur. *Homo-Deus; The Human Arrow; Nora, The Ape-Woman; Ouha, King of the Apes; Pharaoh's Wife*

Didier de Chousy. *Ignis*

Jules Clarétie. *Obsession*

Jacques Collin de Plancy. *Voyage to the Center of the Earth*

Michel Corday. *The Eternal Flame; The Lynx* (w/André Couvreur)

André Couvreur. *Caresco, Superman; The Exploits of Professor Tornada* (3 vols.); *The Necessary Evil*

Gaston Danville. *The Perfume of Lust*
Camille Debans. *The Misfortunes of John Bull*
Captain Danrit. *Undersea Odyssey*
C. I. Defontenay. *Star (Psi Cassiopeia)*
Charles Derennes. *The People of the Pole*
Georges Dodds (anthologist). *The Missing Link*
Charles Dodeman. *The Silent Bomb*
Harry Dickson. *The Heir of Dracula; Harry Dickson vs. The Spider*
Jules Dornay. *Lord Ruthven Begins*
Alfred Driou. *The Adventures of a Parisian Aeronaut*
Odette Dulac. *The War of the Sexes*
Alexandre Dumas. *The Return of Lord Ruthven*
Renée Dunan. *Baal; The Ultimate Pleasure*
J.-C. Dunyach. *The Night Orchid; The Thieves of Silence*
Henri Duvernois. *The Man Who Found Himself*
Achille Eyraud. *Voyage to Venus*
Henri Falk. *The Age of Lead*
Paul Féval. *Anne of the Isles; Knightshade; Revenants; Vampire City; The Vampire Countess; The Wandering Jew's Daughter*
Paul Féval, *fils. Felifax, the Tiger-Man*
Charles de Fieux. *Lamékis*
Fernand Fleuret. *Jim Click*
Louis Forest. *Someone is Stealing Children in Paris*
Arnould Galopin. *Doctor Omega*; *Doctor Omega and the Shadowmen* (anthology)
Judith Gautier. *Isoline and the Serpent-Flower*
H. Gayar. *The Marvelous Adventures of Serge Myrandhal on Mars*
Louis Geoffroy. *The Apocryphal Napoleon*
G.L. Gick. *Harry Dickson and the Werewolf of Rutherford Grange*
Raoul Gineste. *The Second Life of Doctor Albin*
Delphine de Girardin. *Balzac's Cane*
Léon Gozlan. *The Vampire of the Val-de-Grâce*
Jules Gros. *The Fossil Man*
Jimmy Guieu. *The Polarian-Denebian War* (2 vols.)
Edmond Haraucourt. *Daah, the First Human; Illusions of Immortality*
Nathalie Henneberg. *The Green Gods*
Eugène Hennebert. *The Enchanted City*
Jules Hoche. *The Maker of Men and His Formula*
V. Hugo, P. Foucher & P. Meurice. *The Hunchback of Notre-Dame*
Romain d'Huissier. *Hexagon: Dark Matter*
Jules Janin. *The Magnetized Corpse*

Georges Pellerin. *The World in 2000 Years*
Ernest Pérochon. *The Frenetic People*
Pierre Pelot. *The Child Who Walked on the Sky*
Jean Petithuguenin. *An International Mission to the Moon*
J. Polidori, C. Nodier, E. Scribe. *Lord Ruthven the Vampire*
P.-A. Ponson du Terrail. *The Immortal Woman; The Vampire and the Devil's Son*
Georges Price. *The Missing Men of the* Sirius
René Pujol. *The Chimerical Quest*
Edgar Quinet. *Ahasuerus; The Enchanter Merlin*
Henri de Régnier. *A Surfeit of Mirrors*
Maurice Renard. *The Blue Peril; Doctor Lerne; The Doctored Man; A Man Among the Microbes; The Master of Light*
Restif de la Bretonne. *The Discovery of the Austral Continent by a Flying Man; Posthumous Correspondence* (3 vols.)
Jean Richepin. *The Crazy Corner; The Wing*
Albert Robida. *The Adventures of Saturnin Farandoul; Chalet in the Sky; The Clock of the Centuries; The Electric Life; The Engineer Von Satanas*
J.-H. Rosny Aîné. *Helgvor of the Blue River; The Givreuse Enigma; The Mysterious Force; The Navigators of Space; Vamireh; The World of the Variants; The Young Vampire*
Marcel Rouff. *Journey to the Inverted World*
Marie-Anne de Roumier-Robert. *The Voyage of Lord Seaton to the Seven Planets*
Léonie Rouzade. *The World Turned Upside Down*
Han Ryner. *The Human Ant; The Superhumans*
Louis-Claude de Saint-Martin. *The Crocodile*
Frank Schildiner. *The Quest of Frankenstein*
Pierre de Selenes: *An Unknown World*
Norbert Sevestre. *Sâr Dubnotal: Vs. Jack the Ripper; The Astral Trail*
Angelo de Sorr. *The Vampires of London*
Brian Stableford. *The Empire of the Necromancers (1. The Shadow of Frankenstein; 2. Frankenstein and the Vampire Countess; 3. Frankenstein in London); The Wayward Muse; Eurydice's Lament; The Mirror of Dionysius; The New Faust at the Tragicomique; Sherlock Holmes and The Vampires of Eternity; The Stones of Camelot* (anthologist) *News from the Moon; The Germans on Venus; The Supreme Progress; The World Above the World; Nemoville; Investigations of the Future; The Conqueror of Death; The Revolt of the Ma-*

chines; The Man With the Blue Face; The Aerial Valley; The New Moon; The Nickel Man; On the Brink of the World's End; The Mirror of Present Events; The Humanishere

Jacques Spitz. *The Eye of Purgatory*

Kurt Steiner. *Ortog*

Eugène Thébault. *Radio-Terror*

C.-F. Tiphaigne de La Roche. *Amilec*

Simon Tyssot de Patot. *The Strange Voyages of Jacques Massé and Pierre de Mésange*

Louis Ulbach. *Prince Bonifacio*

Théo Varlet. *The Castaways of Eros; The Golden Rock.; The Martian Epic* (w/Octave Joncquel); *Timeslip Troopers* (w/André Blandin); *The Xenobiotic Invasion*

Pierre Véron. *The Merchants of Health*

Paul Vibert. *The Mysterious Fluid*

Villiers de l'Isle-Adam. *The Scaffold; The Vampire Soul*

Gaston de Wailly. *The Murderer of the World*

Philippe Ward. *Artahe; Manhattan Ghost* (w/Mickael Laguerre); *The Song of Montségur* (w/Sylvie Miller)

Victor Margueritte. *The Bacheloress; The Companion; The Couple*

NON-FICTION

Stephen R. Bissette. *Blur 1-5. Green Mountain Cinema 1; Teen Angels*

Win Scott Eckert. *Crossovers* (2 vols.)

Georges Grison. *The Heads that Fell in Paris*

Jean-Marc & Randy Lofficier. *Shadowmen* (2 vols.)

Randy Lofficier. *Over Here*

Brian Stableford. *The Plurality of Imaginary Worlds*

www.ingramcontent.com/pod-product-compliance
Lightning Source LLC
Chambersburg PA
CBHW030406020726
47493CB00003B/963